I0555553

Death in the Time of Ice

Kaye George

A People of the Wind Mystery
Book 1

White City

Press

Also by Kaye George

A People of the Wind Mystery

Book 2
Death on the Trek

Book 3
Death in the New Land

Death in the Time of Ice

Kaye George

This edition published by White City Press
An imprint of Misti Media LLC
https://www.mistimedia.com
Available in both Paperback and eBook Editions
1 2 3 4 5 6 7 8 9 10
Copyright © Kaye George 2024
Paperback ISBN: 9781963479218
eBook ISBN: 9781963479119

Without limiting the rights under copyright reserved above, no part of this publication may be reproduced, stored in or introduced into a retrieval system, or transmitted, in any form, or by any means (electronic, mechanical, photocopying, recording, or otherwise), without the prior written permission of both the copyright owners and the above publisher of this book.

The scanning, uploading, and distribution of this book via the Internet or via any other means without the permission of the publisher is illegal and punishable by law. Please purchase only authorized electronic editions, and do not participate in or encourage electronic piracy of copyrighted materials. Your support of the author's rights is appreciated.

Acknowledgments

Through the many versions of this project, I had so much help from enthusiastic supporters. I count Kathy Waller and Gale Albright among the staunchest and most steadfast. Chris Roerden gave me early guidance. Others who gave invaluable assistance, critiques, and encouragement are Jim Jackson, Daryl Wood Gerber, Cathy Sonnenberg, Kathleen Marsh, Marilyn Levinson, Michelle Martin, Judy Copek, Sally Bartoo, Sharon Wildwind (whose name I unconsciously used for a character), Jean Henry Mead, Sarah Wisseman, and I'll bet a whole lot more that I'm leaving out.

I'm so very grateful to Jay Hartman for believing in my vision and this project and for bringing it to light. The cover artist, Ginny Glass, did a terrific job. I can't imagine a better cover. Thanks, to everyone at Misti Media for making this novel available to readers everywhere.

Prologue

There has always been the wind.

Since our planet began to turn, there has been the wind. This ball of dirt and fire and water started to spin. The air stirred. And Earth's time began.

But the beginnings of the wind are lost in the mists of time. The wind blew before the Appian Way wended through Rome. It blew before the Parthenon crowned Athens. Before pyramids sprang up in Egypt.

Before the Mayans. Before the Incas.

Before Man.

Chapter 1

On current evidence, the Neanderthals lived between about 230,000 and 30,000 years ago—a huge span of time by any reckoning.

—*In Search of the Neanderthals,* Christopher Stringer and Clive Gamble, p. 7

The wind picked up speed over the surface of the ice. It blasted downward off the edge of the frozen field, past tangled masses of spruce and pine uprooted by the relentless, inevitable, insatiable progress of the ice mass. It soared over moraines deposited by the glaciers of the last Time of Great Ice.

A new Ice Age was coming. The wind blew change across the land, howled across a smooth plain crisscrossed by small streams, tore through the forest. It gathered strength, came to an open place, and whipped around a small band of about twenty-five hominids. They gathered around their community fire, singing and telling their history as they did most nights, in order that the young ones might learn it and the elders might not forget.

The song of the tribe lifted to Dakadaga, the Spirit of Mother Sky. The Spirit's many eyes shone down on the tribe, some of her eyes twinkling, perhaps because they were about to fall across the sky in fast, bright streaks.

The wind swept past Enga Dancing Flower, sitting at the edge of the gathering. A gust riffled her long, coppery-colored hair and made her glad of the bearskin cape covering her back and shoulders. A low rumble came from her gut, the sound joining the whine of the wind. She had not gotten enough to eat for several days.

The fire, burning in the shelter of the huts, defended Enga and her tribe from the worst of the wind's assault. But the seasons were turning, as she knew they always did, and the cold, dark one approached, no matter how well tended and warm the fire.

The song had been sung, the Saga had been told. Hama, the Most High Female and leader of the Hamapa tribe, stirred and all eyes turned toward her. Hama's long, thick braid, gray with age, caught glints from the firelight and swung across her back as she stood.

"Hoody! Vav Hama." Hama spoke aloud, entreating the Spirits so they would hear and heed her as she made a rare Official Pronouncement. "Listen! The Most High Female Speaks."

She continued, her voice addressing the Spirits, as well as her tribe. "The Hamapa tribe cannot stay in this place. We must leave our home, our beautiful village. The great beasts are no longer here in great numbers. In the Seed Season we will move."

Enga felt the stirrings of the brothers and sisters next to her.

A mental message, darkened for privacy, came to her from Ung Strong Arm, her twin sister. *Such matters are usually discussed before they're announced.*

Yes, Enga answered her, careful to hide her reply from the others. *This sounds like a serious matter, something new to me. Let me ask about it.*

She sent an open thought, bathed in bright, public color, to her leader. *Has the tribe ever moved to a new place before?*

Hama answered, *Not in the memory of anyone living.*

Nanno Green Eyes shot out a thought. *The Hamapa have lived in this village for generations.* Enga caught a vibrant wave of panic from Nanno and the muscles of her own stomach clenched.

Hama looked around for dissent. When no one offered opposition, she finished speaking aloud. "Mother Spirit of the Sky, Dakadaga, bless the Hamapa." The leader then crouched on the stone between the other two Elders, facing the rest of them.

What will it be like to move a village? wondered Enga to Ung. *I cannot visualize it.*

Ung pondered for a moment. She sat across the circle from Enga, but that was no impediment to their intimate thought-conversation. *It is true, we have not killed much game recently. And we are all hungry.*

Enga shook off her shock from the unprecedented proclamation, realizing nothing had been said about the immediate future, about the next day. She jumped up and thought-spoke to all. *What about the hunt? Will we hold the hunt?*

Hama likewise broadcast her answer to the whole tribe. *Yes, at new sun as planned. And may all the Spirits bless the hunt so we will have enough food for the coming Dark Season.*

An opinion came from the Storyteller, an old, bald male named Panan One Eye. *If we move our village, now, to follow after the herds—*

We will not move our village yet, Hama answered. *The tribe will remain here until Dark Season is over.*

I can see that moving during Dark Season would not be wise. Panan tilted his head skyward and closed his eyes to look inward, into the distant past, where the lore of the tribe resided. *Our Sagas tell of the tribe relocating long, long ago,* he thought-spoke.

The other Elder chimed in. *But we have dwelt here for many ages. Our village, built by the Ancient Ones, is such a fine one. Could we build another village as fine as this?*

Enga had been wondering the same thing, privately, where no one could read her doubts.

Yes, agreed Hama, *the Ancient Ones built well.* She ran her hand over one of the flat stones that had been fitted together so carefully to make the Paved Place, tiny gravel filling the spaces between the stones. *We can build another village. It was done by them and can be done by us. We are the Most High People.*

Enga felt the Elders did not look convinced.

But first we have to survive the Dark Season, Hama continued. *It is almost here. And we need more meat. Much more meat.*

If we have enough meat, there will be no need to move the village, Panan suggested.

Hama skewered him with her look. *Panan One Eye, there will not be more game in the coming seasons than there has been in the recent ones. We will move when warm weather returns.*

Hama rose again, rattled her hollow gourd, and called for the dance to begin.

Enga watched the dancers in the blaze of firelight and waited for a signal from Hama to join in. Chill evening air brushed her bare arms as she shivered and drew her cape closer.

She kept one eye on Hama, their elected leader, who also watched the dancers whirl around the leaping fire. As the tallest female in the tribe, Hama could easily watch over everyone and keep order.

Because of her position, she used moonless midnight hues to shield most of her thoughts from the others. The tribe depended so much on her, to lead them with strength and wisdom.

Enga Dancing Flower. The thought-speak came from Tog Flint Shaper.

She answered him with a fond look.

I am happy you and Ung Strong Arm will hunt tomorrow. I will enjoy watching you, Tog continued.

Hamapa scouts had recently spotted a large herd of mammoth at a nearby watering spot. Hama was too old now to wield a spear, but Enga and the other young, sturdy females could bring down the mammoth. They knew they must bring home a large one tomorrow, an adult. It had been many suns since their bellies had been full.

To point the weapons out to the Spirits for their blessings, Hama shook her gourd toward the tools of the hunt, stone-tipped spears and flint knives, laid out around the fire burning in the center of the Paved Place.

The dancers moved with the solemn beat of the hollow log in a slow circle around the fire. Sannum Straight Hair, the drummer, maintained the rhythm, steady and stately. Soon, Hama bobbed her head at him and he quickened the beat. This dance had to catch the attention of the Spirits.

We are depending on you, Enga Dancing Flower, thought-spoke Hama. *Prepare yourself to dance soon to Dakadaga, the Most High Spirit.*

Enga tingled with eagerness to do what she did best, to dance for the success of the hunt. She stood and bounced on the balls of her feet, waiting impatiently to be called into the circle.

A sudden disturbance erupted between two adolescent males. Enga and the others perceived angry thought waves. She turned her gaze to Kung, a strong, strapping youth, who was standing over little Jeek, threat written in his dark glower.

Kung failed to funnel his thought-speak to Jeek and it radiated out to the others. *No female would prefer you, puny Jeek, to me, big Kung.*

Do not throw those thoughts at me!

I will show you. Gunda would rather be with me.

Jeek scowled and shook his small fist in response, but kept further retorts in check.

Enga thought Kung was developing a swagger that needed to be squelched, but Jeek was not the one who should do it.

Kung's birth mother had died as he was being born. He had been nursed and babied by all the females, but had resisted attaching to anyone. Enga heard he had been a hard baby to cuddle. Very squirmy. It was no wonder his adolescence was proving to be difficult.

Little Jeek, the son of the Healer, was a dreamer. Enga suspected his mind often strayed from where it should be. She carefully sent a private thought to Ung Strong Arm, using the private cloaking color she had learned as a child. *I am not certain Jeek always keeps the good of the tribe in his mind.*

He is impulsive. thought-spoke Ung, using her own dark shade.

Jeek isn't mean. Kung, though....

Ung sent back her agreement. *Kung is young. He'll grow up someday.*

Jeek, at times, seems more mature than Kung, somehow, even though he is younger.

Hama quieted the squabble between the two youths with a stern look and a vivid, cold disapproval they could all sense. The tribe, Enga knew, could not afford dissension at most times, but especially not now.

The dance continued into the night. The males stomped their feet on the hard stones and the females twirled, flinging their hair to get the attention of the Spirits. They wore their best ceremonial finery; wolf and bear capes for the males, soft camel or brown bearskin capes for the females, all flaring with their spins. Their tresses, coppery, brown, blond, and a few gray, adorned with river shells and tiny bird bones, clicked and clanked.

Hama rattled her gourd at the darkness, toward Mother Sky, with her whole body. She raised her arms and her woven hair bracelets fell up to her elbows.

Enga never tired of her tribe's music. Rhythm from the hollow log beaten by Sannum Straight Hair pulsed inside her, excited her. The wooden flute of Panan One Eye and the high, trilling song of Lakala Rippling Water floated the beauty of melody into the night.

But she shivered with something besides the cold. A ripple of distasteful thinking trickled to Enga. She looked around for its source. Her skin crawled as if someone had been watching her, thinking of her in a harmful way. She caught Nanno Green Eyes frowning at her and Nanno quickly looked away, turning her face toward the fire. But Nanno's dislike was nothing new. This felt different. Enga looked on both sides of her, but saw only her fellow tribe members.

Someone crept up behind Enga and put two strong hands over her eyes.

She tensed.

The solid comfort of strong, calm mental waves came to her. She sniffed, then relaxed. *Tog Flint Shaper, you scared me.*

He chuckled deep in his chest. *How could you be afraid of me?*

She laughed at herself for her initial fear. *It is dark time. I am afraid of everything at this time of night.*

The wisp of unkind notion from Nanno floated away. She grabbed Tog's fingers, drew them down to her mouth, and gave a nibble to the thick thumb of the young male who had been so favored by the Spirits at his birth. Tog had come from the body of Hama. The look he gave Enga, and his low laugh, warmed her.

Enga drank in his body with her eyes—broad and powerful, his limbs thick with rippling muscle. She herself had carved the bone that skewered his shiny topknot of smooth, dark hair and had presented it to him at the time of her last kill. She gave Tog the smile she knew he liked, the one that showed her dimples.

But, as she always did, Enga kept part of her attention on their leader. Hama now turned her head. Enga loved Hama's eyes, wise and dark and wide-set in her strong, wrinkled face. Those eyes smiled and summoned her at last.

Enga grinned in return and ran to the fireside so she could join the circle.

Tog sent an individual message after her. *You are beautiful tonight, Enga Dancing Flower.*

You speak fancy words.

You shine like Sister Sun on high. Your eyes are the color of smoke to go with your hair, the color of fire.

Enga sighed at Tog's poetic pictures. In recent days her mind pictures were filled more and more with him. With his sparkling, dark eyes. With his smooth, broad back. With his muscular arms. Sometimes Enga imagined loosening his dark brown hair and burying her face in it. She saw him in her mind while she scraped skins clean to use for hunting, and even when she stripped her clothing off and dipped her body into the stream.

Especially then.

But she yanked herself back from her musings of Tog and their future. Tonight she had a duty. She must concentrate on her dancing so it would be strong enough to win favor for the hunt. She knew she was the best dancer in the tribe. Her people needed her skills tonight.

She tried to empty her mind for the dance. But Hama's Pronouncement had alarmed her. She could not conceive of moving the whole village. Her Hamapa brothers and sisters, she suspected, were all uneasy at the idea. But no one would openly contradict Hama after she had announced an official decision, of course. Enga swallowed with a gulp and tamped down her fears. Their wise Hama would lead them well. She always had.

Enga entered the circle and began to undulate to the rhythm.

Come, join me, she called to Tog, beckoning him with a wave.

I have been waiting for you to ask. He hurried to her side and began dancing next to her, matching her pace and movements. Sannum Straight Hair, squatting at his hollow log, gave Enga a broad smile when she neared him, then hastened his tempo a bit.

Tog wore his ceremonial cape of dire wolf skin. The bushy tails that hung from it tickled her bare arms when he danced near her. She twirled, her own cape of brown bearskin flaring. She shook her long, fiery-colored hair toward Tog, clanking the shells woven into it. She dipped, then rose. Tog kept his deep brown eyes on her. When her breathing became rapid, she didn't know if it was because of the dancing or because of the nearness of Tog.

Enga dreamt of awakening one day soon and going to the wipiti of Hama at first sun, to ask for Tog Flint Shaper in the formal way. A Hamapa First Coupling must be approved by Hama. Enga had not yet coupled with anyone, wanting Tog to be her first. She desired to do what some Hamapa couples did, and stay together all their lives.

These notions had been coming to her for many days. She did not shield these thoughts and knew Tog could see them. Tonight, though, his concepts were not reaching her. Enga suppressed from Tog her desire to see his thinking. He would send them when he wanted to, she knew. His private thoughts, when tunneled straight to her and wrapped in muted, darkened soft shades of night colors to hide them from others, made her feel warm inside, even when a chill breeze blew.

Her glance swung back to Tog and she frowned. He was gazing upon pretty Vala Golden Hair. Enga did a double twirl before him, a wordless scolding escaping from her, and his eyes returned.

My eyes should stay with the object of my desire. His handsome smile warmed her and she returned it.

Then she tried to clear her mind of all but the hunt.

The dancing lasted long into the dark time. Enga parted from Tog reluctantly as the meeting dispersed. When she received permission, she and Tog would couple in the Holy Cave, then would be together inside their own wipiti for many days. Vala with her bright yellow hair would not be near. When Enga contemplated their coupling, the pounding in her chest matched her panting.

*****

Enga Dancing Flower, worn out from the lively dancing, made her way homeward with slow steps. A gust flung a lock of her long hair across her face. Enga inhaled the dusky smell of smoke that lingered in her hair before she flung it back with a snap of her head. Ung Strong Arm had left the meeting early, needing to rest for tomorrow. Enga's twin was the best spear thrower in the Hamapa tribe. Enga sometimes wished she could aim as true and throw as hard as her sister, but, no matter how much she practiced, she could not.

Lost in these reflections, she bumped into someone blocking her path, startling her. She had noticed him at the gathering tonight, standing at the edge of the light cast by the fire, staring at Hama, as he usually did. When Hama had given him a look filled with unmistakable loathing, he had limped away from the gathering, his thin shoulders weighted with rejection.

The Hamapa called him the New One, since they did not know his name. He had been a lone sojourner when they took him in, no doubt cast out by his own tribe.

11

His unexpected appearance here frightened her at first. She kept her fear dark and close so he couldn't read it; then she remembered he did not seem to be able to read her thoughts and feelings. She stood only a few steps from the doorway of the wipiti she shared with her sister. She didn't want to wake Ung, who needed her rest for the hunt. Maybe she would try to get around him and avoid a confrontation.

But he looked so eager to communicate with her, she changed her mind and tried to greet him.

New One. What do you desire of me?

Her thought-speak did not reach him. He only grunted and made odd sounds, as if he were trying to speak out loud, to Pronounce. He accompanied his noises with broad hand gestures, but Enga, grimacing with the effort to follow them, could not tell what he meant.

I cannot decipher your strange sounds. Why can you not speak aloud in our tongue, even if you cannot thought-speak with me?

He reached into the pouch he wore around his neck and drew out a small carving. He ran his pale fingers over it, then held it out to Enga. She took it without touching his skin. Warm from his hand, it fit inside her palm. She turned it over, then held it up to catch the light from Brother Moon. Her breath caught. The smooth wood carving looked exactly like a very small mammoth. Enga was stunned, first at the artistry—she had never seen anything like it—then at the fact that he had handed it to her.

Maybe you hope to bring us good fortune on the hunt tomorrow by carving a mammoth. But why have you given this to me? It is too beautiful for anyone to own.

Enga didn't bother to shield her wonderment, knowing he could not comprehend it. She gazed up at the New One in awe. Could he want her to keep it?

Here, away from the gathering, his white hair did not gleam as it did when in the firelight. But it caught enough light from the beams of Brother Moon to faintly glow. His hair, and his skin, too, were the color of Brother Moon at his most pale. She shuddered when she imagined what it must feel like to touch that skin, almost the color of a fish belly. Then she squelched that notion and narrowed her eyes, trying to read his mind.

What are you feeling on the eve of the hunt, you unfortunate being? You can neither dance nor hunt. His foot twisted inward at such an awkward angle it made his gait slow and jerky.

Enga guessed what he had felt when Hama looked around the circle and beamed her warm smile on everyone but the New One, showing the gaps in her worn, yellowed teeth. To him she always gave a cold frown. Why did Hama not want the New One in the tribe? It was not the Hamapa way to turn anyone away, but Enga suspected that Hama wanted to turn this one out.

After all, the Hamapa had taken in Enga and Ung. They had been found as infants, not far from the village, and had been eagerly taken into the tribe.

What a shame you are crippled. He stood a head taller than anyone else in the Hamapa tribe. *You would make a good runner if your legs were healthy.*

She clutched the carving to her chest and raised her eyebrows in question. *I should keep it?*

He nodded vigorously.

It's a precious possession. But I must share it. Everyone should see this.

Smiling quickly, she tucked it into the pouch at her waist. His return grin split the night with whiteness. Enga paused. She was glad she could bring some joy to this poor creature, spurned by many in the tribe. She felt a measure of kinship with him. *We're alike, you know, New One. We were both cast out by our own tribes.*

Enga knew her thoughts were floating into the air without being received. Pity for him built inside her. But when he tried to follow her into her wipiti, repulsion rose in her throat.

No! You cannot come inside, she thought-spoke in the most definite manner she could. She thrust her palms at him and shook her head to emphasize her motion.

The New One's grin turned nasty. He pushed past her, then turned, grabbed Enga's arms, pulled her to his body.

In a flash her sister, Ung, awoke and jumped to her feet.

Ung Strong Arm! Help me!

Ung leapt to the entrance, twisted one of the intruder's thin arms behind his back, and propelled him out the door. Ung stood at the opening, her thick arms crossed before her, and watched until he disappeared into the cold, windy night. *Go! Do not return here*, she sent after him.

Why did he follow you inside? Ung thought-asked, turning to her sister.

I do not know. I tried to stop him. Her arms burned where his hot hands had gripped her.

Enga showed her the carving. *He handed me this.*

Ung was speechless. She gently took the piece of wood in her rough hands, turning it to get a better look at it in the glow of their fire, which had burnt down to embers for the night. *The New One has a gift for carving.*

It is a marvel. I have never seen such a thing, Enga thought-spoke.

But you had better be wary when you're around him.

Do you think he'll try to grab me again? She rubbed her arm where he had hurt her.

He does not yet understand our ways.

Enga nodded. *I wonder if he will ever learn them. The sounds he makes are so different from ours. And I cannot get any thought-speak through to him.*

I cannot either. Ung returned the carving and lowered herself back onto her warm fur. *Do you ever receive any from him?*

No, I do not think he can communicate with any of us. I thank Dakadaga you are my sister. I could not have a better one.

Ung shrugged off Enga's praise. *You are my twin. I will never forsake you.*

Enga gave Ung's shoulder an affectionate squeeze and readied herself for sleep. After she took off her foot wrappings, she emptied her pouch and lined up the contents on the dirt floor, between her sleeping fur and the wall. Side by side, she set her bone for putting up her hair, her shells and leather thongs she used for hair adornments, her extra spear tips, a smooth rock she had found with an odd shape, and her new carving. As she lay awake, trying to relax enough to fall asleep, she resolved to be on the lookout. This encounter had raised her neck hairs with a whiff of the same distasteful, harmful vibrations she had sensed earlier.

Her mind turned to Tog Flint Shaper, but the New One intruded there, also. Had the New One wanted to couple with her? But she wanted to couple only with Tog. In the future, she would avoid the New One as much as she could.

She did not want anything to interfere with her First Coupling with Tog.

Chapter 2

The high incidence of degenerative joint disease in Neanderthals is perhaps not surprising given what we know of the hard lives they led...
—*In Search of the Neanderthals,* Christopher Stringer and Clive Gamble, p. 95

Well before first sun Enga Dancing Flower stole across the Paved Place toward the wipiti of Hama. She had slept badly, the hunt and this mission preying on her mind.

The Paved Place of the Ancient Ones served the Hamapa tribe well. The Hamapa were proud of their Ancient Ones, and of their own tribe. In fact, *Hamapa* meant "the Most High People," and Enga would always be grateful she had become a member of this clan.

The vast eyes of Mother Sky still twinkled, but Brother Moon had gone into the earth. The central fire, now almost died out, gave her the only light, but she could smell her way to Hama in the dark.

She walked past the dwellings of the others. The domed structures, ribbed with mammoth tusks and covered with layers of animal hides, ranged around the Paved Place in a half circle. The tusks stood in deep holes, and rock piles held the edges of the hides down against the wind and weather. Comfortable body scents clung to all the wipiti.

How could we move all of this? If we do not, though, how could we build a new village? We must have a Paved Place for our gatherings.

Can we carry and set enough rocks, kill enough mammoths for our new wipiti?

Hama's wipiti stood at the end of the semicircle and a little apart. When Enga reached it she hooted softly outside the closed door flap, shivering slightly in the cold, damp air in spite of her mammoth skin wrap. She tugged it tighter and her finger poked through, making a hole in it. She needed a new wrap.

Hama sent out her invitation. *Come inside, Enga Dancing Flower. You are cold.* Her thoughts seemed sluggish and sleepy.

I think I have awakened you. Enga hoped she had not put her leader into a bad mood. This woman had raised her and Ung, and, because of that, they usually had an easy relationship. But Enga was always conscious of Hama's role as leader of the tribe, above that of her adoptive mother.

The next thought from Hama was gentle. *I was about to arise for the day. Come in where it is warm.*

Enga lifted the flap and entered, then squatted beside the fur on which Hama lay, rubbing her eyes to awaken. Enga sat far enough away to convey respect, since this was an official visit.

My Hama, Enga thought-spoke, *I come in the formal way to ask for permission to make a First Coupling with Tog Flint Shaper.*

She kept her eyes on the edge of the fur bed and waited for her answer. No thought waves came from Hama. Enga stole a glance at Hama's wrinkled face. The leader, propped up on one elbow, fell onto her back and gave Enga a gentle smile. Enga leaned forward. Surely this was a good sign.

I cannot give you my blessing right now.

Enga's chin dropped to her chest. She hadn't expected this. She raised her face, blinking back tears. *No blessing? Why, my Hama?*

You must come back tonight after the hunt, my child. If there is food enough, we can celebrate a new coupling. I would hate for your First Coupling to happen without celebration.

She'd been sure Hama would extend her blessing. A weight formed inside her. It almost kept her from rising. Stumbling to her feet, she blurted out, *Can I not be given special permission? Am I not special to you?* Right after she sent the thought, Enga cringed. She was being disrespectful.

These are harder times than we have ever had, Enga Dancing Flower. It is not a time to start babies. We may be facing hunger such as we've never known.

Hama reached to Enga and touched her hand, then let it go. *Everything is changing. I will tell you of news I received. You are the first to hear this.*

Enga felt privileged she was learning fresh news before the rest of the tribe.

A member of the Gata tribe contacted me from afar with thought-speak, late, after last sun. Do you remember the Gata people?

Enga nodded, standing over her leader. *Yes, I remember trading with them once when I was younger. They are beings much like us.*

Yes, they dwell in the direction of last sun.

Why does this concern me?

It concerns our tribe. It tells us how hard the times are now. Their leader died from a sickness and the tribe is quarreling like a pack of coyotes over a piece of meat.

But we would never do that. Where is their new leader?

They are unable to elect a new leader. There is no one to hold them together. They are not hunting.

Not hunting? A tribe had to hunt, Enga knew.

They may starve in the next season, the Season of Dark.

Enga shuddered. *But our tribe would never do these things. We would share our meat. We would hunt. We would elect a new leader.*

I hope we would. The Gata female, continued Hama, *asked me if we could take any of them in. I had to tell her no. I don't know if we can feed our own people in the coming Dark Season. We must hope it is mild and short.*

Enga knew that Hama was more worried than she had let the rest of the tribe know. *So you think these things could happen to us?*

I do not know. I would not like to find out.

It worried Enga for her leader to be so uncertain.

Then Hama opened her mind further to Enga. *I am so sorry about your First Coupling, Enga Dancing Flower. I know you hope to have it soon, and I hope for that also.*

Enga felt a glow inside. Hama did hope for good things for her. And having Hama open her mind so frankly like this felt like the old days when Enga and Ung lived with Hama, then their foster mother. That was before she was elected the leader, when she had been called Jansa Wild Wind.

Hama mused aloud, sharing more of her thoughts. *The wind is pushing the game away from us, pushing us to follow it, away from the Great Guiding Bear who dwells in Mother Sky at dark time. There are difficult times ahead, Enga Dancing Flower.*

Hama's thoughts gave Enga much to consider and she left, deep in reflection, to prepare for the long day ahead. She had danced well. The hunt would succeed. It had to.

*****

At first sun the tribe gathered at the central fire for the hunt. As all raised their voices together, hoping the Spirits would hear them, Enga Dancing Flower and Ung Strong Arm exchanged their private fears.

There was no game to be found the last time we went out, thought-spoke Ung. *Not even hares or deer.*

But Kokat No Ear found a herd at the watering hole where they used to be.

Ung shrugged. *That doesn't mean they'll still be there by the time we arrive.*

The tribe chanted aloud their fervent hope of a kill, asking the Spirit of the Hunt and Dakadaga to bless their endeavors.

Their height was not great, most of them barely over five feet, but their limbs were thick and muscular. The hair on the heads of the youngest members riffled in the wind, some the color of the flames, like

Enga's. The adults who were to participate in the hunt had gathered their locks into hunting braids that hung down their backs.

"Leela tza sheesh. Dakadaga tza sheesh."

Enga Dancing Flower joined the others in chanting for Leela, the Hunt Spirit, and Dakadaga, the Sky Spirit, to bless the kill. Then she crouched to eat from the meager food, taken from the nearly empty storage pit.

Dried fish and dried hare again, complained Ung.

At least we have some stores left, answered Enga. She knew a small amount of smoked peccary and mammoth remained.

That will be enough for, maybe, one more full moon. Then our stored food will be gone.

When they had finished their inadequate meal, Hama addressed them mentally. *If this hunt does not go well, we will consider other options. Even if the hunt brings us food, it may not be enough. In the past, the males have gone on trading trips. We must think about such a trading trip. We have extra knives and our knives are good. Others like to trade for them.*

Several of the females made sour faces. They did not like their males gone.

Enga and the other hunters took up the spears they had laid beside the fire the night before, the ones they had danced around. The males picked up their flint knives, stuck them in the pouches hanging from their loin cloths, and flung the large hunting skins over their shoulders. They would use these skins to drag back chunks of meat and piles of mammoth skin. The two males appointed to guard duty, the Elders, and the young would stay behind.

The hunters filed past their three Elders standing in a line at the edge of the Paved Place, the Most High Female, the Most High Male, and the one-eyed Storyteller. Hama drew herself up to her full height and rattled her gourd in time with the chanting as the hunting party departed.

Usually Hama, the Most High Female, stood shoulder to shoulder with her current mate, the Most High Male. Today, the Storyteller stood between them.

Enga queried Ung. *Do you think Hama is changing mates?*

She has done it before. It bothered no one.

But our tribe doesn't need complications right now. Enga shoved this notion to the back of her mind to concentrate on the hunt.

The blessing of the Elders cheered Enga. The hunt had to be successful. She saw this in all the hopeful faces, read it in all the thoughts.

And if they brought back enough food, Hama would surely grant her request to couple with Tog Flint Shaper. Enga folded these thoughts deep inside, wrapped in dark purple, so no one would discover them. She must not detract others from concentrating on their task.

The Hamapa hunting party trotted over the plain, dotted with lakes and woods, that lay in the direction of last sun, at a steady pace, stopping only at high sun for a few bites of the dried mammoth meat the males carried. They squatted under a stand of tall poplars with leaves of brilliant yellow, almost the color of Sister Sun. Mother Sky blew a soft breath of wind toward them and a few of the branches let go of their leaves, which fluttered down to the grass beside them.

Soon the band rose and began loping through the waving grass toward their destination again. Kokat No Ear, an older male with a puckered face and no ears, his appearance caused by a fire accident long ago, led them toward the herd he had seen on the last scouting mission. His leg had also been injured many summers ago, on the night Enga and her birth sister, Ung, had been brought into the tribe. In spite of this he moved well. The mammoth herd had not been seen near here for several months until Kokat had spotted them.

Mother Sky began to exhale her breath as a brisk northern wind, but Sister Sun still held warmth in her embrace and they welcomed it. Soon, in another moon cycle, her light would hold no heat and the wind would cut into their faces.

Kokat No Ear encouraged them by sending out an image of the area where mammoths took their water, almost one sun's journey from the village. They trotted on and reached their destination well before last sun, just before the time when mammoths would come. Enga and the other females had slain two peccaries—those tasty, succulent pigs—three full moons ago here, at this same lake on the wide rolling plain. That had been the last successful kill.

They rested in the tall spruce and poplar trees at the edge of the lake, waiting until hunting time arrived. As last sun approached, Enga and Ung broke limbs off a spruce tree, crouched in the tall grass, and covered themselves with the fragrant branches. Enga knew this did not take away their odor, but it could confuse the animals. They knelt, clutching their weapons, with plenty of space between them as was their hunting custom.

The other two spear throwers remained in the woods, their bodies pressed close into the needles of the spruce trees. One of the hunters, Fee Long Thrower, was large with a baby, but, for now, she could still spear without hindrance. She was usually a strong and graceful runner, Enga thought, but not so close to birthing.

She waited with her tribal sisters for the animals to come and take water. Her brothers also waited in the woods, staying out of the way until the kill. When she and her twin sister started attacking, joined by the two females in the woods, the males would emerge and attempt to distract the beasts.

This was the most dangerous time. Some of her brothers would try to drive the rest of the animals away; some would concentrate on the animal chosen for the kill, teasing and taunting it so the spear throwers could get close enough to stab it.

After they brought down the animal, the male Hamapas would skin and butcher it, then use their might to drag the hunks of meat home on the large pieces of scraped skin they had brought.

Dragonflies buzzed over the tops of the grasses and two lingering butterflies lit down, flew up, and lit down again. The wind had quieted and the dry grasses no longer rustled, magnifying the silence of the plains. Light faded and Brother Moon appeared.

A scent on the still air made Enga lift her head and peek. The herd was still in the distance, approaching slowly. Enga had seen this herd before, but not for a long while. As always, she felt as she had the first time she ever saw a mammoth. The monstrous beasts never failed to awe her with their huge shaggy bodies and their immense, curving tusks, gleaming now in Brother Moon's light.

A roar split the dusk and the throwers lifted their heads slightly, all senses on full alert. They had heard the mighty trumpet of a mammoth. Brother Earth shook with the ponderous footfalls. Enga's nostrils spread wide, flooded with the exciting animal scent. Her grip tightened on her spear. Ung was the better thrower, but Enga had killed, too. She sent a silent message to Dakadaga, *Give us a kill tonight.*

Eyes wide, Enga peered through the spruce needles of her cover. Brother Moon floated, full-bodied, through Mother Sky. He lit the animals and threw their shadows across the grass. Mother Sky's breath blew the scent of the hidden huntresses away from the herd. Maybe she was trying to help the Hamapa.

Enga sent a thought to Ung. *Do you see the difference? This herd used to have many mammoths, more than the number of all my fingers and all my toes.* Their numbers were noticeably fewer now. Even so, the animals were magnificent, towering over her by at least the height of two Hamapas, one standing on the other's shoulders. Her palms prickled and her chest beat hard against her hunting braid, which had fallen forward and hung between her breasts, reaching to her waist. She wished the braid were behind her. She did not dare make the movement to fling it back now.

A bright yellow warning thought came from Ung. *Quiet. Stay calm.*

Ung Strong Arm was always calm. Enga Dancing Flower was not. Maybe that was why Ung was the better spear thrower.

Her breech cloth bothered Enga. It bunched between her thigh and lower leg as she squatted. A calf muscle jumped. But she did not shift.

The beasts shuffled toward the water hole. Their round feet sank into the mud at the edge of the water with squishing noises. The smaller animals waded into the water to play. A solitary large male stayed behind, guarding them. He would drink last. The huntresses must wait until the smaller ones, the females and young, were close.

Soon. Soon.

Enga heard a strange rustling in the grass near where Ung squatted. Was a small creature approaching? The scent was not that of a mammoth. Enga raised her spear arm slightly. Maybe she could kill whatever it was.

Puzzled, she saw Kokat No Ear rushing from the woods toward them. He was sending a mental message, tinged with the crimson hues of terror. His eyes and mouth were ovals of panic in his fire-scarred face, his arms waving wildly.

Ung cried aloud, "Gaa!"

Enga sprang up with alarm and ran to her sister. Ung lay on her side, both hands pressing her sturdy thigh. A boar fled through the grass, a lone long-nosed peccary, headed for the woods. For a brief moment Enga considered trying to spear it, but she was distracted by the Red of Ung that dripped from the beast's two long, white tusks.

Enga looked down. The Red of Ung also spilled onto the grass, dark colored in the moonlight. Its sharp odor assailed Enga. Anguish and pain radiated from Ung. Enga bent to her twin and saw a wide gash in her thigh. Enga clamped her jaw on her anger and hurled her spear, futilely, after the peccary.

The other throwers and the male carriers ran to them. They barely noticed the herd of mammoths thunder away, across the plain.

Chapter 3

Teek Pathfinder, the youthful son of the Healer, knew what to do. He tore a strip from one of the hunting skins and bound her leg to slow the flow of Red from Ung Strong Arm. Enga Dancing Flower breathed her relief and went to lie next to her twin for the duration of dark time.

Some of them would have to return to the village with Ung, but the group did not want to travel when they could not see the predators waiting for them. Too many had died that way.

Fee Long Thrower shifted her pregnant belly and, taking stock of the troop, began to bed down in the grass between the watering hole and the woods.

Kokat No Ear is not here, she thought-spoke.

A finger of cold walked up Enga's back and she sat up. *Where is he?* asked Enga. *When he rushed toward us, he must have been trying to warn us of the peccary he had seen.*

Tog Flint Shaper read her thought and her fear. He summoned several others. *Help me search the tall grasses.* Then Tog spied a smear of dark liquid in the grass, leading toward the trees.

He must be in the forest, thought-spoke Tog. He ran into the woods, black with nightfall now, following the even blacker trail of Red and summoning the other three males to come with him.

The females squatted next to each other and waited. The males sent no thoughts to them. Enga checked on Ung. She was sound asleep. The wound still bled, but now seeped instead of spurting. Enga felt her shoulders relax just a notch.

Brother Moon moved through the sky, shedding shards of light through the spruce trees, showing the trampled mud of the water hole and touching the small band of spear throwers with its pale glow. The females did not expect good news. They dared not look at each other. Hunting was dangerous. This had been proven to the Hamapa over and over.

Enga reimagined her dancing. Had she let her thoughts stray too often from her task? Was it her fault the hunt had ended badly? She must not think so much of Tog when she danced next time.

At last Tog Flint Shaper relayed back an image of Kokat No Ear. The females held hands and bowed their heads to receive it. He sent them a flash of sorrow. Enga and the others steadied their breathing and closed their eyes to receive the vision.

Kokat lay on his side, on a bed of moss, his arms curled over his head protectively. He appeared asleep, a peaceful expression on his poor scarred face. But just below his face, Red poured from his neck. His Red and his life had left him through that wound. Tog Flint Shaper showed them how he believed Kokat had died. Enga felt Tog's sharp grief and sent him a thought of comfort.

The peccary, thought-spoke Tog, *must have attacked Ung Strong Arm, then gored Kokat No Ear and dragged him here, into the woods.*

Fee Long Thrower answered him. *We were so intent on tending to Ung Strong Arm, we did not even receive feelings of distress from him.*

After the males hauled Kokat No Ear out of the woods, several of them stripped his body of his hunting garments, a lion-skin breech cloth and foot wrappings.

We must notify the tribe, thought-spoke Fee Long Thrower. *Nanno Green Eyes should know. And everyone else, too, of course.*

Fee took it upon herself to do this. Enga stayed out of that stream of thought. Nanno Green Eyes, Kokat's mate, had never liked either Enga or her birth sister. Enga never went nearer Nanno than she had to. Now

Nanno would have more reason to detest Enga and Ung, since she would probably blame them for Kokat's death. Enga gritted her teeth, determined to shield Ung from Nanno's wrath when they returned.

Nanno's outcry drilled into Enga's head, however much she tried to shut it out. It came sharp and piercing and impossible to ignore, throbbing through Enga's mind. After it subsided somewhat, the small band readied Kokat's body for his final resting place.

I will stay with Ung Strong Arm while they go to expose Kokat No Ear, offered Fee.

It is my place to stay with my birth sister, answered Enga.

You might feel better if you assist the final rites for Kokat. You will be with Ung for a long time in the future.

Enga wasn't sure that was the right thing for her to do, but she did not feel like resisting the older female.

Teek Pathfinder and another male, their way well lit by fat Brother Moon, went to find a suitable site. The two males returned soon and Enga joined the dispirited group as they carried the naked body to a large flat rock amid the grass on the expanse of prairie.

The Hamapa would normally smear his body with bear fat so his going would be quick, but they had none with them, so, after sprinkling a few flower petals on him and mourning briefly, they turned away and left. None of them wanted to witness what would now happen to their tribal brother. Kokat's body would return to the natural order of things, feeding the animals that would then feed the Hamapa.

Enga curled up next to Ung, but slept only a little, and fitfully, disturbed by dreams of peccaries and their dripping tusks. She awoke often to make sure the Red of Ung had not begun to spurt again. She knew Ung would lose her life if too much Red departed from her body.

At one point during dark time, Enga jerked upright. She had not danced her best. She hadn't concentrated on the hunt while she danced. Instead, she had tried to impress Tog, had thought of him. Again, she wondered if the hunt was a devastating failure because of her. Ung shifted and groaned and Enga checked her binding, then lay down beside her. She slept little the rest of dark time.

When Sister Sun should have embraced her Mother Sky, she instead hid behind thick layers of gray cloud garments, and Mother Sky began shedding light tears. Hot tears of frustration sprang to Enga's own eyes when she realized they would make their return trip in rain and mud.

Tog and Bahg Swift Feet, another male on the mission, volunteered to carry Ung back to the village. The remaining two males and the other two females would stay and attempt to get a mammoth when the herd came back to the watering place. If it came back.

When Ung had been settled on a hunting skin for the journey home, Tog and Bahg carefully picked up the pallet, shouldered their burden, and started back. On Fee's advice, they avoided sending news ahead of the double tragedy—made even worse by their not having gotten any meat. Kokat's death would be enough for the tribe to deal with now, without Ung's injury.

Enga, carrying the bundle of Kokat's garments, trotted alongside the pallet that held her birth sister and occasionally stroked her waves of short auburn hair. She tried to keep her worries to herself. Her steps sometimes faltered with her tiredness, but she slogged on.

Ung kept pressing on her wound, but it had opened when she was moved and the Red flowed again. Several times, the bouncing of the skin pallet made Ung wince and cry out. But the carriers of the pallet did not slow. They knew they must hurry to get treatment for Ung. They trotted briskly through the light rain along the path to home.

Slogging through the mud, Tog Flint Shaper tightened his grip on the skin that held Ung and mentally reassured Enga. *The wound of Ung Strong Arm is deep, but no bone is broken. It will heal. Our Healer will make Ung Strong Arm whole again.*

Enga shot him a grateful look, but continued to fret. She hoped she was keeping her worries from Ung. She realized she hadn't kept them from Tog. It was hard when she was so weary. Her head ached so.

Even with their accelerated pace, by the time they returned it was nearing the time for Sister Sun to retire. The two guards sensed their approach and broadcast brightly hued public thoughts to alert the tribe. Most of them ran out to greet the hunting party, grinning and noisily cheering, thinking the skin held a slain animal, as it should, and mistaking the intense, jumbled emotions of the hunters for joy. When they saw Ung their jubilation changed to murmuring concern for her. Her leg now bled freely and she held her face tight, her eyes pressed shut in pain.

Nanno Green Eyes emerged from the direction of Hama's wipiti. Spotting the small bundle of her mate's clothing, she ran past Ung, screamed, and snatched up the packet from Enga. She sank to the ground, cradling it and moaning softly. Enga touched her shoulder in sympathy, but Nanno shook her off with a sharp twitch.

Enga withdrew her hand as if a wasp had stung her. Nanno's bitterness almost burnt. Nanno had held Enga and Ung responsible for her mate's crippled leg ever since the night the two little girls had been rescued, but Enga had always hoped Nanno would someday change her attitude.

Other females surrounded Nanno Green Eyes and embraced her, trying to soothe her grief. Enga returned to Ung.

The pale New One approached. He made his strange sounds and put his thin hand on the forehead of Ung. She did not pull away. She opened her eyes to see who touched her. The New One drew back at this, his own odd eyes, as usual, cast down and nearly shut.

Zhoo of Still Waters, the Healer, came running from the woods and motioned for the carriers to put Ung into her wipiti. Enga followed. Zhoo gestured to Jeek, her son of eleven summers, to bring articles of healing from her stores. He ran out of the wipiti, his thin young legs pumping hard.

Ung, my sister, Ung, were the only thoughts Enga could form. Her head throbbed. *Be well, be well.* She dared not think beyond the moment. Kokat No Ear had just died. So many Hamapa died in hunts. She would not let herself think about Ung being one of them.

Sannum Straight Hair came to the doorway and looked in. Enga, grateful to see him, beckoned him.

I would like you to stand beside Ung Strong Arm with me, she told him.

If you wish it, I will gladly do it. The sturdy arms of Sannum had carried the two orphan girls to the village the night Kokat had been injured. That night, a special bond had formed between Enga and Sannum.

Others looked in on Ung, too, and some took seats just outside the door flap.

While Zhoo of Still Waters waited for Jeek to return, she reached for one hand of Ung and one of Enga. The hands of the Healer were cool and steady. Her gaze was steady, too. Her birth mother had been the Healer before her and, when young, Zhoo had been her helper and apprentice. She had seen and treated many wounds.

Her own mate had been killed with the tusk of a mammoth. Zhoo herself had speared the huge beast, then summoned the carriers to butcher it. One of the carriers was her mate. When he approached the animal, it lifted its head, then its body. It was not dead. All the males escaped without injury except her mate. Zhoo of Still Waters never hunted again.

Her calm way now soothed Enga. She felt the pounding inside her head slow slightly. Ung relaxed just a bit, too. But the Red still flowed.

Soon the Healer's young son reappeared with his arms full. He set his burdens down inside the door flap, then handed his mother a sheaf of long grasses. Zhoo laid them on the stump her wipiti was built around and sliced them with her flint knife. After she balled up the cut grasses and stuffed them into the wound, they saw no more Red.

Enga released a loud breath of relief. She reeled with dizziness. Sannum reached out to catch her, and she leaned against him. Ung gave a weak smile, her face almost the color of the New One.

Do not take the attention of the Healer away from my wound, joked Ung.

Enga wanted to give a light answer, but couldn't. Sannum eased her to the ground and they sat together near the inside wall, out of the way.

Next, Jeek handed Zhoo the skin bag of bear fat. His hair, streaked blond-brown by the sun, had fallen from its leather binding into his eyes. He took swipes at it to see what he was doing.

Zhoo, her hair streaked nearly the color of Jeek's, but cropped sensibly short so it would not interfere with her work, dipped bear fat from the bag with strong fingers and smeared the grease over the matted grasses. She topped this with a layer of honey squeezed from a comb she kept in the hollow gourd that had belonged to her birth mother.

Zhoo smiled at Enga. *I think she will recover. It is believed by some that twins are unlucky, but Ung Strong Arm is very lucky today.*

Enga's return smile was weary, barely a smile, but she was happy. The aching in her skull had left and her head felt light enough to float away.

Enga was aware of Jeek's pride in his birth mother's competence. It swelled inside him and spread across his face. The whole tribe took pride in Zhoo of Still Waters. No other tribe they knew had a Healer such as Zhoo, more skilled even than her mother had been. And now, this day, Enga felt a special warmth toward her. If Ung didn't recover from the goring, it would not be the fault of the Healer.

Enga lay down on the dirt floor next to her sister. She felt Zhoo cover her with a thick bearskin and saw her gesture to her son, Jeek, to keep quiet, just before her heavy eyelids dropped.

*****

Nanno Green Eyes, pacing the stones around the fire, wrapped her thoughts in the inky purple of midnight, and they were dark, dark thoughts. She shielded the hot flame of hatred that burned inside her, overlaying it with the grief that consumed her. She would miss her kind, gentle mate. More than she could bear!

Kokat No Ear had been doing his task, going on the hunt, and hunts were always fraught with danger. But Nanno knew the danger was increased by having the twins along. Twins were bad luck. Hama denied it, but Nanno knew it was true.

His death was the fault of those two interlopers, Enga Dancing Flower and Ung Strong Arm. The tribe believed they were exceptional, not unlucky, because they were twins, but Nanno had always thought they were no different than any other stray animal. The tribe should have turned them away. A tiger had clawed Kokat No Ear's leg their first night with the Hamapa, as he rescued them, and he had walked with pain since then. And, if the thought-pictures were true, Kokat had now died because of these two, because he was warning them.

He was gone.

She had never hated anyone as much as she hated those two at this moment. She twisted around and searched for Enga, but the young female remained in Zhoo's wipiti with that bossy, overbearing sister of hers. Nanno hoped Ung would die.

As full darkness fell and the emergency was over, Lakala Rippling Water, the Singer, came to the side of the fire from the Healer's wipiti, where she had been helping keep watch on Ung, and led a Death Chant for Kokat No Ear. A few at a time, the Hamapa gathered and sat broadcasting their own individual memorial thoughts of Kokat.

Nanno sat with them and raised narrowed eyes to Mother Sky, her face tight, her body rigid.

Panan One Eye, the Storyteller, remembered the day little Kokat, as a toddler, fell into the fire. It had scarred his face and burned both ears away. That had earned him his name of No Ear at his Passage Ceremony when he was fifteen.

Cabat the Thick, the Most High Male, who was one summer older than Kokat, broadcast his memories of them as boys, climbing trees, splashing in the creek, running footraces, and filching berries from the storage pits.

Panan and Cabat, as Elders, had quickly donned knee-length mourning cloaks of black bearskin. The rest smeared their faces with ashes as they arrived.

Others floated their memories out to their tribal brothers and sisters, but none came from Nanno. She made sure of that. She received the reminiscence of Enga Dancing Flower on the night she and her birth sister were rescued, how she had cried at the sight of the puckered skin on Kokat's face. Enga also thought-spoke of Kokat growing fond of her and not ever, once, holding anything against her or Ung. Enga thought-spoke of her love for Kokat and her desolation at his death.

Nanno let her head fall forward. No, he had not blamed the girls. She herself felt enough blame toward them for both her and her deceased mate. She clenched her eyes tight in rage.

Chapter 4

New evidence has emerged that Neanderthals co-existed with anatomically modern humans for at least 1,000 years in central France.

—From http://www.abc.net.au/news/newsitems/200509/s14509 49.htm, ABC news article, September 1, 2005

Though Hama had not yet appeared, it was fully dark, time for the nightly council. The rest of the tribe gathered. Jeek, son of the Healer, ambled toward the group and plopped down onto the stones, exhausted but at the same time exhilarated by the work he had done for Ung Strong Arm, assisting his birth mother. It appeared Ung would recover.

The Hamapa tribe sat around their fire on the Paved Place. Akkal, the young, dark-haired Fire Tender, a serious-minded boy two summers older than Jeek's eleven, had done his job well. Jeek edged closer to the fire and its warmth. He shivered in his mind and his body to think what they would do without their fire.

The Most High Male had convened them to ponder their situation and make decisions.

They awaited Hama to lead them in their discussion, but she did not appear. Lakala Rippling Water, the Singer of the tribe, hesitated, then began a Song of Asking. She asked for blessing from Dakadaga, the

Most High Spirit, and pleaded with the Spirit of the Hunt, who had not been kind on the latest outing. Jeek knew what they would talk about. The tribe must decide what to do about the food shortage. The best spear thrower was disabled with a gored leg. Fee Long Thrower, the next best, was very near to birthing a baby. She had not returned from the hunt, having stayed with Vala Golden Hair and two males to attempt another hunt if the mammoth returned to the watering place. But Jeek was sure Fee would not hunt for a while. This was to have been her last hunt before the baby came.

Zhoo of Still Waters stayed with Ung in her wipiti tonight, but Jeek saw that Enga Dancing Flower had awakened for the gathering and sat near Tog Flint Shaper.

The discussion and decision would come after the telling of the Saga by Panan One Eye, the Storyteller. Hama should be there by then. The Storyteller's head always made Jeek think of a bird's egg, shiny and bald, and his cheeks smooth and beardless. He sat near the place where Hama usually sat. Panan had been the mate of Hama once, but now she coupled with Cabat the Thick, who was the Most High Male.

Jeek glimpsed the New One lingering at the edge of the group. Jeek did not believe he could follow any of their thought-discussions.

After the song of Lakala Rippling Water, old Panan One Eye closed both his eyes, the seeing one and the non-seeing one, and transmitted his thoughts to everyone with a deep, important shade of scarlet. The Storyteller held the Saga, the history of the tribe, in his mind. It had been given to him by the Storyteller before him, and all the Storytellers before that, for the Storyteller must always keep the Saga, a sacred thing of the Hamapa people. He told parts of it during their councils.

This night Panan sent a thought-picture of long ago. Long, long, long ago. Jeek watched Panan for a moment, fascinated at how the firelight danced on his hairless head. Then, to better receive tonight's piece of Saga, the lad closed his eyes. He jerked them wide open, however, when the vision arrived. It showed him the land of the Hamapa, but it looked different, strange, and covered with ice.

Yes, young Jeek, came the assurance of Panan. *The Ancient Ones told of a Time of Great Ice. That time happened in a faraway place, before the Time of the Crossing.*

Those are ancient times. Long ago, thought-spoke Jeek. *That terrible Great Ice will not happen now.*

That Ice Time may happen again, answered Panan. *Much snow fell at the most recent Dark Season. The Seasons of Dark and Coldness are becoming darker and colder. And longer. Lengthening as the nights are now.*

Jeek felt the collective shudder of the tribe. Then he caught the scoffing of three adolescent males from across the circle.

These are only the stories of an old one. Crossings. Ice. Ha.

The sturdy youth, Kung, led the trio. They sneered and snorted and squinted, and flung a mocking disbelief back to Panan One Eye. *Maybe your memory is no good, old one.*

The other members of the tribe stared at Kung with frowns and harsh vibrations, and his thoughts faded. But Jeek could tell that he did not bury them deep. If Hama were here she would quell his impudence. Why was she so late?

Jeek shivered again at the Storyteller's vision, still before them. He wrapped his arms around his skinny knees for protection against the cold of the air and of the bleak thought-pictures.

He could clearly see the ice Panan envisioned. It stretched, vast and thick, across the land that now held forests and streams, rolling hills and plains and caves. All was lost under the ice. The air of the vision gripped them with bitter cold, and its sky hung heavy with gray clouds. Snow fell, vast snow that turned to Great Ice.

What could the Hamapa do in such a terrible time? asked Jeek. *Would there be any game?* Jeek envisioned his tribe hungry, crying.

Panan One Eye sent new ideas. *The Ancient Ones lived in a Time of Great Ice. We can live in that time also. We need only prepare. But now, put this Saga away. The Hamapa must hunt again. Soon. Can we hunt with the new sun?*

Nanno Green Eyes waved her hands and thought-spoke with crimson urgency. *We must hunt soon. But some of the hunters are still gone. The Hamapa must have meat to dry and new furs and skins to replace those that are worn out. Tog Flint Shaper caught our last large fish three full moons ago. The dried fish and dried flesh are almost gone. Can we get more fish?*

Jeek had an intrusive, unexpected vision of a giant beaver. He did not know why this occurred to him. The tribe hunted many animals but never touched the giant beaver.

Kung funneled a private, individual thought to Jeek. *Why do you contemplate beavers, stupid boy? That will do us no good. Try to think of the tribe, like you are supposed to.*

Not that Kung put the concerns of the tribe ahead of his own very often, in Jeek's opinion. But Jeek did try to think of the tribe now.

Because the two females most skilled with the long spear, Ung Strong Arm and Fee Long Thrower, could not soon hunt, Jeek knew the tribe was in trouble. No other female could bring down the great beasts. Enga Dancing Flower could throw the spear with some skill, but not as well as the other two. The young girls of the tribe, including pretty Gunda, were being trained, and had, once or twice, brought down small animals. But they were not ready to make a hunt for a large beast.

Panan One Eye, answering Nanno, turned to the subject of the fish traps. He nodded to Nanno and sent an image of a trap with only one fish, and another of a trap with no fish. Rocks, piled in the nearby stream to form a narrowing opening, usually provided plenty of fish for the Hamapa. They need only wade to the place where the rock piles lay a single hand-width apart and scoop up the number of fish required.

There are always fewer fish when we approach Dark Season, thought-spoke the Most High Male, the second ranking member of the tribe, pulling on his fleshy lower lip.

Not this few, shot back Panan. Cabat leaned back, eyeing Panan. Jeek couldn't help but detect the undertone of rancor in the exchange. The air that prickled between them made him squirm.

His mind wandered off again, picturing himself lugging home a huge carcass, enough to feed the tribe until the next Warm Season came.

Kung's sharp scoffing pierced his daydream. *Ha. If anyone can save the tribe, it will be someone bigger and stronger than you, little skinny one. Someone like me.*

Jeek sensed the minds of Kung's two adolescent companions tumbling along with that of Kung. All three funneled in on Jeek so the others could not overhear.

Jeek lowered his head. He needed to guard his thoughts better. More dark colors.

Nanno Green Eyes stood and thought-spoke. *It is time for a decision about our food problem.*

But we cannot decide without Hama, countered Panan One Eye. He swiveled toward Jeek. *You must go and fetch her.*

The young boy jumped to his feet. *He* would fetch Hama? Jeek couldn't keep a tiny grin from his lips. He strutted with exaggerated importance past Kung and his gang on his way to her wipiti. He, Jeek, had been chosen to fetch Hama. Not Kung, but Jeek.

*****

Enga Dancing Flower, fighting her tiredness, watched Jeek leave the circle and head toward the large, set-apart wipiti. But something was not right. A chill swirled through her mind. Wide awake now, Enga sat up straight. Hama would not have missed the intense disturbance caused by the wounds of Ung Strong Arm, or the deep sorrow over the death of Kokat No Ear. No matter how involved Hama became in her narrow, private thoughts, she could not have ignored the profound, widespread emotion of the tribe that night. Especially that of her own birth sister, Nanno Green Eyes, on the death of her mate.

Enga contemplated those around her and tried to read their minds. But whenever she was weary she had trouble receiving the feelings of the Hamapa. Thought waves came faintly to her. As near as she could tell, most were uneasy, like her, without understanding why. If Ung were here she would take action, for she always knew what to do. No one moved. Except Jeek. He drew nearer the wipiti of Hama.

Enga made a decision. She jumped up and hurried across the Paved Place after Jeek, sending him a message to halt. He hesitated. When he turned toward her she transmitted her fear with a subtle, narrowed thought. She felt him understand her concern immediately. A quick thinker, she thought. He must have perceived the unease of the tribe, too. He chewed on a hank of his hair and gave Enga a worried look.

Hama is old, twice twenty. We all know she will die someday, he thought-spoke.

But, Enga somehow knew, the situation was worse than what Jeek feared.

Chapter 5

A rush of intuition, of dread, and of bravery overcame Enga Dancing Flower.

Hang back. I will look in on Hama myself. You stay where you are.

Well before she reached the entrance to Hama's wipiti, a familiar odor drifted out to Enga. The odor of death.

She snatched the tent flap and threw it to the side. A soft sound escaped from Enga and her knees weakened, but held her up.

It was cold. The interior fire had gone out but light from the central fire at the gathering leaked into the dwelling through the open doorway.

She took a step inside. Brother Earth seemed to tilt beneath her feet. The edges of her vision turned gray and she swayed. Then she caught herself on the mammoth rib that supported the wall and sucked her feelings inside.

Something terrible had happened here. Something that went contrary to the order of things. Something that threatened to overwhelm Enga. She must keep herself in control. She must act as Ung Strong Arm would act. Calm, calm.

She shut down her outgoing thoughts, summoned up the very darkest colors she could, moonless night colors, keeping her horror from radiating to the group outside until she could get her ideas in order.

Red spilled from Hama's body. It glistened bright and shiny next to

Hama, but had dried to brown, the color of old leaves, at the edge of a large puddle. Enga stepped around the blood, hoping against her fears that Hama was alive. The little red hairs on her arms lifted and her scalp prickled with fear.

Must not touch the sacred Red of Most High Hama. Only Zhoo of Still Waters, the Healer, can touch this Red. Must see why the Red pours. Must see if there is any life left in her.

Enga knelt beside the bearskin. Hama lay on her side with her face away. Enga gripped the grizzled head and turned it a little. The eyes were closed. It looked as if Hama were asleep.

Her thoughts are usually kept private, unless she is announcing something to the tribe. She had the ability to cloak her contemplations in darkest midnight black. Blacker than Enga would ever be able to. *But she was attacked—someone should have noticed that. Could even Hama keep such distress to herself?* Squinting in the dim light, Enga saw it. Now she understood why no dying emotions had gone out.

A caribou antler prong stuck out of her back.

Her hands froze in midair, hovering over the body. Hama must have been stabbed, killed so suddenly she had no time to form a single inkling. Stabbed with this sharp antler. Stabbed from behind.

Enga shook herself and gripped Hama's shoulders and turned her more. The lifeless body flipped over as much as it could against the antler. Enga drew in air and blinked back the beginnings of tears. Hama's stained moose-fur tunic gaped open in the front. The antler buttons that had been a gift from the New One, and which he himself had fastened to the tunic, were not in place. They lay scattered on the dirt floor around her sleeping skin. Holes in her tunic gaped where the buttons had been torn out.

Enga swallowed with a dry mouth.

I have lost my beloved Hama. She who was the birth mother of Tog Flint Shaper, she who was the leader of the tribe, she who was beloved by me because she raised me. I love her so.

But what had happened to her? Could she have fallen on the antler?

Or did someone stab her?

The vision of Hama standing with the two males in her life, her first mate, Panan One Eye, and her present mate, Cabat the Thick, popped into her head.

The Elders saw the hunting party off, as usual, but they stood out of order. Usually Hama stood next to her mate, Cabat the Thick. Last time, her former mate, Panan One Eye, stood next to her.

Enga remembered wondering what was happening among them, wondering if Hama was changed mates. But then she had needed to concentrate on the hunt. That was the last time she had seen Hama alive.

The vision faded and Enga returned to the sight before her. *Too much Red has spilled. First Ung Strong Arm, then Kokat No Ear. And now Hama.*

Just to make certain, Enga reached down and lightly touched her. Hama's chest did not move. No breath came or went. Her gray-streaked braid spilled into the puddle of Red and stuck there.

Enga fought back the tears that wanted to spring forth while she poked her head out the doorway, motioned for Jeek to stay where he was. With difficulty, because they were so overwhelming, she shielded her dire speculations from him. She balled her fists and kept a mental grip on midnight hues to contain her thoughts. Sannum Straight Hair had risen and was slowly headed this way. She ducked back in to think. She wanted to figure out what gone on and she did not have much time. Was it possible Hama had fallen hard enough onto the antler to kill herself? No, Enga thought. She could not picture that.

A tear finally seeped from the inside corner of one eye. It trickled down beside her nose. Enga reeled while time once again seemed to whirl around her. She took a step. Stumbled, her foot caught on something. She bent to examine it and saw a figure carved from wood, like the one the New One had given her, except it was not a mammoth.

It lay half buried in the hard-packed dirt floor. Enga stooped and dug it out.

What a marvel, she thought, with an intake of breath. *It is even more beautiful than my mammoth. This has to be the work of the New One.*

The New One had carved a figure of Hama, her ample curves, the strong bones of her face, her large, wide-set eyes, her loose, flowing hair, even the woven bracelets at her wrists. The carving held dirt in some of the crevices but Enga could not take time to clean it now. She set it where she had found it. Others would have to decide what should be done with it.

There was no more Hama. How could that be? Hama had been like a birth mother to Enga. Her love for Hama flowed down her face with her tears. Then another idea sprouted inside her.

If someone had killed Hama, who was it? And now, where was that killer?

*****

After Enga Dancing Flower emerged from the wipiti she stood for a moment, gathering herself. Then she used the brightest colors she could summon, the flare of the gaudiest bedding of Sister Sun, to broadcast her message.

Brothers and sisters, our Hama lives no more. Her life has left her.

Enga then sent a mental picture of the leader lying next to a drying pool of Red. She had a faint reply from Ung, but couldn't tell exactly what she was conveying.

Sannum Straight Hair arrived first and put a welcome arm around Enga's shoulder. She leaned into his warmth and rested her head on his chest, still feeling disoriented and shaky.

The rest of the tribe rose and gathered outside the dwelling. Some of the females peeked inside the tent to see for themselves, but most let Enga's mental image suffice.

The birth sister of Hama, Nanno Green Eyes, entered the dwelling and spent some moments inside, alone. When she climbed out, she brushed teardrops from her face. Her hand left a dirty streak on her cheek. Nanno took a few shaky steps before some of her tribal sisters rushed over and helped her to sit by the fire. She stared straight ahead, her light green eyes wild-looking. As much as Enga disliked Nanno, she could not help but share the pain of her two losses so close together.

Enga felt compelled to send Nanno a thought. *I know you are feeling pain. I share it with you, Nanno Green Eyes.* Her answer was a narrowed look with those green eyes, but no return thought-speak.

Panan One Eye, the Storyteller, went in after Nanno, but only stayed a short while.

Cabat the Thick, the Most High Male, arrived with the last of the clan. Even though he was the most recent mate of the slain leader, as well as her second in command, he did not live in this place. Some males lived with their mates. But Cabat, like several other males, single and mated, stayed in the wipiti of the males. He had joined Hama at her place when she summoned him to couple. His steps, always heavy because of his weight, were now also slowed with sadness, Enga thought.

While Cabat was inside, Panan walked around to inspect the outside of the wipiti. He studied the ground and squatted twice, tilting his head to peer at the dirt with his good eye.

A very private thought leapt into the mind of Enga. *Hama's garment has been ripped open. Could her mate, Cabat the Thick, do something like this? In anger? Or a former mate?Panan One Eye?* She could not envision such a thing. She suppressed these speculations and saved them for another time.

Enga squatted with Sannum outside the wipiti and watched her bereft tribe congregate in the darkness. Zhoo of Still Waters, the Healer, stayed with Ung Strong Arm, but the rest of the clan shuffled about or squatted, wiping tears with the backs of their hands. Enga felt unable to move. The two remaining Elders had once again put on their mourning cloaks of black bearskin.

Cabat the Thick emerged from the wipiti and looked around at the group, then came over to Enga and reached for her arm to help her up. *You did a good job, announcing the death of our leader. That was not an easy task.*

Enga nodded to him. He and Sannum led her over to the gathering place. She sat beside the fire, burning low now. Soon they all squatted together and joined their voices to raise a keening lament to the heavens, to whatever Spirits would listen.

Panan sent a message to the hunters who were away. *Our leader, our Hama, has been slain. We sit in sorrow.* Enga, along with the rest of the Hamapa, received the vibrations of the sorrow from the hunters, mingled with that of the village.

Under the stream of sorrow, though, Enga could feel an undercurrent of disbelief, quickly turning to anger. Or was that fear? It grew in strength; it must have come from more than one of them.

Several of the males bore the body out with great care and laid it on Hama's sleeping fur next to the central fire, where the whole tribe could gaze upon their fallen leader. Some rose and stroked her cold, unresponsive skin.

Enga longed for Ung to be conscious enough for her to exchange private thoughts with, although she did not know what those thoughts would be. Her mind was numb.

Lakala Rippling Water, the Singer, started a Song of Mourning above the wailing. Young Akkal, the Fire Tender, scooped up ashes and handed them out so the tribe could reblacken their faces with sorrow. As they had just mourned Kokat, most faces still bore ashen traces.

Since Akkal was a birth son of the dead Hama, by the seed of Cabat the Thick, Enga admired the way he handled himself in his grief. His young, smooth hands shook, but he performed his job. Then he sat and wailed, joining in the chorus of sorrow. Even Kung, not a favorite of Hama, looked saddened, his eyebrows knitted together, his usual surly expression deflated. Her death must come as a serious blow even to him.

Wild, stray vibrations from Ongu Small One did not surprise Enga. Ongu had mated with Cabat after his first mate died, years ago, but he had soon left her for Hama. Their union had not produced any children, and Enga always thought Ongu had wanted him back. No mourning poured from her, just conflicted feelings of losing a leader, one she had not personally liked.

And so the Hamapa, even Ongu in her own way, mourned. Enga felt the unease around her, being without a leader. Tribes fell apart without a leader.

Enga gazed upon Hama's dwelling, the largest in the village. She was the sacred mother of the clan, the highest-ranking female. She wielded a critical vote when the clan needed a decision, although the Hamapa only voted when they disagreed. And when they elected a new leader. Hama was their most important person and was given respect by all. None of the Hamapa would harm her. Would they?

The Hamapa eyed each other, all sitting in a circle. It was impossible for Enga to read any more thoughts. Were they wondering, as she was, who could have done this?

The fire, prodded into life by Akkal, leapt against the night. The older males sat together: Panan, Cabat, and Sannum Straight Hair, birth brother of Cabat. The New One sat near them, his slim fingers drawing a bird-bone stitching tool in and out of a piece of leather held close to his face, pale tears tracking down his pale cheeks.

When the New One joined the tribe he had brought with him, in a pouch around his neck, stitching tools fashioned from tiny bird bones. Enga had never seen such tools before, although she knew the Tall Ones used them. He had also carried a pile of assorted, cured skins. The New One would stick sinew through a small hole he had made in a bird bone and join skins together with it. He had made several beautiful garments this way and had given them to tribe members.

Finally Cabat stood. It was an occasion for speaking. Such a thing must be said aloud so the Spirits could pay heed.

"Hapapa vav. Nonna dy Hamamapapa. Nonna. Tza Hamama. Tza. Dakadaga Hamamapapa sheesh."

The Most High Male Speaks. This is a dark time for the Hamapa. Dark. The Most High Female is slain. Slain. Mother Spirit of the Sky, Dakadaga, bless the Hamapa.

Enga nodded. *Yes, it is a dark time.* Others added similar sentiments.

She bent her upper body forward, feeling pain in her middle. Half listening, she traced invisible parallel lines on the rock beneath her with her finger.

Panan indicated that he wanted to tell another Saga. Cabat sat and nodded at the Storyteller.

Enga raised her head to watch Panan, then bent to continue making the pointless lines. He had been the mate of Hama many summers ago when Lakala Rippling Water, Fee Long Thrower, and Tog Flint Shaper were born of her. Some Hamapa couples stayed together for life, but not all. She had never known why Hama took Cabat for a mate after she had been with Panan for so many years.

She straightened up, startled, when she caught a wave of hatred pass from Panan to Cabat. Did Panan think Cabat had killed her? What had been going on among those three?

She tried to peer deep into Panan's mind. But now it was focused on his task, calling up his stored memories for the Saga. Had she misunderstood the wave? Weariness coursed through her head, sounding like a rushing stream in her ears.

The Storyteller recalled a time when a tribal leader had been killed. *You must know, my brothers and sisters, that a leader has been slain before. In the time of the Ancient Ones, the village was invaded by the Mikino.*

Enga knew these small ones were as vicious as the Hamapa were peaceful.

Panan continued. *The Mikino wanted to take the food of the Hamapa. They also wanted to capture the females and the children.*

At this Enga shuddered. Everyone knew the Mikino ate children and kept females as slaves.

The Hamapa females slew some of the Mikino with their spears; the Hamapa males beat some to death with rocks and clubs. Even the children threw rocks and managed to kill a few. The rest of the Mikino ran. But they had killed the Most High Female and her mate.

At the conclusion of the Saga, Panan One Eye added, *Outside the wipiti of Hama there are small footprints.*

Her brothers and sisters pursed their lips and nodded, considering the Saga.

Are you thinking a Mikino has killed Hama? thought-spoke Enga.

Nanno nodded. *That seems to be what has happened. There are the footprints.*

Even Ongu joined in. *This is something a Mikino would do. They are ruthless killers. Our Storyteller has just related their killing in the past.*

An uncharacteristic boldness took hold of Enga. She surprised herself when she stood and thought-spoke to all of them with an urgent crimson hue. *That was then. This is now. Our leader was not slain by a Mikino. There are no Mikino here. She was slain by one of us.*

Chapter 6

Excavations reveal Regourdou as one sacred site where Neanderthals returned repeatedly to bury brown bear remains, whose bones show marks from stone tools. Yet only a single human [young man] has thus far been unearthed. His people put him on a brown bear skin in a stone-lined pit.

—Sign accompanying a re-creation of this burial in the Smithsonian Natural History Museum depicting the young man with his limbs folded and tied.

Jeek squirmed on the hard stone and searched the grim faces of his fellow tribe members. All thoughts had been tightly shuttered after Enga Dancing Flower had stood and insisted that a Hamapa had slain Hama. Gradually, their minds opened up and Jeek became aware of powerful waves of resistance to Enga's statement, washing over the pretty red-haired female.

You were not born a Hamapa. So you accuse us?

Hamapa do not slay one another.

Panan One Eye has seen their footprints.

A Mikino slew our Hama.

Jeek's birth mother, Zhoo of Still Waters, listening in from her wipiti where she tended Ung Strong Arm's injury, sent her thought out to him. *I cannot visualize a Hamapa killing our leader.* At least she did not send her thought to Enga, nor to the rest of the tribe.

Consider what happened, Enga Dancing Flower pleaded. *No one has been in our village from any other tribe. Only the Hamapa. Only we have been here.*

Roh Lion Hunter, the stocky mother of pretty Gunda, brought up another possibility. *An animal could have killed her.*

Enga answered, *If an animal came into a wipiti, we would all know about it. We would see bite marks, tearing of cloth and flesh, tracks. And smell. We can all smell that an animal has not been in the village.*

It was hard for Jeek to think Hama was gone. *Hama has been the leader of the tribe my entire life. I cannot imagine what it will be like without her to lead us.* Her bright, wise eyes shone in his mind's eye. *But if someone I know has slain her, that will be even harder to imagine.*

Jeek saw Nanno Green Eyes, the birth sister of the slain leader, give Ongu Small One a sideways glance, her green eyes frosty with suspicion. Roh Lion Hunter gave the same look to Sannum Straight Hair, then to one of the youth. Harsh pulses of mistrust throbbed between Cabat and Panan. Jeek was surprised to intercept them. But he was more startled to feel misgivings directed to himself from Kung. Kung thought Jeek could kill Hama?

Soon each Hamapa looked sideways at the others, and they all felt wary gazes turned upon them. Amid the strong waves of distrust, bitterness went out for Enga Dancing Flower. No one wished to think of a Hamapa killing Hama. The fire crackled and sparked as suspicion mounted.

Then, gradually, all thoughts were shielded.

How could someone in our own tribe do that? wondered Jeek to himself. *Who could want her dead?* He dwelt on her last decisions. She had made unpleasant announcements in recent days. Her recommendation to send the males away to trade was unpopular. But if the hunters did not bring back meat, it had to be done, and it was not a reason to slay her. And she had told the tribe they must move the village. This had not been done in anyone's memory and no one wanted to do it. Hama had argued that the large game was moving away. She was right. But could this be a reason to kill her? Despite the flurry of suspicious glares flying around the circle, Jeek did not think anyone in the tribe believed Enga.

Then a thought hit Jeek and he wriggled. Some of them were not natives of the Hamapa tribe. Donik Tree Trunk and Bahg Swiftfeet had both come from other tribes to marry Hamapa females. And Enga Dancing Flower and Ung Strong Arm had come from another tribe. And the New One. He was not even the same kind of creature as a Hamapa. Jeek looked around and did not see him.

The Most High Male took over again. *Nothing can be decided until our thinking comes together. But first we need to bury our beloved Hama. And after that we will elect a new leader. There will be time for other things later.*

Jeek caught a flash from the corner of his eye. The New One stood silent at the border of the woods. His pale skin gleamed in the light. It looked like his skin and clothing, catching a glint from the fire, might be wet. Jeek watched as the New One approached the gathering, his head down, his uneven steps slow and dragging. But Jeek could not read his mind. He sat beside Vala Golden Hair, the Hamapa who had been the most friendly to him. Jeek saw the New One reach over and touch her shoulder. She returned him a slight smile. Jeek wondered if she could be sending him a private message. Then the New One took one of his bird-bone stitching tools and a small pelt from his pouch, bent his head close to his work, and began sewing.

It is a sorrow that all of the tribe cannot see our Hama buried, thought-spoke the Storyteller. *But we cannot wait for the others to return. The body must be put into Brother Earth before bad vapors make us sick.*

Jeek remembered a Saga about a body staying in a wipiti too long and making the tribe ill. He was sad, but also curious and even a little excited to witness the burying of an Elder. He had never seen this done. His foot jiggled as he tried to imagine it.

The burial ceremony for a leader was a special occasion and an important ritual for the tribe. Most dead brothers and sisters were returned to the animals and to the Spirits of the Air, left in the open, he knew, like Kokat No Ear had been, so hungry creatures could devour and use their flesh. The bodies of the leaders, however, were protected from scavengers by placing them inside Brother Earth.

Nanno Green Eyes stood abruptly, ignoring the burial discussion. *We must discuss something else now, while we are in council.*

We are discussing burying our leader. The stern rebuke came from both the Storyteller and the Most High Male.

The Hamapa, continued Nanno, *should think about expelling some members. Enga Dancing Flower is causing trouble for us. Her accusation that a Hamapa is a killer will split the tribe.*

Sit down. Panan's one eye was fierce.

Jeek noticed that the ashes of mourning obscured that dirty streak he had seen on Nanno's face earlier. How could she want to expel Enga? Did not everyone like her?

The tribe agreed to hold the burial ceremony the next day at high sun. The tribal brothers and sisters planned the preparations for the morning, then shuffled off to their tents. Again, the New One had disappeared.

*****

Jeek inhaled the comfortable aroma of his wipiti. It smelled of the furs they slept on, and of his birth mother. The scent of his absent birth brother, Teek Pathfinder, lingered, too. And the smell of smoke from their fire permeated everything. The sound of the wind flapping against the skins walls made him feel cozy inside the warm dwelling, out of the cold night.

Jeek's mother pulled his tattered bearskin over him, smoothed his tangled locks, and put her cool hand on his head.

Tell me again, Mama, how Panan lost his eye, Jeek begged. He wanted to take his mind off Hama's death.

Zhoo of Still Waters gave him an affectionate smile, but answered that it had gotten too late and he had heard the story of the stray spear many times already. *Maybe at the next dark time, tomorrow. I am tired now.*

Do you think I displeased Hama when Kung quarreled with me at the council before the hunt?

No, I do not think so. But, my son, you must not quarrel with Kung and the likes of him. Kung and his friends are young and do not know the way of everything. She ran her soothing hands through his light brown mane. *I know you are too young to bear the sneering attitude of someone like Kung. Yet I hope for you to grow straight. Not to be defiant, as Kung sometimes is.*

I do not want to ever receive those somber thoughts, the ones that the Elders sent to Kung that night, thought-spoke Jeek. *He displeased our Hama.* He caught her hand and rested his cheek on her palm.

Yes, I believe he did. Now I must get some water for Ung Strong Arm. She is sending me a message of thirst.

The thoughts of Jeek at the pre-hunt meeting had not been at all somber for the most part. Jeek had watched pretty Gunda in the shadowy firelight this night, too, as he did at every gathering. She was small and thin, but her light green eyes were huge and deep, the color of forest moss in the twilight, with long lashes that lay on her round cheeks when she looked down. She wore her lustrous red hair braided in the fashion of a girl her age. Females became adults at the age of twelve summers, males at the age of fifteen summers. They also received their descriptive names at that time, at the Passage Ceremony. Gunda had passed ten summers now, and Jeek one more than that. He feared fifteen would never come.

Gunda sometimes looked up and watched Jeek. This pleased Jeek very much. He knew he was not old enough to couple yet, but he yearned for Gunda to choose him as a mate when she became an adult. Kung had jeered at Jeek the other night, thought-speaking that he was sure Gunda would prefer a more mature male like himself. Jeek was proud he had not carried the altercation into a fight.

Pleasure radiated from the warmth Gunda sent him. He hoped they would couple and be as happy together as his own birth mother and father had been before his father had died. Tonight, nestled in his bearskin bed, Jeek forgot about the latest gathering and the troubles of the tribe and fell asleep, feeling warm.

*****

At new sun, after another restless night, Enga Dancing Flower scooped up her possessions, the ones she had lined up the night before, and dropped them into her pouch. She left it next to her bearskin and slogged to the Hama's wipiti where she helped dress the body in a soft camel skin garment, made by the New One. The New One seemed to have a large supply of camel skins. The Hamapa had not been on a long expedition to where the camel dwelt for many seasons. Camels roamed far in the direction of last sun.

Enga was not a birth daughter of Hama, but she and Ung were considered her daughters since she had raised them. The rest of the birth family of Hama helped ready her body. All but Fee Long Thrower, still away hunting, and Ung, healing in the wipiti of the Healer. Enga joined her mind with Ung's so she could almost be there. Others communicated with the males and females on the hunt so they could participate.

What a contrast, thought Enga to herself with a brief scowl. *I am so close to my birth sister, and Nanno Green Eyes did not spend much time with Hama, her own birth sister.* All she had ever witnessed between them were sour feelings and conflict. Could Nanno have killed her own sister? But, if she did, why now?

Enga wondered if Nanno had been in this wipiti just before the death. She had come from this direction when the hunting party had returned carrying Ung and the bundle of clothing from Kokat No Ear.

In the large dwelling of Hama there was plenty of room for all who were there. Lakala Rippling Water, the Singer, her oldest birth daughter, retrieved the special buttons the New One had made. Tog Flint Shaper rubbed her limbs with a soft skin dipped in mint-scented water. The other child of Hama, Akkal, the serious-minded Fire Tender, assisted Tog. Cabat the Thick, her present mate, also joined in and helped. Panan One Eye, her mate before Cabat, sat watching the preparations. The two males shot each other narrow looks.

Enga picked up Hama's hair bracelets. *Shall I put these on her?* she asked Lakala.

Yes, she wore them every day. Lakala reached into Hama's pouch and pulled out a necklack, fashioned of tiny carved bird bones strung on sinew. *And she needs her Death Necklace also.* Lakala adorned her neck with it for the Burial.

The New One was summoned and came to quietly sew the buttons that had been ripped off back into place. His strange pinkish eyes shed tears as he worked.

Enga looked for the figure she had seen, the wooden carving buried in the dirt of the floor. Someone had removed it. She thought it might be good to bury it with Hama, but it was gone. She even looked in Hama's pouch, but it wasn't there either.

Enga ran to her own dwelling to get the carving the New One had given her. She had never shown it to them and maybe it would bring the tribe luck. She would fetch it and place it near the body while they chanted.

When Enga entered her wipiti she stopped for a moment, feeling the silence. It was strange that Ung was not staying there. She would again as soon as she was healed, but Enga was not used to being in a dwelling by herself. She crossed to the pouch she had left beside her sleeping skin and reached into it for the carving.

When she didn't find it she frowned and shook the sac, snapping it upside down. Her belongings fell out, the smooth rock, her hair adornments and spear tips, all but the carving. It was not there.

She sat back on her heels. Dizziness threatened to topple her onto the dirt.

My own figure is gone, and the Hama's has disappeared, too. Did the New One take them back? Someone else could have taken them, but why would anyone do that? I have let no one know about mine except Ung, and, of course, the New One.

She blinked, trying to clear her mind. Had she imagined the carving? She had gotten so little sleep lately she was beginning to wonder what was real. Had she dreamed about the carving? Was it not real? She would talk to Ung about it. If she had imagined hers, maybe she had imagined the figure in Hama's wipiti.

Enga put the flap aside and left her dwelling to return to the activity, staggering slightly.

When the body was ready, Tog and Cabat carried it out to the Paved Place and gently placed it on her own black mourning cape. Pure black bearskins were only used for mourning and burials. But, since death was not uncommon among them, mourning capes were used often. Hama's showed its wear.

Lakala Rippling Water started a Death Chant and the tribe performed a slow dance around the spot where she lay. When Cabat the Thick, the Most High Male, had signaled to cease dancing, he placed the most favored spear tip of Hama beside her. With the help of several others, he bent her limbs up close to her body, rolled her onto her side, and wrapped Hama inside the bearskin. Enga remembered, from her childhood, when the old Hama had died and her limbs had been too stiff to bend.

The dead leader was now the Aja Hama, the Former Most High Female. The three elder males, Cabat the Thick, Panan One Eye, and Sannum Straight Hair, hoisted their burden and carried their leader to the top of the Sacred Hill. Enga and the rest followed at a respectful distance. They murmured a soft chant on their way up the hill, past the Holy Cave where Fee Long Thrower would soon go to have her baby, and on to the burial ground. Enga plucked yellow flowers on her way and the others picked their favorites from among the last of the season's blossoms. Enga held hers to her nose. The smell of their fragrant petals soothed Enga's jagged feelings somewhat.

The males had dug a hole earlier in the day to prepare the gravesite.

The Hamapa threw blossoms into the hole and covered the bottom with flower petals of all colors. Enga was glad there were enough plants still alive to line the grave with color. The breath of Mother Sky whipped some of the petals out of their hands, but most drifted into the pit.

The surviving Elders gently lowered the Aja Hama onto the petals. Enga shivered in the wind, which was growing sharp, and joined in calling out loud the name Hama had been given shortly after birth, the name she forsook when she became Hama, followed by her title, to signify her passing.

"Jansa, Hama, Jansa, Hama."

Now they would select their next Hama and this one would be referred to as either Aja Hama or Jansa Wild Wind. She had been named for her swiftness at her Passage Ceremony.

Tog and the other males placed a few heavy rocks on top of her. Tears flowed like rain from Enga's eyes. She stayed in mental touch with Ung, still confined, and with Tog Flint Shaper, now standing on the other side of the burial hole. The others communicated with each other silently, and they all mourned together.

Even Nanno Green Eyes managed to shed a few tears, but Enga wondered if they were genuine.

The mourners stayed on the windy hill for the amount of time it took Sister Sun to travel two hand-lengths through Mother Sky. The cold kept Enga's eyes open and her head from dropping forward with exhaustion.

They held hands, weeping and intoning, then, one by one, began sifting handfuls of dusky-smelling dirt onto the rocks and bearskin that covered Aja Hama. The males finished burying her, deep enough so coyotes, peccaries, and lions would not smell her and dig her up.

The rest of the sun time was chilly and the Hamapa stayed quiet, except Ongu Small One, who walked about and hummed a light tune. Enga wondered if she was trying to cheer up the tribe. Most of them were thinking of the next step, anointing the new Hama. Enga couldn't think of anyone who would be a good replacement.

*****

Just after Sister Sun went to mate with Brother Earth for dark time, Enga Dancing Flower was roused from her torpor. She had managed to drift into a restless sleep, but now the hunters were returning. The children ran to greet them. Most of the adults had no energy. And they could tell from the hunters' emotions they had not killed a mammoth.

Enga had not been asleep, but she had been comfortable on her bearskin. With a glance of regret at her warm bed, she emerged from her wipiti to see Fee Long Thrower step onto the Paved Place. She held up a small porcupine she had brought down, then turned toward the Healer's wipiti. Fee screwed up her face and doubled over, dropping the animal. Vala Golden Hair dropped the two snowshoe hares she carried and helped Fee to the Healer's. Fee's birthing pains had begun.

*****

The meeting a short time later was short and dispirited. The Saga was one Jeek had heard Panan One Eye tell before, and he did not go into much detail. Only that a short-faced bear, in a time of great hunger, had once attacked the birth mother of the birth mother of the slain Aja Hama. No one mentioned anything about thinking a bear had killed Aja Hama.

Jeek's eyelids were sagging in boredom when Nanno Green Eyes rose.

The males should leave on the trading mission at new sun, thought-spoke Nanno to all.

Jeek was alert now. His mouth pursed into a small circle. Nanno had never brought up something the leaders had not already started a discussion on.

There were two waves of unenthusiastic opposition. Jeek intercepted the thoughts of Enga Dancing Flower.

I do not like the idea of Tog Flint Shaper being gone for several suns. But that would be better than being gone several full moons.

Then Jeek caught the agitation of Roh Lion Hunter, birth mother of Gunda and mate of Donik Tree Trunk, the largest male in the tribe.

It is not good for all the prime males to be away, put in Roh Lion Hunter. *And two of them just returned from a hunt.* She had recently lost a baby and her mood had been irritable lately. Her mate was still doing many things for her, helping with the other children. The rest of the tribe digested her feelings, but didn't agree with her and Enga. The other females thought the trading mission was needed.

Jeek was surprised Roh had spoken out against Nanno, who was her own birth mother. But, after he considered it, Jeek thought Roh was a lot more like the Hama they had just buried than like her own mother, and was closer to her, too.

They discussed the plans until all agreed that a group of four males would depart at first sun for the nearest tribe of fellow beings, strong, sturdy people like them, some with fiery hair also, called the Cuva.

I hope the Cuva have much food to barter for our fine Hamapa knives, thought-spoke Tog.

The tribes of different statures, as well as more who were similar to the Hamapa, lived farther away. Some, the Tall Ones, looked like the New One, slender and even taller than him, but with dusky skin. Others, the Mikino, were tiny and dark-skinned, with small heads on their sharp little shoulders. All these were potential trading partners if, for some reason, they could not trade with the Cuva. The Mikino must be treated with care, but Jeek knew they had been traded with in the past.

Finally the Most High Male stood with a loud grunt. He lifted both arms high before he spoke.

Jeek knew from his teachings that the Hamapa spoke rarely. Only when they wanted to be sure the Spirits could hear them. His mother taught him that thoughts served as their communication with each other. Tribes built like the Hamapa, compact and stout, could generally understand each other. Kin could always understand kin. And the more closely related, she told him, the better and more complete the communication. The Hamapa were mostly kin, so they had no trouble giving thoughts back and forth. Enga Dancing Flower and Ung Strong

Arm, who came from another tribe as babies, had learned the Hamapa thought-speak quickly when they came. Others, who came to mate and stay, adjusted without much trouble.

A decision was going to be Pronounced. Jeek sharpened his hearing and jiggled one foot with excitement. Concentrating, Jeek watched Cabat's fleshy lips carefully. He was proud that he could understand all the words.

"Hoody! Listen! The Most High Male Speaks. The Hamapa trade with the Cuva people. Mother Spirit of the Sky, Dakadaga, bless the Hamapa."

Now, thought-spoke Enga, *since Hapa has spoken it and the Spirits have heard it, it is official. We will trade with the Cuva. Dakadaga, bless our mission.*

Jeek joined the others. *Dakadaga, bless our mission.* He drew a wisp of hair into his mouth and chewed on it, pondering the decision of the tribe. It did not seem like a good time for this mission, so close to so many other things happening. But he knew the journey must be made. Rumbling noises came from his hungry, empty-feeling belly.

The bigger problem he saw was that the Pronouncement had been made without any discussion or vote. And without an official leader. A Pronouncement, heard by the gods, was a powerful thing. Jeek wondered if this decision, initiated by Nanno Green Eyes, was a way for her to assert leadership so she would be elected the new leader.

Chapter 7

The teeth and jaws of the Cro-Magnons are larger than in modern Europeans, as was average stature and (probably) lean body weight. Estimates put early Cro-Magnon height at about 1.84 m (6 ft 1 in) in males and 1.67 m (5 ft 6 in) in females, with lean body weight at perhaps 70 and 55 kg (154 and 121 lb) respectively. So while body weight was comparable with that of Neanderthals, the weight was distributed differently, and the body proportions certainly contrasted strongly...

—*In Search of the Neanderthals*, Christopher Stringer and Clive Gamble, p. 183

Not long after new sun, Jeek awoke. He rubbed his eyes and rolled onto one elbow. The light of Sister Sun, streaming in through the open flap of the mammoth-skin doorway, showed him that his birth mother was not in the wipiti.

Mama, Jeek sent forth, trying to locate her. A moment of small panic washed through his pounding chest.

Fee Long Thrower is having her baby, came the answer from Zhoo of Still Waters, from a distance. The baby was being born. Jeek's breathing eased.

He saw, through his mother, that she and several others were assisting Fee in the Holy Cave, where the new mother and child would stay for a few days after the birth.

Ung Strong Arm is now in her own wipiti, Zhoo added.

He sat up. Sure enough, Ung was not there. He was alone. Jeek grinned and lay back on his warm bearskin. A new baby was a happy time for the Hamapa. They would hold a celebration, with dancing and singing. He visualized the festivity: laughing, lightness, dancing, feasting. But then a somber notion. The Hamapa did not have enough food for such a feast. Now they needed a successful hunt more than ever.

Four males had left on a trading mission very early, before first sun. Jeek had sleepily bade his birth brother, Teek Pathfinder, a good mission. Teek, Tog Flint Shaper, Bahg Swiftfeet, and Donik Tree Trunk had left with a supply of flint knives to trade for food with the Cuva. Jeek had joined the collective supplication of the tribe to the Spirits of Travel and Trade on behalf of the Hamapa males in hopes they would return with food to keep the tribe alive during the Dark Season. Then Jeek had gone back to sleep.

As soon as Jeek's mother sent permission for him to come, he pulled on his moose-skin cape, left the shelter of the wipiti, and dashed across the Paved Place and up the hill to the Holy Cave. On his way he ran a hand through his tangled brown, sun-streaked hair. This day his mother had not been there to comb it. Maybe he should try to groom himself later.

When Jeek reached the top of the hill he shivered in his fur wrap at the cave entrance, unable to see Fee or the baby. Warm air poured out, with so many Hamapa crowded together inside, admiring the infant. There were wide grins at the tiny puckered face and the first smackings as the baby nursed. Jeek crawled through the legs of his tribe to see better.

The cave, which housed their permanent fire, blazed with warmth. The beautiful walls welcomed him with red ochre streaks, painted by former Hamapa brothers and sisters. The cave, big enough to hold the whole tribe, was over half filled. The guests of honor, Fee and her newborn, reposed on a thick pile of fur skins near the warm fire.

Jeek squatted for some time, watching amusing expressions flit across the face of the little one. Every time the baby made a tiny bleating noise, the females answered him with soothing ah-ah-ahs and smiles. Tribe brothers and sisters came and went while Jeek drowsed in the cozy cave, his back settled against a smooth spot on the wall.

Jeek came to when the cave fell silent. He looked at the entrance, where the New One stood, his pale face averted. When the New One looked up quickly and stole a glance at the mother and child, the color of his eyes gave Jeek a shock. They were flower-colored, or maybe the color of clouds, tinged with the rosy light of Sister Sun just after she had gone to rest. He didn't remember seeing the color of those eyes before, since the New One kept them half-shut most of the time.

The New One looked down and took a step inside. He held out a small fur object and Zhoo accepted it. *Your gift is appreciated.* After he had limped out, she unfolded and held up a wrap for the newest Hamapa.

The silence broke as the females admired the wrap, then resumed making soft bird sounds that the baby ignored in favor of his mother's breast.

Wetness gleamed on the cheeks of Roh Lion Hunter, who stood at the rear of the cave. Jeek could sense her pain. It had not been long since she had lost her last baby. It had died on the day of its birth. Her daughter Gunda, ten summers old, leaned her head against her mother's shoulder to soothe her. Jeek grew uncomfortable in the presence of such strong emotions and started pulling at his hair.

Jeek also was not as fascinated with the wrap as the grownups. And now that the child was being fed instead of making those entertaining grimaces, Jeek grew bored watching him suckle and crept out of the cave. Fee would return to her home in a few days. Until then, Zhoo would be tending her much of the time and, with his brother Teek Pathfinder on the trading mission, Jeek would mostly be on his own.

Hunger was starting to cause him pain. He ate at every meal, but there was little to go around, and he did not eat much. Maybe he could figure out how to trap some game while he was spending time alone. The new mother must have enough food, he knew, or the baby would suffer.

He walked down the hill with his head lowered, his hair falling forward into his face, thinking about the baby growing, becoming older, and about the Naming Ceremony that would be held when the child had passed the number of full moons of all fingers and all toes, twenty full moons. This rite of passage included gaining a short name, something to call him. Usually the mother picked it. Jeek grabbed a wisp of hair and chewed it. What would be the future of this tiny boy?

A jarring wave of hatred interrupted these musings just before Jeek reached the edge of the village. He turned, facing toward the bad thoughts, toward the woods.

Ugly little creature. What should a person expect when Bahg Swiftfeet is the seed giver?

At first Jeek could not tell whose thoughts these were. They seemed to be private thoughts that had escaped unintentionally, and the source was not clear.

If I had given Fee Long Thrower the seed, the baby would be beautiful. How can she take seed from Bahg Swiftfeet, with his ugly long legs? Mine are so much sturdier and thicker. How can she couple with him?

Jeek stood very still for a moment, then slunk toward the spruce trees at the edge of the Paved Place. He crouched behind a large clump of sedge.

I want Fee Long Thrower. I want her for myself. Bahg Swiftfeet already has much that is good in his life. I do not. He has a quick mind and all the Hamapa like him. I do not have a quick mind and do not receive the high regard he does.

The speaker was one of Kung's companions, Doon. Jeek knew Doon, as he knew all the members of his tribe. Doon was not given the ability to think like other Hamapa. They realized, shortly after his birth, that he would have to be cared for by everyone. His birth mother did not live through his birth and his seed giver was unknown. He was called Doon because "doondoon" was the Hamapa term for a person who is not able to know many things.

Doon followed Kung like a small child. He had a body small for his age, but he acted even younger than he was. His head was misshapen, flat where it should be round in the back. Hama had let it be known that she did not think Kung a good leader for Doon. But Doon had no other companions.

Jeek had never before heard such things expressed by Doon. He knew Doon considered Fee Long Thrower beautiful. All the Hamapa did. But Fee had coupled with Bahg Swiftfeet. No Hamapa would come between them, unless Fee and Bahg made it known they did not desire to couple any more. That was the way of the tribe. Jeek did not understand the evil that came from Doon. They were not normal thoughts. They made Jeek's insides feel cold and dark.

*****

The Hamapa males on the trading mission made their way through the familiar forest, along the path that led to the nearest tribe, the Cuva. To Bahg Swiftfeet, it did not seem that this tribe had as much ability to speak as the Hamapa had, but that may have been because their oral sounds were slightly different. They made a warning sound like that of a dove, "Cu, cu." So the Hamapa called them the Cuva, or Cu Speakers.

Bahg assumed that the Cuva sent their thoughts to each other as easily as the Hamapa, regardless of darkness or distance, but he had some slight difficulty trading ideas with them.

Bahg's traveling clothes, and those of his companions, were loin cloths and warm fur capes, shaped in circles with holes cut out for their heads. The skins tied around their feet made no noise in the woods, but the birds still sensed their approach and cried out. The pouches slung over their shoulders were light now, holding only dried provisions for their trip and the flint knives for trading. Bahg hoped they would be heavy with meat when they returned.

The baby had been born early enough that Bahg saw him before the group left on their trading mission. It had been hard to leave his mate and new baby for this trip, but he knew it must be done for the good of the tribe.

Along the familiar path, Bahg sighted several new stands of tree fern plants. He signaled his find to Tog Flint Shaper

Tog answered him, *I do not want us to stop now.*

I will take note of the location, thought-spoke Bahg. *We can return to them later, but before they get big and tough.*

Sometimes his tribe chewed the pith of the ferns for food, but they could use only new, tender shoots. Since the mature tree ferns were many, many times the height of a Hamapa, and tough, too, they had to get at them early.

The Cuva tribe lived not far in the direction of the rising sun, less than a half day, but the two tribes did not meet often. The Hamapa usually hunted in the direction of the setting sun and the Cuva toward the rising sun. Cuva hunted forest creatures and Hamapa hunted prairie animals. That way there had always been game enough for both tribes. Bahg fervently hoped game was still abundant for the Cuva.

Well before high sun, Bahg Swiftfeet knew they should be hearing the warning sounds, "Cu, cu, cu, cu." When the Cuva heard and smelled their approach, they called out to make sure the Hamapa knew they were detected.

Bahg walked ahead of the others. It was easy with his oddly long legs, and this day he preferred to walk apart and focus on his mate, Fee, and their new baby. She had been sending him visions of the little one all morning. Bahg and Fee argued back and forth in their thought-pictures about who he looked like.

Those short, fat legs will grow to be long and swift like mine, thought-spoke Bahg to his mate.

Look at his chubby fingers. I am sure they will be long and graceful, like mine.

I look forward to the reappearance of your narrower waist, he teased. He daydreamed about what Fee would look like when she recovered from carrying the baby inside.

Tog Flint Shaper called Bahg back from his reverie. Bahg flinched at the sharp intrusion. *We have almost reached the edge of the village. There has been no sign from the Cuva.*

The little band of traders crept to the edge of the Cuva village with caution, apprehension pounding in their chests.

The Cuva had no Paved Place, but, instead, they had positioned large, flat sitting stones on the bare ground around the fire pit. Their dwellings, made of skin with rocks piled around the outside, much like the Hamapa dwellings, ringed this gathering place. The spines of the dwellings, though, were made of wooden tree trunks instead of mammoth tusks.

No Cuva ran to greet them. Bahg, every sense on alert, followed the others into the village.

One lone male one stood, swaying, on the dirt in the middle of their ring of tents. Bahg Swiftfeet stared at the Cuva, one who was called Goe. The last time Bahg had seen Goe he had been robust, with a thick chest, his hair plaited in one large braid and dressed in a deer wrap in the Cuva way. For a moment Bahg could not move forward. This did not look like the Goe he had seen before.

Goe's large, shaggy head shook, his shoulders slumped, and he was dressed only in a drooping loin cloth against the cool weather. His knotted hair had not been braided for a long time. The bones of his midsection stood out on his bare chest. He appeared too weak to be standing. Bahg did not want to go near him. Maybe he was diseased or carrying bad vapors. Tog Flint Shaper led and the group approached Goe slowly.

Tog thought-spoke for them. *Where are the others? What has happened here?*

The Cuva shook his head and started to keel over. Bahg Swiftfeet ran to him and caught him.

Sit, Goe, said Tog. *We will hear your story.*

Bahg lowered him onto a stone, handling him carefully. Goe felt like a fragile bird, not like an adult male. The rest of the traders took seats nearby. Bahg looked around and now noticed that the dwellings he could see into were empty. The door flaps of most of them stood open. The interiors were dark. The central fire sputtered dangerously low and there was no woodpile.

Goe's story did not take long to tell. *Hunt after hunt went bad. All but one of our female hunters were injured or killed. The males tried to hunt, but got little.*

He took a moment to gather his breath.

There was not enough game for us to keep up our strength, the Cuva continued. *And when our strength was gone, we could not hunt what little game was here.*

Why did you not appeal to the Hamapa? asked Tog.

We waited too long. Thoughts between us do not travel easily, as they do between some others, as you know. But the others we tried never responded. It may be that other tribes have suffered as we have. We were too weak for even a half-day journey to your village. He said only a few Cuva still lived. Most had died of hunger. All of the remaining, but for Goe, who was serving as guard, languished in their dwellings, he told them.

The Cuva looked at Bahg Swiftfeet, Tog Flint Shaper, and the two other Hamapa males, his dull eyes sparked with hope. *Have you brought us help? Can you feed us?*

He gave a great sigh when he understood that they could not. They handed him a small amount of their jerky, but could not spare enough to make any difference. Indeed, they did not have much with them, nor back at their village. Goe told them of another settlement of people who looked like them. *We have traded with them in the past. They dwell to the north, a journey of three suns. But we have not seen them or heard from them for a very long time.*

The spirit of Bahg weighed heavy as he followed Tog and the band out of the village and left the starving Goe. Teek Pathfinder and Donik Tree Trunk had looked, but had not found any more Cuva alive.

Now the travelers had another decision to make. They congregated outside the sad, empty village to decide where to go next.

Should we return home? questioned Bahg.

You know the answer to that, Tog thought-told them. *We must go on farther if we do not get food here. And Goe has said there is another village not too far off.*

But should we consult… the Elders? asked Teek, the youngest one on this mission. Bahg thought he had been about to continue, *…consult Hama.*

Teek had just received his second name, Pathfinder, a few moons ago when he turned fifteen. Teek was gaining a reputation as a follower of game. Now he resisted the idea of making their own decision without tribal input.

No, we are not going to bother them with this. Tog was almost harsh with Teek. *They do not need to know how bad it is here.*

What if the other village is like this one?

It is likely that the Cuva were too weak to thought-speak with them. Why should another village have all the ill fortune this one has had?

Teek grumbled, resisting this, and Bahg was half convinced he was right. But Tog convinced them that they should forge on, and perhaps bring food back for Goe, too. After consuming a little dried meat—their appetites were dulled after seeing the starving Goe—they turned from the direction of the rising sun and headed toward the Guiding Bear who roamed Mother Sky at dark time.

Bahg and Teek went along with misgivings.

Chapter 8

On the remote island of Flores, in what is now
Indonesia, scientists in 2003 made a remarkable
discovery—the remains of a pre-human being, only
about three feet tall, who lived and thrived there until
about 12,000 years ago.

—From ABC news article, "Prehistoric 'Hobbit' Was
Definitely New Species" by Ned Potter, Jan. 29, 2007

The next day it rained, cold and hard, but there was no snow yet.
Jeek stayed inside carving a wooden toy with his small knife. He
wanted to give it to Fee's baby at his Naming Ceremony. It would
appear crude compared to the work of the New One, but the baby
would probably like it.

Jeek's birth mother was still tending the newborn and mother, and
his locks had not been smoothed and bound in several suns. Not since
Ung Strong Arm had returned wounded from the hunt. He tried to
tame his hair, but gave up after a feeble attempt.

Ung had moved back into the wipiti she shared with Enga Dancing
Flower. He would peek in on her sometime today. He and Teek were,
after all, his mother's apprentices.

After high sun, Jeek quit hearing the rain on the skins of his family's
wipiti. He opened the door flap and sniffed. The aftermath of the
shower smelled like renewal. Sister Sun was disrobing quickly, casting

off her cloud garments and scattering them at Mother Sky to consume. She smiled on her mate, Brother Earth. Her grinning beams sparkled on the stone of the Paved Place.

He saw that several others already squatted at the fireside in the center of the Paved Place. Akkal, the black-haired Fire-Tender, headed toward the hill to the Holy Cave where the sheltered fire burned. Akkal tended both fires, the sheltered one and the open one. He held a most important job.

I see the rain has doused our fire on the Paved Place, called Jeek.

Yes, I go to carry new fire from the cave, answered Akkal.

Sometimes Jeek wanted to be Akkal and have the task of tending the fires. The job earned admiration for the boy, and he was not even old enough for his Passage Ceremony yet.

I think, thought-spoke Jeek to him, *a good name for you, when you have your Passage Ceremony, would be Akkal the Careful.*

Akkal smiled at Jeek and continued up the hill.

Jeek put away his carving and peeked inside the wipiti of Enga and Ung, where he checked Ung's wound.

It is looking better and better, he told her.

How long before I can hunt? she asked.

I cannot say. Not long, I think. But Zhoo of Still Waters will know better than I do.

After Akkal returned and stoked the flames, Jeek hunkered near the flames where the stones were beginning to dry.

When all had assembled, the Most High Male and the Storyteller stood before the fire that now leapt in the sunshine, throwing reflections on the damp surface of the Paved Place. The tribe sat in a half circle around the two Elders. At the feet of the Most High Male lay the gourd that had belonged to Hama. In front of the Storyteller lay a pile of small rocks, collected by the Fire-Tender.

Jeek chewed a strand of his hair and wriggled in his intensity to understand what was happening. He knew they were electing a new leader, but had never seen it done. Cabat the Thick, the Most High

Male, signaled for the females who wished to be considered for the position of Most High Female to come to the front of the group.

Jeek held his breath. No one rose for several moments.

Then Nanno Green Eyes got to her feet, walked with solemn steps to stand beside the two Elders, and turned her back to the group. Nanno, who was the birth sister of Jansa Wild Wind, the leader they had just buried, resembled her in some ways. Nanno was tall like her sister, but her eyes were not nearly so wide-set, her scalp showed through her thin hair, and Jeek did not consider her as beautiful as Aja Hama had been. He blocked this idea as soon as it occurred to him, not wanting Nanno to detect it.

The fact that she was the sister of the dead leader would carry weight, Jeek assumed. But he did not think Nanno wise like her sister. The Aja Hama had been calm also, and Nanno was not often calm.

Next, Ongu Small One arose and stood beside Nanno, turning her back to the tribe, also. Ongu was not tall and seemed especially short standing beside Nanno. Jeek looked at their straight backs, knowing they were both nervous. He considered Ongu clever because she liked to try new ways to fix food. Too tiny and slow to be of use in the hunt, she had never gotten injured and her body was whole and unharmed. Her hair grew very long and she wound her braid around her head. Her mate, Sannum Straight Hair, the brother of Cabat, was much older than she was. The tribe looked up to her because she had borne three healthy children who all lived, including the youth, Mootak. Mootak was a member of the gang led by Kung, but Jeek suspected Mootak would not act so bad if he weren't influenced by Kung.

With his mind on Kung, Jeek heard a thought from him. *I wish I could vote, but I am too young. My Passage Ceremony has not come soon enough to vote this day.*

Which female would you vote for? ventured Jeek.

Which do you think, doondoon? Jeek could hear the sneer in the thought-speak. *Nanno Green Eyes, of course.*

Kung's birth mother had died when he was born and Nanno had

taken charge of him, her children being all grown at that time. He had been suckled by whichever female had extra milk, so his childhood had been unsettled, never staying long at any one wipiti. But he had most often stayed with Nanno.

Jeek turned his head slightly to see if any other females would vie for the position. When the two Elders had determined that a sufficient amount of time had elapsed with no new candidates, Cabat stepped forward. He nodded to the group and they began to come to their feet. The females and males who were old enough, one by one, each picked up a stone and walked to the female they preferred.

*****

Enga Dancing Flower was desperately tired. She had not slept soundly for so long. When she did drift off, horrid visions filled her head, visions of beasts coming at her and at Ung Strong Arm, visions of the two of them abandoned in a forest and cold and hungry, visions of one half of a tribe battling the other half, and visions of the earth splitting apart beneath her feet. She sometimes woke whimpering.

She felt a thought touch her, but, rather than the usual warm feeling this gave her, this one caused a coldness inside her. She looked around for the source. The New One sat near Vala Golden Hair, but his pink eyes were aimed at Enga. She shuddered. Was the New One thinking harmful ideas about her? Did this cause the chill that ran through her? She wondered if her tiredness was causing her to perceive things that did not exist.

Then he smiled at Vala, who returned his grin and accepted something small from him. Another of his exquisite carvings? Vala expressed delight to the New One and he bowed his head, humbled by her gratitude, Enga assumed. She wished her thoughts were not so jumbled and confused.

Enga shook her head to clear it and brought her attention to the proceedings. This was a difficult decision for her. She had never cared for Nanno Green Eyes, but she might make a better leader than Ongu Small One, a sweet person, but not a decisive one. Nanno was more abrasive, but maybe that would make her better at governing. Nanno was also older than Ongu, had seen more days, more summers. Enga conferred with Tog Flint Shaper in her mind.

Who do you desire in the vote? she asked. *The two who have stood are Nanno Green Eyes and Ongu Small One.*

I prefer Nanno over Ongu.

She asked from curiosity, as she would not vote for him.

At last Enga went to where the Storyteller stood, picked up a pebble from the pile, then walked to Nanno Green Eyes, bent down, and set her rock by the heels of Nanno. The males who were away sent their opinions back to the tribe, through the Most High Male, so everyone was able to vote. Cabat gathered a few stones and distributed them according to their wishes. Enga watched Cabat place a rock behind Nanno for Tog.

Enga would, however, vote for Ung, who had stayed behind in the wipiti the sisters shared.Enga told her who was standing.

My vote goes to Ongu Small One. I would never vote for that Nanno Green Eyes. You know how much she dislikes us.

Enga put a rock for Ung by the feet of Ongu.

Zhoo of Still Waters tended Fee Long Thrower and the baby at the Holy Cave. These two sent their mental votes to the group and Cabat placed rocks for them behind Nanno.

When all had chosen, the two women turned around. Cabat lined up their rocks so they corresponded and all could see the results. There were a lot more rocks in front of Nanno. The Most High Male handed her the gourd of leadership. A big grin broke out on Nanno's face and a cheer went up.

Enga experienced the crowing triumph of Nanno, the new Hama, as she rattled the gourd toward Mother Sky and whooped aloud. Enga thought Ongu let out a stab of bitter disappointment, but she may have been mistaken. The more tired she became, the more muddled mental signals seemed. She saw Ongu reach over to touch the shoulder of Nanno. To Enga, Ongu's smile looked genuine, but Nanno's wrinkled face gloated. Maybe she was just very happy, though, Enga thought, attempting to see the best side of Nanno, whose thoughts were now opaque.

If these were usual times, there would have been a feast for the rest of the day, but this day they merely nibbled on a bit of dried meat and some nuts and stayed together as dark began to descend.

Enga looked around and noticed the New One had departed from the circle.

At one point during the approach of last sun Enga Dancing Flower stretched up and concentrated. She was receiving a thought wave from Tog Flint Shaper.

Now that the vote is over, he told her, *I must let the Hamapa know our news. The Cuva have no food.*

No food? How are they living?

Most of them are dead.

So you cannot trade with them.

No, we must search farther. We are traveling farther. I want you to communicate this to our new Hama.

Why do you not tell her yourself? asked Enga.

You know she is not my favorite member of the tribe.

She is not mine, either, Enga grumbled, but agreed to convey his message. She ran to tell her of Tog's message.

Hama's brows drew down and she closed her close-set eyes. Enga surmised she was gathering patience to deal with the crisis. Then Hama arose and called the nightly assembly together.

After Lakala Rippling Water sang, the Storyteller started to relate a tale Enga had not heard before. It was from their past, when more neighboring tribes lived close and there was more trading. He squinted his good eye and told of the Cuvas, and others, and of trading flint knives for suet and flesh. Then he told of the Mikino. Their diet was vastly different. They ate mostly grains and plants, which the Hamapa detested. They also kept large cats captive, but did not eat them. They traded their beautiful pelts for knives. Next, he mentioned the Tall

Ones, where the New One had come from, and started to describe their garments, wonderfully woven and sewn.

The new Hama chopped her hand at him, stopping him in mid-thought. Her rudeness shocked Enga. She could tell it shocked Panan One Eye, too. And irritated him. He pulled at his lower lip, then rubbed a hand over his hairless scalp.

Hama motioned for Enga to stand, so she rose and relayed the dismal news from the traders. When she finished, Hama gave her a curt nod and motioned her to sit. Enga knew the dead Hama would have thanked her for delivering the message.

Frustration emanated from her brothers and sisters, then fear. Enga waited for Hama to calm them.

The tribe's muttered consternation blended together. They disliked the news, but knew the males had to go farther. They sent sympathy and mourning to Goe, the Cuva, hoping good fortune would befall him. No answer came. Enga wondered if Goe was too weak to receive the wishes.

Hama, instead of reassuring her tribe, proposed that a hunt by the children should take place at the next first sun.

Four of our males are gone trading, thought-spoke Hama, *and Fee Long Thrower, as well as Ung Strong Arm, are disabled. Someone must try to bring meat home. We have speared caribou in the forest in the past.*

And how will we spear caribou with no spear throwers? shot back Ongu Small One.

The children, Hama answered. *They have never hunted before, but now, in this hard time, they must try.*

Enga thought Gunda was brave to offer. *I will try. I have been training and can sometimes hit the target.*

Kung stood up and transmitted his feelings. *I can do it with Mootak and Doon. We are larger than Gunda and we should throw the spears.*

Enga ignored this, as males never used spears.

Roh Lion Hunter, mother of the little ten-year-old female, Gunda, gave her opinion. *The young girls should try. They at least have training. The young males have none.*

Jeek, the son of Zhoo of Still Waters, nodded agreement at this.

My Gunda has trained for years now, Roh thought-spoke. *She is ten summers old and will be ready for her Passage Ceremony in only two summers.*

Hama countered that their training might be spoiled by hunting when they were not yet ready. *Maybe the young males can take an animal. They have no future as spear throwers and so cannot ruin their education if they fail, or are injured.*

Ongu protested. *My boys are too young. They will be hurt. Maybe killed.*

Her oldest child was Mootak, the companion of Kung and Doon. She had two males younger, ages six and eight. None of them had ever been on a hunt.

This is what we must do. The young males must hunt. Hama frowned at Ongu. *They must do it for the tribe.*

Many of them grumbled and disagreed, but none had another solution. Enga noticed that only Hama considered her idea good. Cabat managed to convince Hama to wait for the space of one sun, to prepare for the hunt tomorrow and to hold the hunt just after Sister Sun appeared the next day. A few Hamapa would scout for recent signs of caribou and point the hunters in the right direction. The deer usually returned to the woods nearby for mating at about this time in the cycle of seasons. Also, spear shafts had to be fitted for the youths.

Sannum Straight Hair tried to reassure Enga. *The decision of Hama is not a bad one. And no one has a better idea. She has a point about ruining the training of the girls. Perhaps soon we will have enough food for the Dark Season and we can all relax for a time.*

Enga loved her adopted tribe and feared for them all. She gazed at them in the flickering light. They studied the sparks of their communal fire, their wide-set eyes in their strong, broad faces clouded and serious, and Enga tried to picture the next hunt, led by the rebellious youths.

Then Hama held her rattle high and declared an opinion, but not aloud. She sent a depiction of the nearest tribe of Mikino, who lived several suns' journeys toward the place where Sister Sun retired at the end of the day, opposite the direction the traders had taken. Her vision of the Mikino was soaked in blood and death.

The Mikino killed the Aja Hama. A Mikino must be killed.

Enga sent an objection back. *No! The Mikino have not been here.* Sannum and Panan joined Enga in protesting.

Kung stood, and Doon with him. Kung agreed that the Mikino had killed their leader and so the Hamapa should kill one of them.

Attack the Mikino! Attack the Mikino! thought-screeched Doon.

This is not what we need now, mused Enga privately, narrowing and darkening her mind to keep the idea in, *not more agitation and fear. Is there no wisdom in our leader?*

It startled Enga that most of the others heeded the new Hama, however. Maybe they were relieved to stop thinking about whether or not one of them had killed their Hama. Maybe it was just easier to go along with the leader.

Cabat the Thick, the Most High Male, stood to thought-speak. *It does appear there are a few small footprints near the wipiti where Hama died. Panan One Eye has told me this. Although most of them were covered by those of Enga Dancing Flower. Even if the Mikino did kill our leader, we will wait until the rest of the males are back to confront them. We are too few without them.*

Enga admired his adept sidestepping of the real issue of who killed their leader. But was there an undercurrent to what he thought-spoke? Did he think she deliberately obliterated some footprints?

Panan, the Storyteller, confronted Cabat. *Are you throwing suspicion where it does not belong? Are you hiding something? Did you want Hama dead because she was returning to me?*

Cabat ignored the accusation and turned his back on Panan. *A Hamapa would not kill another Hamapa. A Mikino did this.*

Fear for her tribe welled up more strongly yet inside Enga. What would happen to them if they could not agree on anything? They needed a wise leader, one who considered her opinions before she announced them.

The council ended with no decision on doing battle. Most wanted to wait until the males returned. Then they would have adequate food, and could gather enough strength to make the journey and, if Hama could not be deterred, engage the Mikino in battle.

Chapter 9

Only one extant weir has been described from the
Midwest, a stone structure located on the Chariton River
(near its confluence with the Missouri River) in
Missouri (Connaway 1982:156). Shields (1967:490)
presents evidence that this was indeed a prehistoric
structure, and that it was originally "V"-shaped (with a
gap in the center), but was reconstructed (and its design
altered) by European Americans sometime after 1837.
—From Prehistoric Fishweirs in Eastern North
America, Master's Thesis by allen lutins. Found at
http://www.lutins.org/thesis/

Soon after first light the child-hunters spread out at the edge of the
spruce forest. Sannum Straight Hair had scouted and found a
caribou herd that had returned to the forest. He had heard the males
rutting, he reported, clanking their horns together and grunting. The
Hamapa did not hunt caribou as often as they hunted mammoths since
one mammoth provided so much meat and fur, but as the mammoths
were moving away maybe they could hunt caribou more often.

Jeek eyed his young companions and squared his small shoulders,
then flung his long tangled hair behind him.

The adolescent males, Kung, Doon, Mootak, and young Akkal, held
the spears that Sannum Straight Hair and Enga Dancing Flower had

fashioned for them. The shafts were short, for their smaller arms. They would attempt to use them for the first time. Jeek looked up at Kung, the tallest of the four spear holders, and down on Doon, the smallest. He saw Kung and Akkal wipe sweaty palms on their garments. Jeek felt his hands sweat, too, even though he held no spear.

Kung bragged, *This spear seems light. It should not be a problem for me to get a big caribou.*

No, it shouldn't, answered Jeek. *Since we will drive them right at you.*

To himself Jeek wondered, *Why does Kung think spearing should be easy? Has he ever used one? Did he stab the Aja Hama? Could that be why he thinks spearing an animal looks easy?* A chill came over Jeek when this occurred to him. Doon's bragging echoed Kung's, but Jeek did not consider Doon at all capable of using a weapon.

His mind wandered further. *I do not understand why the rest of the tribe thinks Enga Dancing Flower wrong when she says a Hamapa killed our leader. That has to be what happened. But who? Kung? Maybe it was.*

Jeek reeled in his speculations and returned to the task. He and Gunda gave each other nods. Normally he would be thrilled to be this close to little green-eyed Gunda, but their mission was too important for him to even think about this now. Enga had felt she needed to stay with Ung, so she was not here to help. Enga had little experience hunting caribou, so she had not felt the need to go along and, as she put it, be in the way.

But what was this? Why was Gunda standing next to Kung, tilting her head up at him, and smiling at him with such glee? He tuned in. He couldn't catch the substance, but Gunda and Kung were flashing thoughts back and forth. Was Gunda admiring Kung? Did she not know he was full of talk only? Jeek balled his fists and clenched his teeth.

I will show her how skilled I am at flushing game. After all, I can do this because I have done it before. Now she will see who is competent.

Sannum had found signs of a herd deeper into the woods, so they headed that way, leaving the spear holders where the trees began.

With Roh Lion Hunter leading them, Gunda, her two sisters, Jeek, and the two birth brothers of Mootak crept into the woods to flush out the caribou. Roh, recovered enough now from losing her baby to help them, had been on several caribou hunts in the past. Three of the flushers, Gunda and her two younger sisters, were her birth children.

Jeek and the others stole through the brush, seeking the animals with their eyes, their ears, and their noses, hoping to hear the clashing sounds of the males vying for females. Forest birds called out in alarm as they passed and rodents rustled in the fallen leaves and needles underfoot.

They searched for a long time. They walked through the spruce, tilting their nostrils up to sniff for scent of the animals, and casting their glances from side to side, watching for signs they had been there. The herd sighted yesterday must have moved deep into the woods. They did startle many small animals—hares, shrews, and one porcupine—but no caribou. A cat of long-tooth lounged on a ledge outside a cave, but didn't bother the children. Jeek took note of where the cave was. Maybe later one of the real hunters, an adult female, could spear this cat. *Or could I spear it myself? That would impress Gunda.*

At last Roh halted, held both arms up, and silently sent out a strident signal. *Straight ahead. Near the edge of the water.*

Jeek sucked his breath in, then worried that he had made a noise. But the herd did not turn toward them. The two males were making too much noise. They lowered their heads and swung their impressive racks at each other, connecting and stepping back in a kind of dance. They snorted and grunted as they clashed. The female caribou and a few more males stood in a huddle watching the competition. The caribou could not have been more fascinated than Jeek was.

All of the children crowded in close to Roh. Jeek stole up next to Gunda to watch. Roh grinned and thrust up all the fingers of one hand and two of the other hand. That was the number of adult females. The Hamapa would concentrate on the females since they and their antlers were smaller and there would be less chance of getting hurt if the animals challenged the hunters. She poked her tongue between her teeth and motioned her plan partly with her hands and partly with thought-signals. Jeek hoped it would work.

The children half circled the animals. The two little brothers went behind the herd, and Gunda's two sisters took one side. Roh went with them. Jeek and Gunda took up position on the other side and crouched, waiting until all were in place.

His chest thumped like a herd was stampeding inside it. To calm himself he grabbed Gunda's hand and took several deep breaths. She returned his look with her soft green eyes. His chest thumped again. One more deep breath. Then he was ready. She nodded. She was ready also.

Roh Lion Hunter remained motionless a few moments more, then gave the mental signal. *Go!*

The children leaped up, waving their arms and shouting, "Yiy yiy yiy yiy," as loud and as fast and as high-pitched as they could. The male animals stopped, tossed their heads, then fled through the trees. The females jerked their heads up, looked around in panic, and started to stampede.

The children trampled after them.

Over there! Jeek pointed. *I'll get the female who is leaving the herd.*

He put on speed and brought her back to the stampede so the caribou would meet the hunters when they emerged from the forest.

The deer had been found deep into the woods and ran a long distance with the six Hamapa children chasing them, yelling and flapping their arms to keep the creatures moving. Two or three young males split from the stampede.

Should I get them? asked Gunda.

No, let them go, answered Jeek. *They are small. We must concentrate on the adult female caribou.*

Suddenly, Jeek's toe caught in a root and he sprawled on his stomach. Blushing furiously, he jumped up and continued the chase.

88

Had Gunda seen him fall? Roh had. She sent him a wave of encouragement with a kind smile. He hurried to catch up with Gunda, gritting his teeth and scolding himself for being clumsy.

When the does finally burst from cover, Jeek relaxed a bit to see the spear holders waiting. He let one arm drop to his side for a moment. The two large males had veered off and had not made it this far. If they had, the waiting spearers knew they should let them go, as Roh had prepared them.

The chasing children halted, staying in position, still waving their arms and yipping, in case some of the animals turned and tried to run back into the woods.

Even though the caribou were smaller than a mammoth, they were much larger than a Hamapa. Their hooves and horns were sharp and could do a lot of damage. Jeek smelled terror in all the young males holding the spears. Female spear holders sometimes gave off the scent of fear, too, but this emotion was far greater.

The eyes of stupid Doon grew huge. He gave a strangled cry and threw his weapon down, then fled. Kung trembled. His arm wavered. He threw a spear but it wobbled and fell short, not far from his own feet. Mootak saw Kung's spoiled throw, trembled with his whole body, tossed his spear aside, then ran after Doon. Kung followed them.

Akkal, the young Fire Tender, was the only spearer left. He stood his ground, his legs planted wide. He let his spear fly and it hit a doe in the shoulder. But she swerved and the spear fell to the ground, landing beneath the trampling hooves of two other animals.

After the entire herd had rushed past the hunters, the echoes of pounding hooves grew dimmer and dimmer, until they were heard no more.

Akkal walked with deliberate steps to pick up the unbroken weapons. The children who had flushed the beasts stood in place, their breathing heavy and their thoughts heavier. They tried not to transmit blame to the throwers, but Jeek thought the shame of the throwers radiated with such intensity that the censure of the smaller children would not be noticed.

They sat to compose themselves. Roh told them they should wait until Sister Sun had journeyed one hand's length through her Mother Sky to recover.

This herd is gone, she thought-spoke, then reassured them. *Another day we can try again.*

Jeek watched as, one by one, they lay on the ground and closed their eyes, giving in to their exhaustion. He had not slept the night before from excitement. Maybe the others had not either.

Then an idea arose, lifting his spirits. He darkened his thoughts, crawled to the pile of spears beside Akkal, lifted the smallest one, and headed back into the forest.

He was remembering the young caribou males that had first broken from the herd. He was also remembering spying on Gunda when she had spear practice with the other girls. Maybe he, Jeek, could spear one of the small male caribou.

He raced back to the stream where they had spotted the herd, covering the distance in a shorter amount of time, now that he wasn't being careful and searching. There, he picked up the scents easily, a trail of acrid animal fear. He followed the direction they had fled, then found the place where one had split from the other.

But, in the end, the animal had reversed, then crossed the stream. Jeek knew he couldn't cross it; the current was too swift.

He drew his arm back to throw the spear into the water in his frustration.

Wait!

He whirled around. Gunda walked toward him slowly. *Do not waste a spear, Jeek. I feel your rage. We will now continue to be hungry. But do not throw the spear away. We need it.*

Jeek nodded at her. He knew she was right. A feeling of fluttering arose inside him as she took his hand and they walked back to the group.

The others were awakening as Jeek and Gunda approached. Roh did not ask where they had been. Jeek assumed Gunda would tell her mother later. His stomach rumbled in hunger. The small band started their long trudge home. There would be no feast, no food, no hero's welcome.

*****

After Lakala Rippling Water had sung a blessing to begin the nightly meeting, she went to sit next to Ung Strong Arm. This was the first outing for Ung since her injury. Enga Dancing Flower touched Lakala's arm. *I am grateful to you, Lakala Rippling Water, for taking such good care of my birth sister. It relieves my burden.* She had even gotten in a short nap earlier.

The children had returned and Roh Lion Hunter had depicted the failed hunt for the rest of the tribe. She had cast her own spear at several animals on the way back, but had not hit any.

Hama stood to lead the meeting. She held her head high and steady with no sign of nervousness. Enga tried to imagine being a Hama. She didn't know if she would like it. She was certain she would be shaky and uncertain of herself at first. One creature she knew she would not like to be was the New One. She didn't see him at the gathering tonight.

Enga could not quite see what Hama clutched in her fist, but it looked like a carving. She squinted to see better. *Did she take the carving from the wipiti of Aja Hama after her death?* Enga kept her eyes narrowed in suspicion. *It looks as thought she did. Did she take my own carving also? But what would she want with them?* Enga shook her head in puzzlement.

Even though the topic for the night was the food shortage, Enga wanted to address another topic first. She stood.

It is time to discuss the slaying of the Aja Hama, thought-spoke Enga.

The rebuke of Hama came swiftly. *We will not discuss this now. There is no point in going after the Mikino while the males are still away.*

But we have not decided who killed her! Did Hama really think a

91

Mikino could manage to sneak into their village undetected? Enga was sure they could not. The Hamapa would sense them, smell them, hear them. Hama was not seeing this thing as it was. She was seeing something else. And Enga was not almost certain Hama held the carving the New One had given to Aja Hama.

So you think you know better than your leader? Hama's thought-speak felt harsh. She tucked the figure into her waist pouch. *If a Mikino did not slay her, who did? You are so sure a Hamapa did. Maybe the Aja Hama had decided to expel you and your birth sister and you killed her in order to stay in the tribe. You are not a true Hamapa.*

Enga stared. The beating in her chest stopped. She dropped to the ground and tried to draw a breath. *No!*

Hama gave Enga a sly glance. *I heard that Aja Hama did not want you. Twins bring bad luck to the tribe. She always wanted to get rid of you.*

The venom of Hama's lies struck her like a snake bite to the stomach. Enga sprang up and ran from the circle of light. She could not stay here and receive those thoughts. They were not true!

She ran into the cold woods, but soon stopped. Her tears blinded her in the darkness and she was afraid she would run into something. Maybe even a dangerous animal.

The Hamapa tribe has to know how much Ung Strong Arm and I loved our old Hama. She was not our birth mother, but she was our true mother. She loved us. Why does this Hama torment me this way?

Enga stumbled, then sank to the damp earth and curled her body into a round shape.

If an animal eats me, maybe then Hama will feel guilt, and shame. Maybe the Hamapa will expel Hama herself.

She knew she could not stay alone in the woods at dark time. Her sobs quieted bit by bit. She sat up. The wind moaned above her, sending gusts across her face and drying her tears.

Soon, thought-feelers broke through the darkness in her head. Old Sannum Straight Hair had followed her. He reached her and she rose and fell sobbing into his strong, warm arms.

He stroked her hair and crooned a low, audible note that rose and fell. *Come back, Enga Dancing Flower. Cabat the Thick and Panan One Eye have both told her she must not say such things.*

But do any believe her? That I would do such a thing? That I am not a true Hamapa?

Most do not.

Do any? Do some Hamapa believe her?

He did not reply. But that was her answer. There were some who did.

*****

After Enga Dancing Flower returned and everyone calmed down, Jeek's mind wandered far from the deliberations of the tribe. The commotion of Hama's charges, and Enga's distress, both were over for now. But Jeek knew the animosity would surface again. This was not finished.

Jeek gnawed on his hair and considered what he had heard so far. Gunda, sitting halfway across the gathering from him, had a worried look on her face.

What do you think about all this? he asked her.

I do not know. I have never seen a Mikino.

I haven't either, but we know they eat babies.

He saw Gunda shudder. *It's hard to imagine eating a baby.*

But Jeek knew that traders had brought stories of them from far away, stories that put fear into Jeek, fear into all the Hamapa. Hamapa loved their babies. Panan One Eye, the Storyteller, often said that the babies were the future of the tribe.

The new Hama, still in charge of the meeting, invited solutions to the problem of too little food for the coming Dark Season.

We need meat and fish. Soon ice will form on the streams and prevent catching fish. Even now there are few fish in the water and none in our traps.

Cabat the Thick, the Most High Male, was silent. The others were silent, also. Even Panan One Eye, the Storyteller.

Enga sat in brooding silence, her face flushed darkly, almost matching her auburn hair. Jeek had not seen her dimples lately and he missed her smile of sunshine.

The pain in his stomach turned his mind to food. Again, the image of a sleek, fat beaver appeared to Jeek. It made spit pool in his mouth. In Jeek's daydream, he sought the watery home of the giant beaver, the fearsome beast no one hunted, the dreaded animal as long as two and one-half Hamapa males laid head to feet.

Panan One Eye entered Jeek's thoughts.

I will tell of the Saga of the Giant Beaver of ancient times, he told Jeek, then began his tale.

In the times that are the dimmest in the memories of Storytellers, there lived a Giant Beaver, an Enormous Beaver, greater than the ones who live now. He was given a task by Dakadaga, the Spirit of Mother Sky. Her child, Brother Earth, was covered with swirling waters and there was no dry land. Dakadaga and Beaver dove to the bottom of the waters and brought up piles of mud. They shaped the mud into hills and valleys.

Then Dakadaga built mountains and caves while Beaver made paths for the water so it could run in rivers and streams. Beaver sent water over the mountains to make waterfalls, and dug deep holes to make lakes.

Jeek had never heard this Saga before. He tried to imagine such a time, with no land. There could have been no Hamapa, no land animals for them to eat. Jeek remembered a Saga of Brother Earth Shaking that Panan had told not long ago. In that Saga, Brother Earth, angered by the Hamapa, tried to get them off his back. But how could there be a time with no Brother Earth? He knitted his brow trying to imagine it.

When Dakadaga declared the work finished, Beaver rejoiced in what they had created. But then males and females were placed into the creation by Mother Sky. Beaver was jealous and did not want to share his creation. This Beaver invaded the villages and devoured males and females.

Jeek sat very still. Every Hamapa eye was on the one eye of Panan to see what came next from inside his mind. Mother Sky exhaled and a sudden gust of wind sent sparks into the sky. One fell on the bare head of Panan. He absently brushed it off and continued his tale.

Dakadaga despaired of her creation and declared that beavers would only eat fish in the future. And so people survived and the beaver does not eat them in these times. Now the beaver eats only fish.

Jeek cocked his head when a new idea occurred to him. *The beavers do eat fish. Many, many fish. The trouble we are having finding fish is because the beavers have eaten so many fish.* Cabat the Thick stepped into his thinking.

That is a true thought. I have had the same one. Beavers eat so many fish there are not enough left for the Hamapa.

And I can fix that, shot back Jeek. He imagined himself stabbing the beaver until it died. He pictured a huge store of meat from his kill and a large, thick, warm pelt. Countless garments would be made of this pelt. It would be called The Pelt of Jeek.

Jeek drifted off into another daydream. In this one he had passed fifteen summers and it was the day of his Passage Ceremony. His tribe was so proud of him for having saved them by slaying the beaver. Dakadaga had given his new name to Hama, and it was Jeek Beaver Slayer. Or maybe Jeek Master Beaver Slayer. Hama raised her gourd, then lowered it toward the shoulder of Jeek, Master Beaver Slayer. He caught Gunda's eye, then bowed his head and smiled to—

NO! This stern warning was from Cabat the Thick.

Jeek looked up and Cabat's gaze caught him and held him. His fleshy lips pooched out with the frown he gave Jeek.

No, Young One. You cannot slay the beaver. Our best female hunters cannot slay the beaver. He stays in the water. We cannot get to him.

And, even if we could get to him, Cabat continued, *our Saga says we must not eat the beaver. He helped create the land and it would be wrong to eat him. It would anger Dakadaga.*

Jeek's dream vanished. He would not be able to save the tribe. He would not be able to bring home meat from the beaver. He knew his vision, if it had continued, would have next included Gunda, looking at him with admiration, her green eyes large and glowing under her thick lashes. Most of his daydream visions ended that way.

Gunda had heard his scolding and avoided his eye for the rest of the meeting.

As Jeek shuffled to his wipiti to ready for sleep and the time of no sun, an agitation spread to him. The trouble again came from Doon.

How will it now be possible for Fee Long Thrower to look upon Doon with favor? I failed to bring meat home. I failed to win favor from Fee Long Thrower. Can there be a way to make her eyes shine on me?

Doon was not sending this out, but its emotion was strong and Jeek was close by. Sometimes slow-witted Doon could not control his feelings as well as the other Hamapa could. Even though Doon's thoughts were somber colored, flashes of bright excitement kept them from being private. Jeek apprehended a clear golden picture of Doon, standing tall before the tribe, the stoop in his shoulders gone, convincing them to kill the giant beaver. Had Jeek's own daydreams been influenced by wisps from Doon? Or maybe Jeek's musings had been taken up by Doon?

In Doon's vision, Fee Long Thrower smiled when she looked on Doon. His head did not look nearly so flat in the back. Then there was a scene with the baby, bloodied and dead. Doon depicted the giant beaver killing Fee's baby.

Jeek scrunched his eyes shut and closed his mind off before he could hear more. Doon's thoughts were not good. They filled Jeek with fear, made him afraid of Doon. Could those thoughts bring a beaver to harm the baby?

Then his eyes flew open wide. He must do something. Fee was in the Holy Cave, surrounded by females and safe as long as she was confined. After that she would be vulnerable. He could stay near Fee after she went home from the Holy Cave so that she was not alone. Or he could stay close to Doon. He must ponder this.

Another notion occurred to Jeek. Doon had betrayed feelings of violence. And Jeek believed what Enga Dancing Flower contended, that a Hamapa had slain their leader, not a Mikino. It must take deep, deep violence to be able to slay a person. Could Doon have done it? But Doon was not smart enough to sneak up on a Hama and kill her. Was he?

Jeek's spirit weighed heavy that night. His mother came to check on him before she returned to the Holy Cave.

I must tend Fee and the baby, but I know there is a sadness in you.

I'll be all right. Jeek turned to the wall.

His mother stroked his head. *Do not be too bothered. Our tribe has always made it through times of little meat. We will this time, too.*

He knew his sadness bothered her, but he didn't want to tell her what he had overheard, or to share his suspicions with her. His mother needed to tend the new mother and didn't need other worries.

Maybe he would talk to Enga Dancing Flower about Doon. Her mind was clever and she always listened to Jeek when he wanted to say something, even though he was not yet an adult.

His birth mother held him, hummed to him, and swayed back and forth to comfort him for a few moments before she left. Jeek kept his thoughts close and, in spite of the rumblings in his tummy, he eventually fell asleep. But his dreams were not good during that dark time. They held giant beavers, even bigger than the ones he'd seen, and bloody babies, and Doon with a huge gaping mouth and wild eyes.

*****

It was dark time and Enga Dancing Flower was almost asleep. But an odor aroused her. She didn't associate this smell with her wipiti. She sniffed again, then knew who it was. The New One. He stood near, she could tell, but not inside her dwelling. She thought he must be just outside.

What did she think of this creature? One moment she admired him greatly, the next she was repelled by his appearance. She, along with many in the tribe, valued his talents for sewing. At times it occurred to her that he must be terribly lonely, being isolated by not being able to read thoughts. Vala Golden Hair spent a lot of time with him. Maybe she had figured out a way to communicate with him.

Enga liked the carving he had given her. It had lain in a place of honor, next to her spear, until it disappeared. He seemed to desire to stay and be a member of the tribe. And, usually she was glad he was with them. He would have died if they hadn't taken him in. But she wasn't the only Hamapa to be repelled by him. Enga couldn't make up her mind.

She shuddered and thrilled at the same time to think of touching that milky white skin. And those eyes were so pink. Strange, that those eyes were wide-set in such a narrow face.

Enga rose from her bed on one elbow, concentrated, and sent the New One a question. *What do you want?*

No answer came. Enga drew her brows down. She didn't know what to do. Did he wish to communicate with her? If she felt more alert could she receive his thoughts?

After she heard him depart she lay awake a long while, feeling thunder booming in her chest and pounding in her ears, fearing he would return. And afraid of what she might want to do if he did.

Chapter 10

Neanderthals build homes with mammoth bones... The bone structure was found near the town of Molodova in eastern Ukraine on a site that was first discovered in 1984. It was constructed of 116 large bones including mammoth skulls, jaws, 14 tusks and leg bones.

Inside at least 25 hearths filled with ash were also discovered, suggesting it had been used for some time.

—From http://www.telegraph.co.uk/science/science-news/8963177/Neanderthals-built-homes-with-mammoth-bones.html

The Hamapa traders reached the site of the next village after a journey of three suns, as Goe the Cuva had said they would. The sparse trees were mostly birch. When they thinned out, the land opened into a rolling plain of short, blasted grasses. On the tundra, the breath of Mother Sky blew harder and colder with every step. She seemed angry.

Bahg Swiftfeet lagged behind the others as Sister Sun dipped low, focusing his mind on his warm mate and his soft, chubby, newborn son, until Tog Flint Shaper summoned him. Bahg sent a quick loving message to Fee Long Thrower and ran to catch up with the others.

He almost bumped into his tribal brothers at the edge of the village. Sister Sun had gone to sleep, leaving the bosom of Mother Sky, but

Brother Moon, becoming slim now, had come out early this night. He shone his eerie half-light on the village. Goe had not told them the name of this tribe. Maybe the Cuva called them by a name they made up, as the Hamapa had done with the Cuva.

This is as deserted as the Cuva village, thought-spoke Bahg.

Maybe more deserted, answered Tog. *I don't detect anyone here. Nothing is stirring.*

Even the wind died down suddenly. The puzzled males, their necks prickling with the eeriness, stepped softly across the central meeting place, paved like that of the Hamapa. The stones, the color of dark blood rather than the snow white of their own, absorbed Brother Moon's pale beams.

I smell no life here, thought-spoke Bahg, his nostrils distended.

The empty homes were wrapped in skin and piled with reddish rocks around the bases, and the staves were of mammoth tusk, like those of the Hamapa. Bahg stepped closer to one.

Look at this, he thought-spoke to Teek. *It is not whole.*

Teek, at the dwelling next to that one, agreed. *Not a single one of these could shelter anyone for the night.*

The skins were torn and some of the sturdy tusks snapped into two and three parts. Bahg walked from one to another, trying to see what had done this.

A set of parallel rips in one of the skins told him a long-legged, short-faced bear, a fearsome animal with huge, dexterous claws, was probably responsible.

Tog saw him examining the skin and overheard his pondering. *But this bear usually lives on scraps that other creatures leave. Why would it attack a living being?*

Do you remember a Saga by Panan One Eye recently? asked Bahg. *We were on the hunt, and we sat and received it. He told of a time of great hunger, when a short-faced bear attacked the birth mother of the birth mother of our Most High Female who was just slain.*

They recalled that Saga, and they cringed, half expecting a bear to rise up from the silent, empty space surrounding them.

Bahg sent a thought. *I hope these people were gone when the village was attacked.*

I'm not sure they were, answered Tog. They all looked to where he pointed, at a pile of bones, white in the moonlight, beside the cold, black fire pit. Bahg ran over and saw the bones had been snapped apart and gnawed upon.

More evidence of a bear, Bahg thought-spoke.

He saw terror in Tog's tight jaw. Would a bear attack them soon? They all searched the surroundings for scents.

But look at these, thought-spoke Tog, relaxing a notch and running his fingers over the rough edges of the bones. *They are not new. They are old and have been in the dirt.* He sent a picture of a bear digging the bones up from the dirt, then gnawing on them.

When Bahg bent and picked one up, he saw what Tog meant. Dirt clung to the fissures in the dry bones. The bears must be very hungry to dig up old bones like this. Is there not even food for them? he wondered. *Let us try and locate their burial ground. We can see if these bones came from there.*

Let's look for it at new sun, suggested Tog Flint Shaper. They all agreed they were tired and hungry and it would be best to rest for the night. Tog picked a place to camp among some aspen saplings next to the nearby stream. Bahg had trouble falling asleep, hungry from eating very little jerky for several suns now.

*****

Enga Dancing Flower rose early, to be ready if Ung Strong Arm needed anything. It had been many suns since the goring of her leg, and Ung was getting restless spending most of her time inside.

Help me to sit outside, Sister, requested Ung after they had braided each other's hair and donned cloaks. Enga fastened the door flap open and the light of Sister Sun poured in. The air was crisp and clear, carrying the scent of drying leaves and needles, a beautiful day for this season of shorter sun times. *If only we weren't so hungry,* wished Enga.

Lakala Rippling Water sat nearby, braiding strips of leather together.

Would you like help? Lakala thought-asked.

Enga, grateful for the assistance, noticed, with a flood of inner warmth, the tenderness growing between her birth sister and the official Singer of the tribe. She had seen Sannum Straight Hair smile at those two, also. At least Enga could rely on the support of Sannum and Lakala, even if the rest of the tribe turned against them. Enga still stung from Hama's accusation in the last meeting. How many of her Hamapa brothers and sisters would side with her? Could some of them suspect she killed Aja Hama? Did more than their new Hama want to expel her and Ung?

You can help me get Ung Strong Arm to a seat by the fire, Lakala Rippling Water, thought-spoke Enga. *Ung can not yet put much weight on her injured leg.*

Of course I will help.

We are grateful for your help, put in Ung.

Enga and Lakala supported Ung across the square and got her seated close to the fire. The tribe was gathering for the first meal of the day. At the edge of the flames, a thin gruel of nuts, seeds, and water sat warming in a wooden trencher, a hollow log smeared with mud on the outside to keep it from burning.

This brew smells vile, remarked Ung.

We have this and some dried fish, thought-spoke Lakala. *That is all we have for this meal.*

Enga made a face. Like all Hamapa, she disliked eating anything but meat, and occasional berries.

Gruel should be for elders who have lost teeth and can no longer chew meat, she thought-spoke.

I remember chewing meat for the mother of my mother, thought-spoke Lakala. *But I do not remember eating this stuff.* She tucked a skin around Ung.

Sannum carefully scooped up some gruel in a hollowed half-gourd and brought it to Ung.

Enga knew that Sannum and Lakala and, of course, Ung, would always stand at her side if needed.

Zhoo of Still Waters trotted down the hill, ate quickly, then took some food with her for Fee Long Thrower, still in the cave with her baby. Enga watched her go. This nurturing female with the caring hands surely would not turn against her either.

The New One arrived after Zhoo left. His eyes, usually merely pink, were an angry red today, like the robes Sister Sun sometimes wore when she was ready for sleep. Enga tried to penetrate his mind, but could not, as usual.

Cabat the Thick grunted as he crouched and scooped out a large portion of food into an eating gourd, then carried it toward the wipiti of Hama, who had not joined them. Cabat had to know there was no truth to what Hama had said, that she and Ung were not unwanted by Aja Hama. The only one who had never wanted them was Nanno Green Eyes, now Hama.

Panan One Eye jumped up, very quickly for a male of his age, which was more summers than twice the number of fingers and toes. He planted his feet wide in front of Cabat, blocking his way.

Enga Dancing Flower watched the two carefully, fear vibrating inside her. Panan, while muscular, was not nearly as big around as Cabat, and a little shorter. After the spear had destroyed Panan's eye so long ago, a fall had caved his head in slightly on the same side. This was even more obvious because of his baldness; his head was as smooth as a river rock. If Cabat's head had possessed dents, they would not have been visible through his glossy curls. The thickness of Cabat, while it slowed his walking and running, gave him an aura of physical power that Panan did not possess.

Panan nevertheless drew himself up to his full height and confronted Cabat. *There is no need to take so much for Hama. She is one person. Several of the tribe have not yet eaten and there is almost nothing left.*

Cabat stuck his arm out and pushed at Panan's chest. *Get out of my way,* he thought-spoke.

I will not let you do this, thought-screamed Panan, and he grabbed the gourd. The two males struggled until it clattered to the ground, spilling the precious food onto the stones.

Why are you waiting upon this Hama? asked Panan. *She is not your mate. She is your leader.*

I waited upon Aja Hama, shot Cabat, bending to retrieve the gourd.

The good eye of Panan narrowed. *Yes, you did. Although she was going to send you away and take me back.*

Cabat froze, then straightened up, the gourd dangling in his hand. Enga closed her eyes and willed them to quit quarreling.

She was not! I was so good to her. Cabat waved the gourd at Panan, flinging flecks of gruel onto him.

But you were ignoring her too much. And she wanted to return to me, the seed-giver who gave her the most children. I think you knew this and waited upon her the day she died. For her last meal, the evening meal.

Yes. Yes, I was there. I saw her before she died. Cabat's face sagged. *We fought.*

And you killed her? asked Panan. *You were angry so you killed her?*

Enga's fists clenched in her lap. She wanted to scream at them to stop. The group could not remain together if the Elders quarreled with each other. Cabat had assaulted Aja Hama? She had to keep paying attention, had to know if Cabat killed her.

No! No! We fought, yes, we fought, and I even ripped her clothing open. Those antler buttons popped off her tunic. But I did not kill her. We were both angry with each other. But I would never harm her. She was alive—and still angry—when I left her.

Cabat had laid hands on Hama! He had assaulted their leader and ripped her clothing. What else had he done?

Cabat turned and slowly waddled away, heading for the woods, still clutching the empty gourd.

The tribe froze, everyone motionless for a moment, no one blinking an eye or daring to draw in breath. Then Enga joined Panan and several others in trying to push the spilled food into another gourd. They saved some of it, but it was cold now. The salvaged gruel was returned to the wooden trencher, to warm near the fire.

Eventually, after everyone else had gotten a share, Hama arrived. She peered at the gruel, frowned at the quantity, then scooped up what remained and began to wolf it down. She did not comment on the absence of Cabat.

Young Jeek, the son of the Healer, squatted beside the fire. He hunched his shoulders and chewed rapidly on a strand of his hair, then spit it aside and shoved the last of his own gruel into his mouth. Enga wondered if something besides the Elders' argument was bothering him. After he had gulped his last morsel, he arose and approached Enga with slow, uncertain steps, his brow furrowed in his smooth face. She liked the young lad, his energy and enthusiasm. He had been one who had helped retrieve the spilled gruel.

Before Jeek reached her, though, Hama finished eating and stood up. She rattled her gourd to get their attention.

It is now time time for Fee Long Thrower to return to her own wipiti.

Jeek's eyes sent Enga a lost, worried appeal and his little chin quivered. She would make time to see what troubled him as soon as she could.

But now she must pay attention to Hama.

Enga nodded with the others over the announcement. Yes, it was time for Fee to return home. The baby, thanks to the blessings of Dakadaga and the Spirit of Birthing, was healthy and getting plumper. It was enough days, the number of one handful of fingers less one, since his birth. Sometimes new mothers stayed in the cave longer, but the tribal sisters agreed that Fee was ready to travel.

Why do we not try to get to the bottom of the slaying of the Aja Hama? wondered Enga to herself. She wanted to share her thought with Ung, but, after what had happened at last dark time, she guarded this idea carefully from Hama, and all the others as well. *There is a killer among us. It appears that Hama will not pursue this matter, other than to accuse me. But someone should find out what happened. I will tune in to all the sisters and brothers as much as I can and try to discover their innermost secrets.*

As Enga rose to go up the Sacred Hill to help get Fee, she swayed. Little gray dots swam before her eyes, then slowly disappeared. She was so tired. A scrap of ill-guarded thought from Ongu Small One, the female who had not won the election for leader, floated to her. Enga could not be certain, but she thought Ongu was thinking that Nanno, the new Hama, should not be their leader. She, Ongu, would be better suited for the position and—here Enga's eyes widened and her breath caught—the Hamapa would be better off if Nanno were not a Hamapa, if she were not alive.

Enga told herself she might have misunderstood the faint notions. They were just wisps, and complicated, and Enga was not clear in her mind. She would tuck away what she had just overheard. If Ongu never again had thoughts like these, Enga would ignore them.

But she could not disregard the tension among the three Elders. The situation could not work for the good of the Hamapa tribe. A person alone could not live. The tribe must stay together, must work together. And they must have good leadership. It was the only way they survived.

*****

Fee Long Thrower gave her tribal sisters a grateful smile and settled into her own furskin bed with the baby. She was well supplied with soft coverings for her infant. Enga Dancing Flower could tell Fee was happy to be at home.

But not happy to have Bahg Swiftfeet so far away, Fee thought-spoke.

Yes, we all miss the males, answered Enga. *I will be glad when Tog Flint Shaper is back also.*

Hama frowned at their interchange. Enga could not penetrate her mind, though, to see why she frowned. Maybe Hama assumed they were criticizing her for sending the males on the trading mission. Enga turned her mind completely inward and imagined, for a brief moment, the baby she would someday have after she mated with Tog, a pink and

106

chubby baby like this one. Would it have her red hair or the dark mane of Tog?

The women fussed over Fee awhile, then left her to be alone with her baby for the first time. The Hamapa went about their daily business. Some went to the stream to see if their traps held any fish. Some ground the meal they were presently forced to eat.

Enga could not shake the prickly, frantic feeling she had had ever since Hama had spoken out against her. The terrifying vision of being thrust into the woods with Ung would not leave her mind. She pictured the tribal sisters and brothers screaming at them, throwing things, hurling harmful thoughts after them. Drops of sweat sprang to her palms.

But she had not killed Aja Hama. And she must prove she had not. The best way to do that would be to find out who had. She was certain a Hamapa was responsible.

Enga remembered Jeek trying to tell her something and looked around for him, to see if they could discuss what was troubling him now, but couldn't see him. She tried to ponder the killing of Hama, but her hunger soon prevented her from concentrating. Doing something about the meat shortage was more pressing. The young girls had not had spear practice since the mammoth hunt went wrong. Fee was their usual instructor. Enga had only assisted her a couple of times and felt unqualified to lead the practice, but she would try. They girls should resume their lessons. She took a deep breath, squared her shoulders, and summoned the girls.

*****

The Hamapa buried their dead leaders on the top of the Sacred Hill, but there was no large hill nearby.

There are no hills here to bury the dead, thought-spoke Tog Flint Shaper. *So where would this tribe with no name bury theirs?*

They have to put them somewhere, answered Bahg Swiftfeet.

If we find a graveyard, and these bones by the fire have been dug up from there, we can rebury them, thought-spoke Teek Pathfinder.

107

They spread out and combed the rolling grasslands, seeking anything that might look like a graveyard. As they searched, Bahg joined his companions in wondering where all the living ones had gone. He climbed a small rise and searched through the growth of stunted willow bushes on its side. No burials here. Maybe if they found the burial ground it would give them a clue about what happened to this tribe.

Soon young Teek gave a shout and Bahg ran in the direction of the sound. He crested the next rise. Teek stood in a depression that was deeper than the others in the area. He held a bone in one hand and waved his arms, jumping up and down and pointing to his feet. Wisps of his streaked blond hair, refusing to stay bound, bounced on his forehead.

Bahg Swiftfeet paused at the top of the knoll, rooted to the spot, unable to move. The view to the north spread out before him. Beyond the rolling hills spread a vast, windswept grassy plain. Beyond that rose high ridges of broken rock mixed with uprooted birch, willow, and pine trees.

Looming far off in the distance, many more days of travel away, a massive field of white shone in the cold sunlight. The visions of the Time of Great Ice, given to him by Panan One Eye, the Storyteller, paled before this sight. This ice struck him with awe and brought shards of cold to his insides.

This is what is coming. It will destroy everything in its path.

At the top of the rise, the icy breath of Mother Sky tore at his back. After his brief glimpse of the future, the wind impelled him down the slope. But, halfway to the bottom, he halted again.

The dirt at Teek's feet was deeply furrowed. Piles of bones, torn from their careful resting places, lay like small snowdrifts around him. He had found the burial ground and animals had obviously disturbed it. Either this tribe had buried many, many leaders, or they had buried everyone in the tribe as they died, instead of exposing and giving back the bodies as the Hamapa did.

Tog Flint Shaper and Donik Tree Trunk came pounding down behind Bahg. They, too, were halted and sobered by the sight of the bones. The three started to draw closer to Teek, using caution in this strange place, the only sounds their harsh rasps and the rustling of the tall grasses in the bitter wind. At least Mother Sky's breath was not as fierce lower in the hollow.

A roar sounded above the whine of the wind. Bahg jerked his head toward the sound and flared his nostrils. No smell could come against the blast of cold.

Then a shrill squeal came to Bahg from a nearby stand of stunted willow bushes. A small cub bawled and ambled from the bushes, his long, ungainly legs and his cute, short snout giving him a harmless appearance. At another time, Bahg would consider trying to kill the animal for food. But not now. They were between the cub and source of the roaring.

The four males braced themselves for what would come over the hill.

Chapter 11

The girls made their way to the meadow, trailing Enga Dancing Flower. There had been no spear practice for too many suns. The last one had been on the day before their instructor, Fee Long Thrower, had gone hunting.

Jeek watched the girls file into the woods, especially Gunda, the oldest. They all looked eager to learn to hunt. Gunda had confided to him she was a little worried about her Passage Ceremony, which she would have in only two summers, since she was ten now. She would become an adult and acquire her adult name at that time, and she wanted to be able to hunt well enough for an impressive name. She would not like to be called Gunda Bad Aim.

I hope, Jeek thought, *she will be ready to hunt well by then. She must.*

Jeek followed them, undetected, and observed from the edge of the field, hiding behind a stand of tall ferns, glad he was slim enough to do this. He loved to watch the concentration on Gunda's face as she aimed her spear. Her braid, shiny in the sunlight and the color of ripe red berries, swung as she bent to pick up a spear, and again as she flung it toward the target, an old, battered gray wolf skin. His breath caught when she stretched and heaved another spear across the clearing.

Males did not throw spears, only females. Jeek knew this—his birth mother had told him many times—but he could not understand why. He wanted to throw spears. He had always wanted to. He knew Gunda would be impressed if he could do something no other male could. But he had no spear. Only females had them. He supposed the caribou hunt had demonstrated that only females should. Still, he wanted to spear, too.

My little goose, his mother would thought-speak to him, stroking his tangled hair. *Males do not possess the patience that females do. And they could not throw straight. And look at the mess your hair is in.* She spent every night, when there were not patients to tend, smoothing out his hair and binding it up. He knew she wanted him to crop his hair as she did, but he would miss it if he did. When he became the Healer he would chop it off with a flint knife the way his mother did.

Jeek often followed the girls to watch Gunda. His mind was also on the spears and how it must feel to throw them. He was so very hungry and the girls were missing the target more often than they hit it. Could he do better? Enga Dancing Flower seemed nervous instructing them. Maybe she did not know how to teach them. He pulled a strand of his blond-streaked hair out of its twist and chewed on it as he watched.

Gunda ran to the target and picked up the spears. Jeek kicked the ground around him, searching, then picked up a straight stick, almost the length of a spear. He watched Gunda and held the stick just as Gunda held her spear. She sighted the center of the skin and held the spear straight out before her, then drew her arm back and hurled it. It fell short. Enga Dancing Flower sent her a kind message of comfort, smiling warmly at her, showing her deep dimples. Enga held Gunda's arm and guided it, trying to correct her throwing, but it did not improve in three more tries. The next girl took her turn.

Jeek watched for a few more moments. It was obvious to him that none of the young girls would be ready to hunt soon. The youngest, only six summers old, could barely hurl the spear halfway to the target.

He traveled farther into the forest with his stick. On the edge of the stream he found a thick bush with dark purple berries, the sour ones called softberries. He concentrated on one small berry and threw his stick at it. He hit a berry, but not the one he had tried for. He made another attempt. The stick missed all the berries and traveled deep into the bush. He crawled into the bush to get the stick, groping in the shadows for it. Something sharp pricked him and he drew it to his mouth to suck the Red that formed a little bead on his fingertip.

Looking more closely he saw a pile of antlers, looking as if someone had hidden them there. He briefly wondered if he should let the tribe know so they could use them for something, but then he saw his stick next to them. He was eager to practice, so he dragged it out and kept throwing it until he hit a targeted berry. A huge grin split his face when he did. He threw and threw and threw, hitting more and more of the berries he aimed at.

Now he wanted to try it with a real spear, no matter what his mother said. He returned to the practice area to watch from behind the ferns.

After the group broke for a rest, he thought-called Gunda to him, softly and narrowly, so the others could not hear. *Follow me into the woods,* he told her. *And bring your spear.*

I should tell Enga Dancing Flower I am leaving, answered Gunda. She glanced around for Enga, but didn't see her.

Come on, Jeek urged. *I must show you something. It's not far.*

Just for a minute, Jeek. I don't want to miss practice. Gunda left her group and joined Jeek.

It won't take long.

The warmth of Gunda beside him almost made him dizzy. He took her hand, small in his, and led her. When Jeek reached his softberry bush he asked to borrow Gunda's spear. She was confused.

What would you do with my spear, Jeek? Males do not throw spears.

But maybe it is a time for something new. We have no meat and no spear throwers. I have been watching your practice. None of you can throw well enough to bring down an animal.

Gunda frowned, but handed her spear to Jeek. The renewed touch of her soft little fingers stopped him for a moment. Then he threw the spear at the bush. It went too far.

Gunda looked a question at him, but he retrieved the spear and tried a few more times. When he hit the berry he aimed for, Gunda's small mouth fell open, then smiled. That smile brought sunlight into this dark part of the forest.

We should tell Hama, Gunda. I can hunt for the tribe.

Once more Gunda frowned. *But we use more than one hunter to bring down a large beast. You cannot get a mammoth alone. Maybe you should keep practicing until you can throw three spears at once.*

Remembering the pile of antlers in the bush, Jeek started to send a thought to Gunda. *I have another surprise. Look what I found.* He took a step toward the bush.

Just then Gunda received a message from Enga Dancing Flower which she shared with Jeek. *They are resuming practice. I must return.*

She grabbed her spear and hurried away to rejoin the group. Jeek followed behind her, mad at himself for bragging, and for saying she didn't throw the spear well. What if she didn't like him anymore? She had frowned when he said that.

At the clearing, the two children halted. The spear throwers had left. Jeek and Gunda opened their minds and caught an urgent summons. They trotted toward the village.

The light was fading, the time of darkness was coming. All Hamapa knew they could not be in the woods during the darkness. They must be near fire. The fiercest of the predators roamed at night, but the animals feared fire.

Jeek asked Gunda if he could carry her spear. She said no.

Gunda thought-spoke, *The others are just ahead. Let's run to catch them.*

As he ran Jeek considered telling the elders of his new ability. *But I do not think I will be allowed to hunt. It has never been done that a male throws the spear.*

Gunda looked at Jeek and pondered. *Do you really think you could help the tribe, Jeek?*

He turned to face her as they jogged, slowing now as they drew near enough to the village to smell the smoke from the fire. *I want to hunt.* He waved his arm like a spear thrower to emphasize his thoughts. *But maybe I won't ask permission. If I ask and I am denied, then I cannot hunt.*

Gunda stopped and turned her eyes on him. They were the color of new spring leaves, even in the gathering dusk. *You want to hunt without permission? Alone?*

Maybe not alone, he answered.

Suddenly, a clamor met them. Many Hamapa were wailing aloud. Jeek and Gunda looked at each other, puzzled. What could be the trouble? Jumbled thoughts were flying, too many and too distraught to make sense. Some of them sent pain and some sent a vision of brilliant, flowing Red. The two children broke into a run.

One vision emerged above the others: Fee Long Thrower, unconscious, followed by the face of her baby, screaming. Jeek's chest grew cold. He ran faster.

Gunda's mother, Roh Lion Hunter, met them as soon as they entered the village. She had sensed them coming. She drew Jeek and Gunda to her and squeezed them against her soft breast. Roh was not much taller than Jeek, a stocky, solid female. She was not tall like her birth mother, who was now the Hama. Trying to rest his head on her shoulder was awkward as she gripped them both in her strong arms.

Our beautiful baby! Her voice wailed high and sharp. *The baby has been hurt! And Fee Long Thrower also!* Roh gave them a thought-view of Fee's wipiti. They understood Roh was seeing this through Jeek's mother, Zhoo of Still Waters, who was in the wipiti.

A small inside fire burned near the doorway, throwing as much shadow as light on the support tusks and the walls of mammoth skin. The baby lay kicking and squalling on the dirt floor, his tiny pink hand mangled and crushed, his cozy bed of camel skin empty next to him. Fee lay very still on her bearskin, and her Red was flowing from a wound in her hair. Zhoo knelt near Fee, radiating calmness.

Jeek closed his eyes and touched his mother's mind lightly to see Fee and the baby better. Several Hamapa females, led by his mother, were in attendance. Zhoo was finishing wrapping Fee's head wound, who was not awake. Two of the others bent over the baby, picked him up and carried him to Zhoo. She placed him in his nest of soft camel skin and examined his crumpled little fist. The baby and Fee both smelled of milk, overlaid by the hard smell of Red.

Then Jeek's mind filled, unbidden, with Doon's vision he had seen, the vision of the beaver attacking the baby. Was it possible Doon could predict the future? He had vowed to keep track of Doon and make sure he didn't follow through on his dark thoughts. Jeek had failed. He had gone off into the woods to watch Gunda, forgetting all about Doon.

What is this new thought, Jeek? This came from his mother.

Doon had notions of the beaver hurting the baby of Fee Long Thrower. I heard them. Could Doon know the mind of the beaver? he asked.

I do not believe so, she answered.

He guarded his thoughts about Doon from the others, not sure what meaning to give to them. He wanted to find out more before sharing his speculation with others.

Wait! thought-spoke Roh to Gunda and Jeek. *I have just received a message from my mate, Donik Tree Trunk.* She eyed Jeek, then continued, *This must wait for later.* Jeek wished she would tell the news, because his brother, Teek, was on the trading mission with Donik and he had not had communication from him since two suns ago.

A summons to gather at the Paved Place was issued by Hama. The Most High Male went to stay with Fee and Zhoo during the meeting, and the rest of the Hamapa plodded with heavy feet to the gathering place.

Hama stood and delivered a thought. *Doon had a message for the Hamapa.*

Jeek jerked his head up, surprised. Doon, giving the tribe a message?

Doon strode slowly to stand beside Hama. When everyone had squatted and turned their full attention on him, he thought-spoke.

This baby, and Fee Long Thrower also, they have both been attacked by a giant beaver. I saw the beaver enter the wipiti of Fee Long Thrower and Bahg Swiftfeet. I saw the beaver leave the wipiti.

Thoughts tumbled toward Doon. *Why did we not see this? There is no scent of beaver. When did you see this? Where is the beaver now?*

He answered only partially. *The young girls were shooting, the males were gone trading, the rest were gathering nuts in the forest. And now Fee Long Thrower and the baby are dead.*

Jeek's eyebrows shot up. Fee Long Thrower was not dead, but Doon had just said she was. The others did not heed Doon's last thought. Jeek found this curious, but that last thought-speak was softer and more obscure than the rest, and they were always used to ignoring many of Doon's thoughts. The tribe was terrified at the idea of a giant beaver coming into their village. Jeek could tell this consumed them. They shivered and clutched each other. He wished his mother were beside him.

This has never happened since ancient times, the Storyteller told them. *The giant beaver no longer eats Hamapa. Has anyone seen tracks?*

Hama spoke aloud. This was her second Official Pronouncing. Every male and female took notice.

"Hoody! Listen! The Most High Female Speaks. The Hamapa will slay the giant beaver. The Spirit, Dakadaga, bless the Hamapa. The Spirit of the Hunt, bless the Hamapa."

So, with no discussion and too much haste, Jeek thought, it was decided. The Pronouncement made his empty stomach feel queasy. The Hamapa would hunt the giant beaver. The Hamapa seemed too stunned to object to Hama's quick decision.

Maybe we can eat the meat, thought-spoke Cabat. Jeek shuddered.

Lakala Rippling Water started a Song of Blessing to Dakadaga, the Spirit of Mother Sky, but Jeek heard her voice, usually fluent and beautiful, waver and crack. She next sang for healing for Fee and the baby and the tribe did a dance for them, accompanied by Sannum Straight Hair's slow drum and Panan One Eye's flute.

Then the Hamapa laid out their weapons and danced around them for a pre-hunt blessing, but their feet were heavy. Their minds were turning, one by one, to consider if it would be wise to hunt the beaver. Not all the thoughts were guarded.

Lakala continued with a Song of Blessing to the Spirit of the Hunt. This one was more intricate than the Song of Healing and Lakala stopped several times to sip from a water gourd in the middle of the chant. The New One held the gourd out to her.

Jeek sat at the edge of the dejected gathering, wrapped in his moose skin and his dark thoughts. He heard the confused thinking of the tribe as if at a distance.

How can we hunt and slay a beaver?

We have never done such a thing.

And if we do slay it, what do we do with the carcass?

Eat it? We have never eaten beaver.

And for good reason.

Some of them wanted to go see the tracks at Fee's wipiti.

In the front of his mind Jeek reasoned that Doon held twisted emotions regarding Fee and her baby. Doon thought about the baby being attacked. And then it happened. He tried to think of a benign explanation. Maybe Doon did not predict the future. Jeek did not believe he could. No one could predict the future. Maybe Doon made his vision come true.

A heavy hand gripped Jeek's shoulder.

Shut your mind! You are thinking harmful things of Doon.

He looked up into Kung's handsome, sneering face. *Bad things happen to those who wish ill to my friends.* Kung's words ran a chill up the back of Jeek's neck and made the hairs on his arms bristle like a porcupine. Kung's fingers dug into Jeek's shoulder, hard; then Kung released him and strutted away.

Now Jeek had a new thought. Had Kung helped Doon with the attack? He must discuss this with someone. He ran toward the wipiti of Enga Dancing Flower and Ung Strong Arm. Before he reached it, however, Cabat the Thick stepped in front of him.

Where are you going in such haste? Cabat asked.

I want to, I want to see if Enga Dancing Flower needs anything. To see if she needs help with Ung Strong Arm. Some instinct told him not to confide in Cabat.

She does not. And she is busy now. Do not disturb her.

It occurred to Jeek that Cabat was the birth father of Kung. Had he overheard their exchange? Could he tell that Jeek wanted to talk about Kung with Enga?

What are you plotting, young Jeek?

The shrewdness and accuracy of Cabat's question made his breath catch. His thoughts whirled and muddied. *Plotting? No, no plot, no plan. I just want, I just want to speak with Enga Dancing Flower.*

Cabat narrowed his eyes. *What about?*

I told you. Jeek spun away and went to sit by the fire. He watched until time to go to sleep, but Cabat did not get far enough away from Enga's wipiti for him to approach it.

*****

The males heard another fearsome roar, then a beast's head appeared at the top of the hill above the desecrated graves.

Bahg Swiftfeet's knees gave way. He caught himself with his hands before he hit the ground. He, Tog Flint Shaper, and Donik Tree Trunk, halfway down the hill, had not yet reached Teek Pathfinder, who stood in the middle of the dug-up graveyard at the bottom of the hill, holding the bone he'd discovered. Teek was nearest the bear cub, but had not yet seen it. He was too busy gaping at the huge mother bear.

Bahg knew that animals sometimes seemed to intercept thoughts and he did not want to send one to Teek. He also did not want to panic the boy.

So he crouched, rooted to the spot, as the fearsome beast crested the hill, slowly revealing her massive body. She reared up on her long hind legs to a height greater than that of two large Hamapa males, stacked up. Her mighty roar stood his every hair on end. Her stout curving fangs dripped with saliva and she waved enormous, sharp claws in the air, then thumped down onto all fours.

This propelled Bahg. He shot toward Teek, to protect him, but saw that even he, with his swift gait, would not reach Teek in time. He skidded to a halt. The mother bear pounded toward her cub. The other two males on the hill knelt and cowered in the tall grass. There was no way they could outrun the bear and there were no trees to climb. The three sent their dark despair to Teek and tried to send him strength. Teek now saw the cub and stood immobile between the two bears.

Bahg sent a frantic message, *Drop, curl up, play dead!* Teek threw the bone he was holding at the bear. He dove for the ground.

She reached him before he made it.

She swatted, hooking a claw into one of his arms.

Teek spun to the dirt, screamed, clutched his wounded arm with the other hand.

In less than a blink she was beside him. She swatted again.

Teek flew into the air.

Bahg felt the jolt through his feet when he landed.

Teek curled himself into a tight ball. The she-bear came at him again, batted him, then sat back. He rolled across the littered graveyard, bumping over the mounds of dirt and the piles of dug-up bones.

It grew quiet. The three males on the hillside held their breath, afraid she would hear them if they drew any air.

The wind current brought her stench of rank, damp fur to them. Bahg opened his mouth to keep from gagging on the smell. Then he could taste the odor on his tongue.

The mother animal ambled over to where young Teek lay, unmoving, utterly still. His blond-brown streaked hair had come loose and hid his face. She loomed over him on her hind legs and roared.

Then she dropped down and raked the claws of one paw down his back, cutting deep furrows through his mammoth skin cape. The groves immediately filled with blood.

Bahg absorbed Teek's pain, but took in his bravery, too. *Don't move. Stay still,* thought-spoke Bahg. Teek lay limp and motionless, barely breathing, even through his pain. Bahg could feel Teek clinging to the hopeful, almost prayerful, thoughts Bahg and the others were sending.

The bear sniffed, curling her lip, snorting with moist, slurpy sounds. The breeze swirled through the valley and lifted Teek's hair, ruffled the bear's fur. Then she batted him with her powerful front paw one last time, rolling him over again.

Still, Teek did not flinch. Neither did the three on the hill. Bahg held his mouth open and breathed shallowly, silently. He heard a roaring in his head like a waterfall.

The mother bear took one more deep whiff of Teek, nudged him with her snout, then ambled away the way she had come, the baby scooting along behind her.

The Hamapa males maintained their still, silent positions for a long time after the bears left, in case they came back.

Chapter 12

The giant beaver was the size of a large black bear and weighed 330 to 440 pounds (150 to 200 kilograms). It measured at least 9 feet (3 meters) long and stood about 3 feet (1 meter) tall at the shoulder. In comparison, the modern beaver measures up to 3.5 feet (more than 1 meter) long and weighs from 20 to 86 pounds (9 to 39 kilograms).

—*Ice Age Mammals of North America: A Guide to the Big, the Hairy, and the Bizarre*, Ian M. Lange, p. 120

Young Jeek plodded home at the end of the evening and lay down in his empty wipiti to sleep. He would have to confer with Enga Dancing Flower about Doon and Kung later.

Resisting Hama's undesirable idea of a beaver hunt, he tossed and turned for a long time. His bearskin felt hard and scratchy that night. But he knew her order must be carried out. They would have the hunt. No matter what the Most High Male said, Hamapas would never eat the meat. He could tell that much from stray thoughts during the meeting. Such a waste of time and energy, Jeek thought, carefully guarding his mind with midnight-purple hues.

His birth mother, Zhoo of Still Waters, finally came to the wipiti, but only for a short time since she must keep tending the injuries of Fee Long Thrower and the baby.

Do not be alarmed, she told Jeek. *But I have received a message from Roh Lion Hunter about your brother, Teek.*

Jeek sat up. *What of Teek? Is there danger to him?*

Zhoo closed her eyes and two tears squeezed out. Her lips trembled and she nodded her head. *Yes. He is in danger. I want to tell you before the others do. I experienced it at the time but did not know what it was. The attack on Fee Long Thrower happened at the same time and I was not able to sort it out right away. The mate of Roh Lion Hunter, Donik Tree Trunk, sent her a message telling her that Teek was attacked by a bear today. The males are bringing him home as quickly as they can. He is alive. Now I must return to tend the two injured Hamapa.*

Jeek did not get much sleep that night.

*****

The adults knew where the huge beaver dam was, near the swampy area in the direction of the rising sun, but away from the direction of the Guiding Bear of Mother Sky. The whole tribe now realized that neither Fee Long Thrower nor the baby was dead, despite the message of Doon. But Fee did not awaken and the baby's hand was mangled badly. It might happen that Zhoo of Still Waters could not fix it. She had treated it and bandaged it heavily with the inside of a soft rabbit skin.

Now, the next morning, Enga Dancing Flower and Roh Lion Hunter led the way to the dam with the girl children, Gunda and her two younger sisters, following. The youth also came, Kung, Mootak, and Doon, plus Akkal. Jeek had begged and pleaded until he, too, was allowed to go along, but Hama told him to go last and not get in harm's way.

I know I am younger than the others here, but Mootak has only seen twelve summers, one more than I have. Jeek scowled, stung with resentment. He saw there was no way he was going to be able to confer with Enga about his suspicions of Doon, Kung, and maybe even Cabat the Thick.

As they had left the village, filing past the elders who wished them good fortune, Cabat had thought-whispered with Hama, who had then made it clear to Enga that Kung was to be given a good position in the hunt. Cabat's whisper was not very private, nor Hama's instruction.

The five females carried spears; the five males brought large pieces of skin, in which to bring back the raw pelt of the beaver. The windy breath of Mother Sky, a constant for so many suns now, was still and Sister Sun gave them just a bit of warmth on their way through the woods.

Roh must be feeling much better, thought Jeek. She seemed to be completely recovered from the loss of her baby. He was glad of that. He liked Roh, and not just because she was Gunda's mother. Roh was an easy female to be around, sweet and caring. And not at all like Hama.

He was glad of the recovery of Ung Strong Arm also. She had walked unaided to Lakala Rippling Water's wipiti to spend the day there while Enga was away on the hunt.

But there was much he was not glad of. The favoritism to be given to Kung was not the custom of the Hamapa. There was something rotten in the leadership.

His other concern was personal and had nothing to do with the good of the tribe. It was petty of him, and he kicked at the mud clods on the path with the thought, but he wanted to carry a spear. He knew he threw it better than Gunda. And she was the oldest of the girls. On the other hand, he did not think the beaver should be speared. He thought the plan to hunt the beaver was not a good one. The animal could easily escape and hide inside his lodge or just under the water. Even if he were injured or killed he would go there. How would they retrieve such a huge body from those places? They needed a better plan.

Gunda fell back to walk beside Jeek. He took joy in the thrill her slim body made him feel and in her lustrous fiery hair, tamed into braids today. In just few years she would be a fine-looking adult. Her soft green eyes sought his.

Jeek, I want you to know how sorry I am about your birth brother, Teek Pathfinder. Maybe he was not injured too badly. He is still alive, at least.

The males had not sent any thought-pictures of Teek, which Jeek desperately wanted. Jeek took her hand and pressed it.

I am happy to receive your good thoughts. I cannot get him out of my mind, even though I do not know what he looks like right now, or how he is feeling. It was kind of her to express her feelings this way. But he wondered if she still thought he was a jerk for bragging about his spear throwing.

Just now I overheard you. About the beaver. Others are also complaining about the decision to hunt the beaver, you know. But Hama does not think it necessary to bring anything back. If we merely slay the beaver we will prevent future attacks and we will have more fish. It could be that her idea is good.

Jeek sent her a picture of the inside of the beaver lodge as he imagined it. It held many giant beavers.

Gunda took a moment to think about that. *So you think there are many?*

There has to be more than just one.

Then we will have to slay the largest one, thought-spoke Gunda. She gave Jeek a look of impatience and ran back to walk beside Enga Dancing Flower, giving Kung a smile on her way. Did she think Kung would be better at slaying the beaver than he would be? Jeek was by far the braver of the two. He knew that. Some day Gunda would see it. And, besides, what good would it do to slay just one beaver?

The trees had thinned during their journey and were now scarce. The marshy land, the kind preferred by the beavers, made them tread with care, finding hillocks and stretches of dry earth to walk on. Sister Sun shone warmer here. They progressed toward a line of trees that indicated water.

Jeek still kept to himself the feeling that there had not been a beaver attack. It was possible he was wrong and Doon did see it. If so, if there really had been a beaver attack, Doon had foretold it. Or at least thought about it before it happened. Jeek kicked at the dirt harder. He hated all this confusion. He bit down hard on a strand of his hair.

A thought-shout sounded in his head. They were at the beaver dam and all were to be quiet. A cautious statement came from Enga. *Now we must decide how to proceed. Shall we try to draw them out of their dwelling?*

Jeek and the others hunched down and crept ahead until they could see the pile of twigs and saplings, looming larger than a Hamapa house. The beaver lodge stood in a small lake created by the nearby dam, which bridged a narrow spot of the water.

On the other side of a boggy area below the dam, Jeek caught a glimpse of a black snout before it ducked under the water. Was that the beaver? He held his eyes so wide they felt dry, hoping to get another sighting. He had never seen a beaver before, just projections from other people's minds.

The air, still and stale, smelling of rotting vegetation, drifted from the surrounding swampland. Jeek wrinkled his nose and strained to look through the murky water for another glimpse of a beaver.

But he had missed some thoughts. He'd better pay attention to what Enga was conveying. *The idea of Gunda is a good one. We shall surround the dwelling of the beaver.*

Wait! Jeek could hold his thoughts no longer. *It would be better to trap the beaver, not try to spear it.*

The others laughed and he heard scraps of phrases: *stupid idea, how could a trap be that big, who could build it, how long…*

Jeek's cheeks burned. *I could build it,* he countered, not knowing how he would. *Give me a period of two suns and I can trap the beaver.*

Enga smiled and soothed him with a wave of softly colored thought. *We will attempt to spear it today. If we fail, you may build a trap, Jeek. For now, stay back.*

This was a small consolation, but at least Enga was pretending to take him seriously. He was grateful for that.

Then he saw it.

The creature climbed the bank to the wooded land on the other side of the swamp, revealing an expanse of wet, glossy fur as it pulled itself up with large, but delicate-looking, clawed feet, webbed between the toes. Its length was that of one and one half Hamapa males. The mental pictures he had seen had given him an idea of its size, but he hadn't quite imagined it this large. Its long tail was dark skin, having no fur.

It turned its head and Jeek saw the gleam of two front teeth, wide and white, curving outside its mouth for a length greater than Jeek's hand-span. A hard lump rose in his throat.

The creature turned its dripping body, faced them, and sat. It eyed the Hamapa band with cautious curiosity. Jeek wished he could see inside the mind of the majestic beast. He gazed into the small, bright eyes, but they were opaque to him. He tried to swallow the lump in his throat.

His brother and sister tribe members started to fan out slowly, but, with the movement, the beaver lumbered to the pond above its dam, slipped into the water, slapped the water with its long, curious tail, and disappeared under the roiling surface.

The hunters continued moving until they surrounded the pond and lodge, then hunkered down to wait. Jeek felt they would never spear the beaver. It would probably wait inside its lodge until they left.

They waited. Sister Sun traveled far, throwing a lengthening shadow of the lodge across the pond. No beaver appeared. The water lay still, its surface unbroken.

A thought came from Kung. *We have to prod it out of its dwelling. I will take a long stick and climb on the structure, then poke him and make him come out.*

Jeek could feel the adult females, Enga and Roh, resisting this idea, but the rest of the youth thought it might work. The older females capitulated and gave Kung permission to try to move the beaver. How much did the Hama's desire to give preference to Kung influence them? Jeek wondered. Roh told Kung that there was a place at the top of the lodge that was not as sturdy as the rest, to provide ventilation. Maybe he could get at them through that place.

Jeek saw a thought of Kung. *My Passage Ceremony will be soon. I will be named Kung Beaver Slayer.*

He countered back to Kung, *You are not slaying the beaver. You will be Kung Beaver Poker.*

Kung did not like that. He shut Jeek out and went toward the trees edging the water upstream to find a stout limb. He returned with a long spruce branch, stripped the needles, then stole toward the lodge.

He had no trouble wading through the chest-high water. He stopped when he got to the pile. A soft breeze had sprung up and carried the odor of the stale water to Jeek. It also carried the strong musk of the animals that must lie waiting inside the lodge.

It carried one more odor, too. Jeek smelled fear in Kung, but not as much as the fear Kung had radiated on the caribou hunt. Jeek decided to send good wishes for Kung. If this did work, and the beaver were speared, it would be a very good thing for the Hamapa. Kung disdained the well-wishes of Jeek. He turned his head toward Jeek and gave him a sneer.

With one foot, his skin-wrap dripping with pond water, Kung tested the wall before him. It held. He took a step, then another, then put his hands down and started climbing the wall of domed sticks on all fours, still gripping his stick. He moved so slowly Jeek knew his fear was holding him back.

At last Kung neared the top. Jeek felt lightheaded from holding his breath. Kung straddled the top of the mound and began prodding it with his stick. Jeek heard a few twigs snap. Kung jabbed harder. More pieces of the shelter dislodged and fell.

He looked around and grinned, then attacked with his full strength. He brought the stick down again and again. But not on the beavers, on the lodge.

The females were sending him advice. *Start poking. Poke the beavers. Don't hit the walls.*

Jeek was about to add his message to theirs, advising him to go for the smallest one, when it happened.

A section of mud and twigs gave way.

Kung fell into the beaver lodge.

Jeek and the rest of the Hamapa sprang up. Stood paralyzed for a moment. Then they all dashed toward the screams and skirmishing coming from inside. Roh reached the lodge first, scrambled up the slope and, peering into the structure, began thrusting her spear downward. Enga soon joined her.

All Jeek could see from the minds of Enga and Roh were confusion at the dark interior, and worry that they must not stab Kung.

The large beaver Jeek had seen earlier surfaced near the dam, clambered over it, and splashed through the swamp, escaping the hunters. Jeek could see several cuts bleeding through its fur, but the animal did not look mortally injured. Two smaller beavers followed the big one. They appeared unhurt.

Kung was injured, however. Enga and Roh lowered themselves to the floor of the lodge, then tore down its walls. They carried him, dripping a great quantity of his Red and still screaming, out of the ruined beaver lodge and to shore. Enga gripped Kung's shoulders and Roh his legs. Kung's head was carried higher because Enga was taller than Roh. He appeared to be clutching his arms together across his chest. They set him gently on the ground and tried to soothe him.

Jeek tried to see the source of all that Red. Kung was losing so much Jeek thought he would not live. Akkal and Mootak hacked at some of the hunting skins, peeling them into strips. With shaking hands, Enga grabbed a piece of skin and wiped at the blood.

Then Jeek saw that Kung's hand gripped the end of his other arm. It was severed just below the elbow. The beaver must have bitten it off. Jeek reeled. Felt dizzy. But he could not take his eyes from the horrific sight. He swallowed the bitter bile that rose in his throat and managed not to vomit.

Shame washed over Jeek for having felt animosity toward Kung earlier. How could he have let petty personal feelings rise above the good of the tribe? He felt deep dishonor, unworthiness. He did not deserve to be a Hamapa. He stared at the crimson stump.

As fast as Enga dashed it away, more Red appeared and gushed from the place where Kung's arm should have been. Akkal and Mootak worked quickly. They wrapped strips of hide tightly around his arm, then whipped some more skins over the wound.

Jeek felt the jagged agitation of everyone, but Kung's fierce, vivid, screeching agony overrode their swirling emotions. Enga took a deep breath and straightened her back, then leaned in toward Kung's face to focus his attention on her.

We must get you back to the village, Enga told Kung. *You must stay calm until we reach Zhoo of Still Waters.* Jeek didn't think Kung heeded Enga's thoughts. He might have heeded her horror at his mutilation, though. Or that of Roh, or any of the rest of them. They couldn't conceal it.

The other young males hurried to fashion a carrier from the remaining hunting skins, then the failed hunters slogged through the swampland and rushed into the woods.

Kung screamed for a while, then stopped his screeching, moaned and thrashed for a short time, and finally fell still and quiet. All they heard was the pounding of their feet on the dirt trail and their heavy panting as they ran. Jeek could tell he was not the only one feeling broken inside.

Chapter 13

It was too bad, Enga Dancing Flower thought, that Kung's burial ceremony was not what it should be. Aside from the fact that there was not enough food for a feast, and hunger gnawed at her belly like the teeth of the giant beaver, there was not enough grief for a proper mourning.

Kung had no living birth mother, only Cabat the Thick, his seed-giver. Akkal had also come from Cabat's seed, but he had been born of the Aja Hama. Two males could not be more different than Kung and Akkal. Still, Akkal came to help. But with only two family members, it fell to others to help attend Kung. Doon and Mootak, with some of Mootak's birth family, as well as several others who, Enga surmised, were trying to atone for not liking him, gathered in the wipiti of the single males where Kung had lived.

Enga joined them, she, too, feeling guilty for disliking Kung.

Cabat squatted near the body of his son. He reached out to stroke the cold, lifeless hair, then sat back and let the others do the work.

The Hamapa stripped his handsome body and rubbed his skin with mint-scented water. Enga braided his hair, then they carried him out to the Paved Place.

The tribe had sat around the fire with ashes on their faces last night and had gone through the motions of mourning Kung. But true grief, the kind that dripped with black, came only from Cabat and dim-witted Doon. Even the grief of Mootak, Kung's other follower, was edged with a tinge of relief. Cabat's loud wails had screeched on and on until Panan One Eye had told him to stop. That, however, had only made Cabat escalate his keening. It battered Enga's ears until very late.

Kung's birth mother had died shortly after he was born. And he was born just before the two toddler orphans, Enga and Ung, were taken in by the tribe.

Poor Kung, thought Enga. *How awful to go to death with so few true mourners*. Enga wondered if their arrival had taken away attention that the baby Kung had needed. Would he have been easier to get along with if he had been cared for more? She held these thoughts in dark blue to keep them private.

Now, as high sun neared, the New One sat with them on the Paved Place, next to Vala Golden Hair, sewing, as they sang a Death Chant for Kung. The New One puckered his flat brow. Enga thought he probably didn't understand what was going on. He looked up from time to time, his pink eyes sometimes avoiding hers, sometimes searching for them. Enga was beginning to think of him as Skin Worker.

He could do almost miraculous things with his tiny stitching tools, made from bird bones with a hole drilled in one end, the other end sharpened to pierce the hides he sewed. He held the skin and the stitching bone close to his face, occasionally putting it down and resting his eyes. The Hamapa made neck adornments from bird bones, but had never used them for stitching. Enga had seen Vala holding the bird bones once or twice and wondered if she was trying to learn to use them.

At high sun most of the tribe trudged across the prairie to the rock they used for laying out their dead. It was far enough away from the village they did not have to see the raptors feasting on the body, but close enough so the Elders could walk there and back.

Enga's face, like the other broad faces, had been cleansed of ashes at new sun, and, like the others, she wore her hair loose. Hama led the procession, her strut parading her consciousness of her position. Just behind her walked the two elder males, Panan One Eye and Cabat the

Thick. Panan's bald pate shone in the sunlight. Enga thought his round head matched Cabat's round belly. He seemed to drag his squat, heavy body through the thick grasses.

Normally, four sturdy adult males would bear Kung's body, but the adult males were still gone on their trading mission. So Akkal and the adolescents, Mootak, Doon, and young Jeek, struggled with the body hoisted onto their shoulders, trying to step in rhythm. Sannum Straight Hair, his long dark locks mingling with his beard, carried his small hollow log. He beat it with a stick to keep time. The rest of the tribe streamed after them, walking to the beat and lightly chanting, along with Lakala Rippling Water, a song to the Spirit of Death.

Enga paced behind Ung Strong Arm. The sun glinted off her sister's short, fiery tresses, and off Lakala Rippling Water's long light-blond locks that swung to her shoulders. Lakala walked beside Ung and reached to steady her when she occasionally faltered.

Most of the tribe were wrapped in cold weather fur capes of mammoth, brown bear, and moose. The New One, though, limped along in a fitted garment of camel skin he had fashioned for himself. The clothing accentuated how much slimmer and taller his body was than theirs, how much narrower his shoulders, and how thin his arms and legs. The only pale skin that showed was his face and his hands.

At the rock, gleaming smooth and flat amid the waving grasses, they halted. The drum and the chanting stopped. The four who had carried him lifted Kung onto the rock in silence, then rubbed the bit of bear fat they had brought over his skin. Enga joined the others in casting fragrant crushed leaves and pine needles onto the body. Very few flowers bloomed this close to Dark Season. For Kung, there were not enough flowers, not enough grief, and not enough food for a feast.

Hama worked her way over to stand beside Cabat. The way she touched his shoulders and caressed his face made Enga wonder if Hama desired to mate with Cabat. Hama had taken her birth sister's position in the tribe. Did she now want her sister's mate?

Hama and Cabat turned and left before everyone else.

After they had gone, Enga was startled to feel ripples running through the group amassed around the rock. Ongu Small One's soft thought-speak rose above the others, but narrowed so it would not reach beyond the group.

She is not the right leader for us.

She was answered by several others, agreeing. *Bad luck has been ours since she has led us... The future does not look good... There are others more qualified...*

Should Enga mention the dirt on the hands of Nanno Green Eyes after her birth sister's death? Did it mean they had struggled, fought over something? For now she kept quiet. Her last comments on Aja Hama's death hadn't been welcome.

After the rites for Kung, Enga tried to take a nap, but her mind would not quit working, so she joined the tribe members back at the fire on the Paved Place. She looked around for Jeek. Her thought feelers found him in his own wipiti, staying there for the rest of the day and helping his mother with her patients. He said he couldn't meet with her now.

They clustered there in silence, not sharing thoughts. Hers strayed to the absent traders. She hadn't received any messages from them for several days and wondered why that was. She tried to send a loving thought to Tog Flint Shaper, but didn't feel it reached him. If only she could feel his arms wrapped around her.

Then she turned her mind to the death of Aja Hama. It was time to think seriously about that. If a Hamapa killed her, which Hamapa would that be? Nanno Green Eyes became the new Hama on Aja's death, and was enjoying her power. But she could not have killed her own birth sister. No Hamapa had ever done that.

Ongu Small One had contended for the position, but hadn't won it. Could she have gotten rid of Hama, hoping to become the new one? Panan had once told a Saga of a male Hamapa who killed another male, but that happened in ancient times.

The two elder males had both liked Hama, although Cabat has quarreled with her and even laid hands on her.

Enga couldn't think of anyone else with even a remote reason for wanting her dead, let alone anyone who would kill her. She had seen Kung exhibit violent thoughts and dislike of Hama, but he was now dead. Most of the tribe had loved her, and most now wished she were still leading them. Enga, as usual, kept these musings very, very private.

When she saw Ongu leave to go to the creek, Enga decided to follow her and try to talk about this. She saw Ongu squat beside the stream and heard the splattering as she added her own water to it.

Wait, thought-spoke Enga quietly and narrowly, so only Ongu could hear her. *I want to ask you something.*

The look Ongu gave her was not friendly, but was not unfriendly. *Then ask me.*

I think you did not like Aja Hama.

You are correct. And I do not like Nanno Green Eyes as Hama either.

I, too, think you might have made a better leader, Ongu Small One. Enga did not know if she truly thought this. Probably not, since she had voted for Nanno. But the sentiment served her purpose at this moment. *What do you think happened to Aja Hama? Who do you think killed her?* Enga watched with all her senses open to see if she could tell whether Ongu would tell her the truth or not.

Ongu narrowed her eyes, pondering. *It is possible a Mikino killed her. But our leaders do not agree on this. I cannot say what they cannot know. Their disagreement is distressing and is not good for the tribe.*

Do you think that our leaders are unwise?

No, not all of our leaders. Only one of them is foolish.

Ah yes, you would not think Cabat the Thick foolish, since you were mated with him once. Or do you think he is foolish for mating with Aja Hama?

What I think of Cabat the Thick is no concern of yours, Enga Dancing Flower.

After Ongu brushed past her abruptly, bristling with hostility, Enga could not decide if she could have killed Aja Hama or not. She had more questions for Ongu, but wondered if Ongu would speak to her about this again.

She would try to question some others.

*****

We are near, Tog Flint Shaper thought-spoke. *We should reach our village by last sun, or maybe just after full darkness.*

The traders, Bahg Swiftfeet knew, were as weary as they had ever been. The fast, thumping pace necessary to get Teek Pathfinder back as soon as possible, and the weight of carrying him, wore at them. The wounded young Hamapa male occasionally cried out, the raw bear-claw wounds on his back raging with burning pain.

Their foot wrappings of tough skin were shredded from the pounding of their feet on the dirt, and they had no more spares. Tog, Bahg, and Donik Tree Trunk took turns bearing Teek on their backs until he could no longer grip them. Then they had to carry him two at a time.

They reached the stand of young ferns, but stopped only to slurp up water when they came across it, pulling out jerky to chew as they ran. There was no time to stop if Teek were to survive.

Their heaviest burden was mental. They all agreed they should not worry the tribe with the bad news they bore. Not only Teek's serious injury, but the failure to find anyone to trade with. There would be no more food when they returned than there had been when they left.

Something is getting through, came a thought from Tog. *I'm trying to keep my thoughts locked down, but one with strength is coming from the tribe. From Enga Dancing Flower, I think. She is greatly troubled by something.*

No! Bahg gripped one of Tog's shoulders as they jogged. Usually thick and strong, it felt thin, almost frail. They were all losing weight. *Keep your thoughts to yourself. We will worry them soon enough. They do not need to learn of our disasters until they have to.*

Why do you not want to be the bearer of bad news? countered Donik. *What does it matter whether they learn now or later?*

Bahg didn't know what it mattered, but he wanted to shield his tribe.

138

He, too, had been getting urgent thoughts from his own mate, Fee Long Thrower, that felt almost tragic. He was afraid of what they would find when they returned. Something bad had happened in the village. He had gotten several visions of his beloved Fee and his rosy pink baby and the vision contained pain.

*****

In the late afternoon, Enga Dancing Flower lay down for a few moments; Kung's funeral had worn her out. Even without deep grief for his passing, the motions of mourning were tiring. Maybe pretending made it more tiring, she thought.

She lay on her bearskin, trying to relax, but still unable to stop her spinning mind. She kept quiet because Ung was beside her, fast asleep. Already exhausted from many nights of sleeplessness, the long, slow walk had further drained her.

Hama's killer had never been found. The tribe had never even looked for the killer. Was she the only one troubled by this? The business with Doon telling the story of seeing the beaver disturbed her, too. Had no one taken note of him telling them Fee Long Thrower and her baby were dead when they weren't? If he did not see their deaths correctly, had he seen a beaver correctly?

Enga sat up with a feeling of ice in her chest. Maybe Doon harmed Fee and her baby. Did he tell that story to draw attention away from himself? She lay back and pulled a light lavender shade down on her thoughts so they wouldn't carry.

Then she smelled the New One. Again, he must be just outside her dwelling wall. Why did he do this? It was mid-afternoon, not dark time, like the last time he stood there. She decided to see if she could tell what he wanted.

Enga rose from her bed, careful not to disturb Ung, and crept out her doorway. The New One stood at the back of her wipiti. He looked down into her eyes as she approached. She tilted her face up to return his gaze. His eyes were such a curious color. He rarely held them wide open, but now he gazed on her, his red-pink pupils darting back and forth.

She sent him a question. *What do you want?*

There was no answer. There was no sign that she had sent a thought to him. His eyes continued to seek hers. Back and forth, back and forth. Enga drew her brows down. She did not know what to do. How could she communicate?

It was such an odd feeling that she couldn't send or receive thoughts with him. It was like gazing upon the side of a huge rock, or the surface of a still pond. She kept her gaze on him and still he returned it, no expression on his face. Was he trying to communicate something to her? She didn't know how to ask him.

Enga raised her eyebrows and shrugged. He stared at her.

That direct look from those unusual eyes thrilled something inside her. Enga wasn't sure if she welcomed this or not.

He turned and limped along the path behind the dwellings, his turned-in foot dragging with every other step, until he came to the end of the row. Enga followed him.

Maybe he wants to show me something. If I learn how to communicate with him, it might be a good thing.

He avoided the Paved Place and kept walking until he was at the edge of the village. Enga slowed her steps. Now she was not sure she should follow him. They were heading toward the Holy Cave. He turned and made a motion with his head for her to continue after him.

He must know not to enter the Holy Cave, she thought. *Surely he has seen how we revere it. How we save it for special occasions. A female's first Red Flow, a place for First Coupling, and a place for Birth. Our sheltered fire is kept there. A male must not go inside, uninvited by a female, after his Passage Ceremony. And then usually for his First Coupling only.*

But he kept going up the Sacred Hill. His strides, in spite of their uneven rhythm, were long and Enga had to trot to keep up with him. She did not want him to defile the Holy Cave. She remembered him hovering at the entrance when he delivered the gift for Fee's baby. But

140

he had not entered. She had thought he understood.

He reached the entrance and stopped to look back at her. She sped up and reached him just before he ducked inside the Hamapa-sized entrance.

Wait! Halt! You cannot go there!

But the New One didn't heed her thoughts. He was making soft, garbled sounds, but they didn't mean anything to her. They were like soft Pronouncements, but did not consist of Hamapa sounds. She thought he was sending her communication, but they were not thoughts.

The fire that burned here was the main reason the cave was held holy. The central village fire could always be replenished from this one. Of course, a new one could be kindled by striking flint, but it would be considered terrible bad luck if this one went out.

The fire's heat warmed the cave, made it a good place to birth babies and to have First Couplings for new mates.

He took his tunic off over his head and stood before her with his chest bare. Since his skin and hair were so light, Enga Dancing Flower had always assumed his body was hairless, but now she could see that he had a great deal of it, especially on his chest, much more hair than a Hamapa male would have. But it was all snowy white.

The New One must be warm in here.

When he reached for her she was surprised. His touch on her arms was gentle. He pushed her cloak up and ran his long fingers along her arms. It tingled. His hands and arms bore short hairs, again, more than a Hamapa.

When he tried to put his mouth on hers she suddenly knew his thoughts, even though she could not see them.

For just an instant, Enga returned his kiss, the warmth of those pale lips thrilling, deep inside her, down low. Then she moaned aloud and pulled back. He was not Tog Flint Shaper.

Enga twisted away with a grunt. His grip tightened on her arms and his sounds rose higher. She knew her arms would be bruised later. He let go of her with one hand and slapped her face so hard her teeth hurt.

She landed a blow with her elbow to his middle body. He crumpled onto the floor of the cave with a great roar. Now his expression clearly told his thought. He was puzzled. And mad.

She didn't stop to see if he got up, but ran down the hill. She passed Hama on her way. The memory of Hama, back when she was Nanno Green Eyes, always following her and tattling on her sprang into her mind. What would Hama tell the others if she found out Enga had gone to the Holy Cave with the New One? If she found out what they had done there?

When Enga reached her wipiti she stopped outside the door, remembering Ung, sleeping inside. Her anguish flew toward Tog, trying desperately to touch him. There was no response.

When her breathing slowed a bit she went inside.

You are breathing hard. You are troubled. Ung was awake.

All is well, my sister. Enga tried to hide her anguish, but couldn't. Ung was her twin and could see what had just happened to her in the Holy Cave. It was laid out for her as plain as the light from Sister Sun.

Do you think the New One meant you harm?

Enga did not know. *Maybe he did not intend to harm me at first. If I had coupled with him I don't know if he would have struck me or not. But I also harmed him.*

We will keep a watch on the New One, thought-spoke Ung. *You will not be alone with him again. You are promised to Tog Flint Shaper. The New One does not understand our ways yet. Maybe, with the Tall Ones, the males chose mates rather than the females. I have heard that.*

Was that true? Did the New One just not comprehend that she was promised? Was this the way coupling was done among Tall Ones? With mates chosen by males? With slapping and hurting?

Ung, I am grateful you are my birth sister. I will not bring this up with the tribe. It would cause bad feelings toward the New One. Maybe he deserves them, but maybe he does not.

Ung considered, then agreed with Enga. *He might be cast out and die.*

Enga had to discuss her suspicions with someone. *Do you think a Mikino killed our Hama?*

I think we should listen to what the Elders say. If they decide it is so, then I will believe them.

Ung was a better Hamapa than she was, Enga thought.

*****

After dark, the trading party stumbled into the village. Enga, sitting outside by the fire with Ung, leapt to her feet and dashed to them.

Tog, Tog! You're back.

Then she saw that his arms were occupied. He held the bare shoulders of Teek Pathfinder while Bahg Swiftfeet held his ankles. Tog shook his head at Enga and pushed past her. *We must get Teek Pathfinder to the wipiti of Zhoo of Still Waters for healing.*

The Red of Teek seeped from the skin wrappings around his body. Tog cast a glance back at Enga before they entered the wipiti. He sent her a swift, incomplete picture of Teek's young back, raked with furrows from a bear's claws.

Enga knew from that vision that Teek was in great danger. When a Hamapa was injured by an animal, the wound often became red and fiery hot, then oozed white poison. If Zhoo could control these reactions, Teek would live. If she couldn't...

It was not a good thing that Zhoo must see her own son this way, but she, and she alone, could help him.

Bahg hurried to his own wipiti to find his unconscious mate and injured son. His grief billowed from the wipiti.

Jeek came running with his arms full of the materials Zhoo would need, her dried grasses, bear fat, and honeycomb. His eyes were streaming with tears for his birth brother. He plowed his way through the gathering, the Hamapa parting for him when they realized he was on his way.

The New One stood to the rear of the crowd around the door of the Healer's wipiti. He looked over and caught Enga staring at his eyes.

They looked colorless in the darkness. He made no movement toward her. He appeared to have recovered from her blow. Her arms were still sore from his vicious grip. Then her attention was drawn back to Teek.

Low moans of pain came from the Healer's wipiti. They vied with the hungry cries of Fee's baby, coming from her wipiti a few doors away. The Healer had elected not to move Fee after the attack, which meant she had to be checked on often. Enga knew Bahg was cradling the infant, but the baby was hungry.

The ones standing and squatting nearest the opening of the Healer's wipiti conveyed to the others what they were seeing. Zhoo, after pouring clear water over the tracks the bear claws had made down Teek's back, had taken the long grasses from Jeek and was trimming some of them on her indoor tree stump. She stopped occasionally to put down her flint knife and run a hand through her short-cropped hair. Her hands were steady in spite of the storm Enga saw raging inside her. The Hamapa sent her admiration and encouragement.

She is Zhoo of Still Waters, thought-spoke Enga Dancing Flower. *She is the most skilled Healer we have ever had. She will save her son.* Her entreaties to the Spirit of Healing joined those of the whole tribe. She lifted her face up to transmit her prayer.

Zhoo left most of the grasses uncut, gathered them up, and bent over her son. She laid the rustling grasses in Teek's long wounds, smearing a thin layer of bear fat over them. Bear fat, like food, was running low. Through Tog, Enga saw Jeek hand the gourd that held honeycombs to his birth mother, then watched her top the grass and fat mixture with the squeezed honey. The Hamapa had not yet had to use the bear fat and honeycomb for food. But one day soon they might.

There was a commotion behind Enga. The New One was making his way through the watchers and, since he couldn't tell them he was coming, had to touch their shoulders with his thin, pale hand to move them aside. She turned and saw the expressions of those he was trying to move. They did not welcome his intrusion. But Enga saw what he carried.

He has soft skins to bind the wounds, Enga thought-spoke. *Let him through. Let the Skin Worker through.*

Enga had some private thoughts, too. *Maybe he really meant me no harm. There is no way to tell him that the cave is holy. Many caves are not. And there is no way to tell him I intend to become the mate of Tog Flint Shaper. I must ask the tribe how we can talk with him. Maybe they will have some ideas. And I will ponder this also.*

Chapter 14

Jeek's mother, Zhoo of Still Waters, told him to go to the nightly gathering. Teek Pathfinder, his brother, was finally asleep, though his face sometimes twisted in pain through his slumber.

I must stay here with my poor wounded son, as well as look in on Fee Long Thrower, who still sleeps, and her baby later. She gave Jeek a soft pat on the head.

You will not need my help?

There is no reason for you to be here while he is not awake. Go and see what is discussed at the council. See if there are any more ideas about how to feed the tribe. I am so weary I would rather not listen to the tribe tonight.

Jeek joined the gathering at the Paved Place. He pulled his moose skin cloak tight and scooted close to the fire. Mother Sky breathed down hard on them, whipping up the flames and sending them dancing in wild swings and swoops. He was worried about his birth mother. She was so tired. And worried, even though she didn't show that to most.

Lakala Rippling Water began with a Song of Asking to the Spirit of Healing. She tilted her face upwards, her blond hair bound in a knot at the nape of her neck. Sannum Straight Hair beat the log drum to her rhythms and Hama occasionally shook her gourd. She did not have the sense of timing her birth sister, the Aja Hama, had possessed.

The Storyteller took a deep breath, then started a Saga. He aimed his thought, and his one good eye, in the direction Sister Sun came from when she awoke, the direction the traders had gone without success. Then he turned toward the place where Sister Sun had just bedded down. The firelight shimmered across his shiny dome as his head swiveled.

This is where we must go next. It is the land of the Little People. The Mikino.

Jeek perceived a shiver coursing through the tribe.

Mikino, thought-whispered a few of the Hamapa.

Jeek pulled a strand of hair out of its binding and chewed it rapidly.

Yes, continued Panan One Eye, glaring at those who uttered the word. The firelight caught the whiteness of his blind eye and it gleamed. *Yes, they are a vicious people. But we have tried others. Now we must try them.*

He sent them a vision of the Mikino, since the youngest had never seen them. They were short beings with small heads. They wore untreated animal skins for warmth. Their village consisted of crude shacks, built of sticks and grasses. But, a short distance from them, were the caves. The Storyteller let them hear a mighty roar, then took them to the caves. These were barricaded with thick logs and were far sturdier than their dwellings. They had to be, for they held jaguars. The ferocious cats were larger than the tigers Jeek had seen in the forests around his village.

It was hard to tell, through the chinks in the logs, how many were in the enclosure, but there were at least four or five. A gap in the ceiling of the cave let in a little light. Their yellow eyes glowed in the glow of Brother Moon, for the Storyteller had taken them there at dark time, and the Mikino had no fire. They ate their food uncooked. And they sometimes fed their enemies to the cats.

In the distant past, thought-spoke the Storyteller, *the Hamapa traded with the Mikino. Some of them will remember us. There's a chance we can get food for the dark time from them, perhaps one of their cats. They need good knives and we have them. The Mikino do not make knives since they hunt with large stones and wooden clubs.*

148

They have always been eager to trade for our knives.

Jeek shuddered along with his tribe brothers and sisters. This seemed a very risky undertaking. And the Hamapa were growing weaker by the day.

Hama took over. She stood up, using her height to make herself more important. *It is settled then. We will send a trading party to the Mikino. But if they will not trade, we will get revenge for the death of our leader.*

Ongu Small One, the mate of Sannum Straight Hair, broke in. *How far away are they? Do our traders have the strength to reach them? They have just returned. How could they fight them if they need to?*

This made Jeek sit straight up. What was happening? Hama had just decided, but there had been no discussion, no tribe consensus. Then, Hama had not made a Pronouncement aloud. And finally, Ongu had just openly challenged Hama's decision. Jeek had never seen such things happen. A ripple of surprise went through the startled minds of the tribe.

No! burst from Panan like thunder. *We will not fight the Mikino! If we make the trip, we will trade.*

I agree, added Cabat the Thick. *But I do not think we can accomplish a trading mission now. The males are worn out.*

Jeek stared at the Elders. Hama did not answer them. She ground her teeth, then continued as if she had made no decision. *There is one matter we must attend to now,* she commanded. She turned her frosty eyes to Doon and bade him rise.

Doon looked around from where he sat and radiated confusion. Jeek caught his thoughts. *What did I do? What's the matter? I didn't do anything.*

It is about the beaver that we hunted, continued Hama. *The beaver that killed Kung. We must learn a bit more about it. Come, Doon. Show us exactly where you saw the beaver that attacked Fee Long Thrower. Maybe it is the same animal.*

Doon cast his thoughts about. They were not coherent, but confused bits of worry and apprehension. Jeek did not blame him for being perplexed at this moment. So much unusual was happening this night. Then, after a short hesitation, Doon stood up and shut down his tangled thinking.

Yes, I will show you at first sun. There are tracks, but we cannot see them clearly now. They go into the woods.

Hama made one more surprise announcement. She thought-spoke that Doon would have his Passage Ceremony the next night at the council.

The last startling declaration was again from Panan. *The murder of Aja Hama will be discussed at the next council also.* He looked at Cabat for support. He gave it with a grudging nod. Then Hama whirled and strode to her wipiti without formally ending the meeting.

Jeek followed Doon as the Hamapa left, hoping to hear some of his poorly guarded thinking. He was rewarded. Jeek could not decipher the strains of thought, but did receive the emotions of triumph and gloating. Doon started toward the wipiti of the single males, where he lived, but veered off into the woods before entering it.

Jeek stopped following. There was no way he would go into the woods at the time of full darkness. What in the name of Dakadaga was Doon doing?

*****

At first sun, Jeek, curious as to what Doon had been doing in the dark, made his way to the edge of the village after he had eaten his meager morning meal. He saw Sannum Straight Hair and Panan One Eye returning from the stream where the tribe set their fish traps. Sannum carried three small fish, the kind that would be bony.

Vala Golden Hair came out of the woods from the main path, carrying an armful of tender young ferns. She smiled at Jeek.

The traders saw these, she thought-spoke, *and told me where to get them. At least it is something to eat, other than jerky and gruel.*

He turned his head away before making a face. He did not like fern shoots. But he would probably have to eat them. After Vala reached the

Paved Place, Jeek continued his quest.

Before Jeek could find the place where Doon had entered the woods, however, Hama summoned the tribe to the Paved Place.

It made Jeek feel good inside that all the males were back with the tribe. The tribal family felt complete. He squatted with the others to receive Hama's thoughts.

She stood and raised her arms for attention. Then she pointed at Doon and he rose to stand beside her, facing the group. Doon looked around with a flicker of fright in his dull eyes, then squared his shoulders and thought-spoke.

A very large beaver attacked Fee Long Thrower and her baby. He made tracks into the woods. I will show you these tracks.

Doon turned and marched toward the woods. Jeek looked around at his fellow Hamapa and they all looked as puzzled as he did.

A few thoughts floated around: *Why did we not see these tracks? How did we not notice a beaver here, in our village?* Jeek could tell others were giving mental nods, agreeing with the asking of these questions. But they all rose and trailed after Doon, who now walked side by side with Hama. He was undersized for his age of fifteen summers and looked especially short next to her.

The two stopped at the edge of the Paved Place and Doon pointed down. Jeek struggled to edge forward through the knot of onlookers and see the tracks. They did look like beaver tracks. He could make out claws and even a suggestion of webbing. That seemed to settle it for the tribe. Bahg Swiftfeet and Tog Flint Shaper walked into the woods, following the trail of the tracks, but returned after a short time.

Jeek saw Tog give Enga Dancing Flower a private look. He longed to know what they were discussing. For himself, he wanted to see where the tracks ended. He wasn't sure Hama would approve of him doubting the word of Doon, since she was eager to accept it. So he would wait until later, then see how far the tracks went and where they led.

He was interrupted when Hama gathered them again after a very short time.

This is a happy occasion, she informed them. *It is time for the Passage Ceremony for Doon. He has seen fifteen summers and can now be called an adult.*

A ripple went through the Hamapa. Doon was born just about the same time as Kung. Kung, who should be having his Passage Ceremony also. This would make it a happy and sad time.

She had more to announce. *A name has been given to me for him by Dakadaga and I will bestow it at our council when first dark appears. There may be an unexpected event or two also.* Her smile let them know it would be another happy event. Maybe two happy occasions would blunt the loss of Kung.

Chapter 15

Neanderthals, an archaic human species that dominated
Europe until the arrival of modern humans some 45,000
years ago, possessed a critical gene known to underlie
speech, according to DNA evidence retrieved from two
individuals excavated from El Sidron, a cave in northern
Spain.

—*The New York Times*, Neanderthals Had
Important Speech Gene, DNA Evidence Shows, by
Nicholas Wade, October 19, 2007

Enga Dancing Flower sat with her sister, Ung Strong Arm, and
Lakala Rippling Water outside Lakala's wipiti. The three females
twisted leather straps into braids they would give to Doon for hair
adornments at his Ceremony, which would take place soon. Sister Sun
was dipping toward her beloved mate, Brother Earth. This night Sister
Sun was arraying herself in rosy, glowing cloud garments for her tryst.

Ung Strong Arm, thought-spoke Enga, *I am worried about what
Hama said about us.*

That we were not wanted by Aja Hama? Ung chortled. *No one can
believe that. Sannum Straight Hair was one of the males who brought
us to the tribe from the woods. The other Elders, Panan One Eye and
Cabat the Thick, were also there. Many who are still with us can say she
willingly took us in and raised us.*

And even if some did say you were unlucky, put in Lakala, *Aja Hama would not have wanted to expel you from the tribe.* She bit off a leather strip and tied the end.

But we must do something, thought-spoke Enga, *to show Hama we have worth to the tribe. That we are true Hamapa and did not kill Aja Hama.*

But do you think she will bring this up again? asked Ung.

I believe she will try to get rid of us, answered Enga. *She has always hated us. Especially me.*

A long shadow fell across Enga and she looked up and gave a wave to Jeek as he passed. To rest her eyes from the close work in the waning light, she watched him saunter to the end of the row of dwellings. Jeek would make a fine-looking male soon. He was built sturdy, like his mother, Zhoo of Still Waters and, like her, his disposition was calm and sensible.

He stopped and looked around. Enga perceived a desire, directed only to her, for her to follow him.

I wonder, she mused to herself, Ung, and Lakala, *where young Jeek is going. Something has been bothering him lately. Have you noticed?*

Besides hunger? asked Lakala. *And young Gunda?*

Enga smiled. The growing attraction between the two young ones made her happy, as it did the rest of the tribe.

I'll be back soon, answered Enga as she put down her handwork and got up to follow Jeek. Ung's puzzlement trailed after her.

Where was that boy? Enga stood on the path in the woods. She had tracked him by smell for a distance, then lost him. His odor wasn't on the trail at this point. He had left the trail. Why would he be going into the woods at this time of late sun? Soon the Passage Ceremony for Doon would begin. Could this have something to do with Doon?

She pictured Doon being named, standing with his stooped shoulders before the Hama to receive the touch of her gourd. Then she remembered that he had showed them the beaver tracks this morning. Tog Flint Shaper had noticed her doubting that the tracks were actually made by a beaver and had let her know his opinion that they looked authentic after he and Bahg Swiftfeet followed them. At the time she had wondered if they had followed them far enough.

I wonder if Jeek is checking the beaver tracks. He is a clever child.

Enga retraced her steps back to the point where Doon had shown them the large prints leading away from the village, down the trail. Now that she pondered it, why would a beaver follow their trail? It did not go to a beaver lodge.

The beaver tracks left the narrow footpath at the same point Jeek's scent did. Branches were broken where the tracks had gone, and she saw the footprints of Jeek's wrapped feet in the moist earth of the forest floor, beside the beaver tracks. Now she was sure her thinking was right. Jeek doubted the tale related by Doon. Enga did also. Jeek was not hiding his passage through the underbrush. He probably left a trail for her to follow.

She put her feet in Jeek's footprints to hide hers and crept through the dense growth of tender ferns and young trees. Somehow, she did not want anyone to find out she was here, checking up on Doon's tale. Enga kept quiet, not knowing exactly what Jeek was doing, and suspecting he didn't want anyone else to know but her. She stole through the woods, noticing the light starting to fade rapidly with the bedding down of Sister Sun.

Then she came upon Jeek. He stood gazing at two huge old tamarack trees. Their trunks were bare of needled branches at ground level since they grew close together. A youth like Jeek would be able to squeeze between them, but a grown male like Tog Flint Shaper would have a hard time.

Jeek sensed her behind him and slowly turned. His lips trembled and his eyes shone with tears. He pointed at the tracks he had followed to this point. Enga saw the problem at once. The tracks led between the trees and continued on the other side.

This cannot be, Jeek thought-spoke, just to her.

You are right. If those tracks were made by a beaver, it would be a large one, like the one that attacked Kung. The tracks are large. No beaver, not even a small one, could go between those two trees. Enga felt cold inside. A dull ache gripped the back of her head.

They both used their personal dark colors to funnel their thought between just the two of them. Jeek's thoughts came to Enga through a narrow, grape-tinted tunnel.

Shall we see where the tracks end? asked Jeek. He had worried half his brown-blond hair from its leather binding and chewed on a thick strand.

There is no need of that. We need to get back before Doon goes through his Passage Ceremony. The Elders will have to decide what to do about him. If he becomes a Named adult, his punishment for deception might be much worse. Maybe, if he has not yet passed into adulthood, he can be dealt with as a child and his offense can be pardoned.

Enga held the colors of midnight wrapped around her mind as she and Jeek crashed through the forest. This misdeed needed to be announced in person, not transferred by thought. The light of the forest was approaching the hue of her mood. Her head pounded with pain.

At last they neared the village. Darkness was complete in the woods. A glow came through the trees from the Hamapa fire. From a distance, Enga caught the last haunting notes of the song of Lakala Rippling Water, singing Farewell to Childhood. They stepped up their pace.

We will be too late, thought-spoke Jeek.

Maybe the Passage can be undone.

They stumbled onto the edge of the Paved Place. Enga ran through the sitting Hamapa and slid to a halt in front of Hama just as Hama placed her gourd on the shoulder of Teek Pathfinder, who knelt in front of her, looking up to Dakadaga, the Spirit of Mother Sky. Cabat the Thick squatted beside him to steady him.

Hama spoke:

"Hoody! Listen! The Most High Female Speaks."

What was this? This was not Doon. Enga blurted her surprise to the

156

whole tribe.

Hama shot a thought at Enga and Jeek, who now stood beside her.

Why are you late? Where have you been? Sit down. We will talk later. It is now time for the naming of Teek.

But Teek is already named Pathfinder, thought-spoke Enga.

Sannum Straight Hair tugged on the edge of her mammoth cloak and she sank down beside him. Jeek joined her.

Sannum sent a private message to Enga and Jeek. *This is the surprise of Hama. Teek is receiving a new name because of the ordeal he went through. You missed the other surprise, the naming of the New One.*

The New One? He is now a tribe member? This surprised Enga. She looked around for him. He was close at hand, on the other side of Sannum. A wide grin split his long, pale face. Enga tried to think his grin made him look foolish, but there was something appealing about his happiness.

Yes, the New One is now named Stitcher. He will just have that single name, our Hama declared. Can you see the carvings he did for her? She showed them to us when she named him. They are sitting on the ground next to her.

Enga's shock flared. She had seen both those carvings. The little mammoth was the one the New One, now Stitcher, had given her. The other had disappeared from Aja Hama's wipiti after her death. Another Pronouncement jerked her attention back to Hama.

"Dakadaga sasa vav Teek. Rowah Klack."

Dakadaga has given the name for Teek. Bearclaw.

The Hamapa approved of the new name. They nodded and sent thoughts and hoots of congratulation to Teek Bearclaw. Enga joined in. The name was fitting.

But those carvings! They did not belong to Hama. Stitcher may have stolen them and given them to her, but he did not make them for her. But what could Enga do about it? She could not say that Hama was lying. That would make her hate Enga and her sister even more. She almost whimpered.

But what of Doon?

The Hama nodded for Teek Bearclaw to rise and return to the group. Cabat and Sannum helped him as he was still weak.

Then Hama summoned Doon. He jumped up and walked to her with a puffed-out chest.

"Nasa!" called Enga Dancing Flower aloud. *No!*

Hama glared. No one thought-spoke, let alone spoke out loud when Hama was Pronouncing. She turned slightly away from Enga and spoke.

"Dakadaga sheesh Doon shensoha. Hamamapapa vava Doon Wadunk Fada."

Dakadaga, bless the adulthood of Doon. The Hamapa name Doon Beaver Tracker.

Enga was on her feet, waving her arms, Jeek beside her. She sent her thought as urgently as she could. *Wait! Halt!*

Stiff vibrations came from her tribe, telling her to sit down and be quiet.

Hama glared at Enga, touched her gourd to his shoulder, and continued. "Shensoha Doon."

This is the adulthood of Doon.

Enga interrupted again, sweat springing to her face and her palms at the audacity of what she was doing. No one had ever faced down a Hama in the middle of an Official Pronouncing.

Doon did not track any beaver. He made the tracks. Her knees shook, but she stood her ground.

You are not telling the truth, thought-spoke Hama.

I am telling the truth. Doon is not, answered Enga, leaning forward, trying to impress Hama, feeling her face contort in fear.

Jeek sent her a surge of encouragement.

Panan One Eye jumped to his feet and Cabat the Thick heaved himself up.

You defy Hama? Cabat sent amazement with the thought. It was one thing for him, the Most High Male to do it, but quite another for her.

But Panan heeded Enga. *Why do you think this? We all saw the tracks. Fee Long Thrower and the baby were injured. Surely a beaver did this.*

Jeek and I followed the tracks into the woods. If you see where they go, you will know a large beaver did not make them. Enga sent them the picture of the tracks going through the narrow passage between the ancient trees.

Chaos broke out. Everyone leaped up and swirled around Enga and Jeek, pressing so fiercely she feared they might be crushed.

Chapter 16

Bahg Swiftfeet gazed on the sleeping form of Fee Long Thrower, his beautiful mate, and feared for her future. This was the fifth new sun she was unconscious. Her dark hair, the same dark hair of most of those related to Hama and Aja Hama, lay damp and matted around her peaceful-looking face. Bahg pulled back the bearskin that covered her and stroked her silky white arm, peppered with soft, downy, dark hairs. He leaned close and crooned a low, desperate, humming chant into her ear.

His meditation was interrupted by the awakening squeal of his son. The baby was hungry. Some of the females had assisted the baby, held him to Fee's breasts, at first bulging with unexpelled milk. Bahg thought the baby had gotten a little bit the first day. But the second day of Fee's coma, he seemed unsatisfied. He squalled as he tried to suck. Bahg guessed that Fee was not producing much milk. The baby cried for most of the second and third days of Fee's coma; then Roh Lion Hunter had come to help.

There had been no babies born to the Hamapa for six years, no babies who had lived, that is. Roh had lost a child a few moons ago and she had tried yesterday to nurse the infant. The suckling had soothed the baby somewhat, but Roh did not think he was getting very much milk, if any. The baby only occasionally cried now. He was exhausted.

Fee needed to awaken very soon. She had been attacked by what Bahg, and everyone else, had believed was a beaver. But how could they have been so stupid? Beavers do not attack people.

Bahg hadn't been paying that much attention to the discussion at the meeting last night, exhausted as he was from getting Teek back to the group the day before, then dealing with the infant. He had been overjoyed, as the rest of the tribe was, that Teek was well enough to hobble out to the meeting and receive his new honorary name, Bearclaw. Dakadaga knew he had earned it. Teek was proving himself to be a valuable asset to the Hamapa and Bahg was glad they were not going to lose him.

The Storyteller had told the Saga of the Time of Crossing. The Hamapa never tired of that vision of their distant ancestors making the long journey across the narrow strip of land to reach the place where they now lived. Many other journeys were made, of course, before they ended up here, but that Crossing had been what brought them to this land of many animals and streams.

Their old land had been a good one, too, but other beings competed for the game. The others battled the Hamapa ancestors and drove them away from the best hunting places. Those other beings, taller and darker than the Hamapa, more like the Tall Ones, used dogs for hunting and were able to kill more game, and more easily than a Hamapa ever could.

So the Ancient Ones had left the old land and had journeyed many, many seasons, summer and winter, warm time and cold time, until they came to a land they liked. They had been led by the Guiding Bear of Mother Sky.

In this new land there was more space, and enough game for everyone. The Tall Ones had followed later, but there were never as many living in this land as there had been in the old one and there was no fighting here.

Bahg Swiftfeet has told us of seeing Great Ice on their latest travels. That Great Ice will drive game away. It is what will make us move our village.

Bahg once again shared the vision of that vast, gleaming expanse and the other traders joined in with their versions.

After the Saga ended, Hama began the ceremonies, surprising them all by giving the name Stitcher to the New One. Then by renaming Teek to Bearclaw. They marveled at the carvings Hama said Stitcher had given to her.

Then, just as Hama was bestowing his Passage name on Doon, Enga Dancing Flower and the boy Jeek had burst into the meeting with the disastrous news of the fake beaver trail.

Bahg replayed the scene in his mind for the tenth time. He had attended with the baby and witnessed all of it.

Hama had screeched in a high, thin wail. She had reached for the face of Doon with her fingernails and managed to give him a couple of deep scratches before the two males nearest her caught her arms and held her until her rage subsided.

Cabat the Thick, who had raised Doon with his own birth son, Kung, after both Doon's birth parents died in his infancy, had screwed up his pudgy face and started blubbering.

Hama had thrown thoughts of disgust at him.

Old Panan One Eye seemed to be the calmest. He took it upon himself to interrogate Doon. *Is there truth in what Enga Dancing Flower and Jeek tell us?* he thought-spoke.

Doon stood resolutely mute. Nothing came from his mind.

Will the Hamapa all sit now? And tell me, Panan continued, *how a beaver can fit through such a small space. This is not right, Doon. Did you make these tracks? Did you try to tell us an untruth?*

Still nothing from Doon. His face, usually slack-looking, took on a stony aspect and he gritted his teeth. Even he, with his slow wits, must have known what was about to happen to him.

Bahg, knowing fully what was going on, had shifted the weight of his baby in his arms and stared at Doon. A moment ago Doon had been named Doon Beaver Tracker. Now he was about to be disgraced. The baby started to whimper. Bahg stuck a finger into his tiny mouth for him to suck and held him close.

Panan gave Doon a look of gentle sorrow. *Would you like to go with me to the place where the tracks travel between the trees, Doon?*

Still no reaction from Doon.

And why did you make the tracks, Doon? There was no beaver. Is that true? The volume of his thought-speech rose, strands of scarlet radiating with his thought-words. Panan clenched his fists. *Was it you? Did you do this heinous thing, this hateful thing? Did you harm your sister and brother Hamapa?* Panan stepped close and put his face in Doon's, his red-hot anger rising, fury distorting his usually gentle, wrinkled face.

Doon took a huge, shuddering breath and looked around at the wide-eyed, disbelieving faces, all turned up toward him. Then he broke.

Bahg was nearest and caught Doon one-handed as he crumpled to the ground. Doon's body shook with his great sobs. He didn't bother to cover his face with his hands, just let his tears flow onto the paving stones.

Something snapped inside Bahg. He handed his baby to the nearest Hamapa and gripped Doon by the neck. Bahg's sky-blue eyes blazed and bored into Doon. *Did you do this? Are you responsible for what happened to my Fee Long Thrower and my baby?*

Doon's silence was his answer. He shook Doon by the neck. Donik Tree Trunk and Tog Flint Shaper ran up and, after a struggle, peeled Bahg's fingers from Doon's throat.

This is not the way to do this, thought-spoke Tog. *Doon will be dealt with.*

Bahg then collapsed and sobbed next to Doon.

Now, the next day, the whole tribe walked around subdued, their heads down, their mood grim and desolate. Doon had been turned out of the tribe that night with his clothing and one knife. He would have to find another tribe to take him in if he were to survive. Bahg knew he would not find one. The nearest tribe was nearly dead of starvation and the next nearest had disappeared.

Two summers ago, when Bahg had joined the Hamapa to mate with

Fee, he had traveled from his native tribe, many moons to the south. Doon did not have the mental capacity to survive long enough on his own to make it to that tribe, or any other.

Doon would die alone.

Chapter 17

Michael Richards, now at the University of Bradford in England, and his colleagues recently examined isotopes of carbon (13C) and nitrogen (15N) in 29,000-year-old Neandertal bones from Vindija cave in Croatia.... The analyses show that the Vindija Neandertals had 15N levels comparable to those seen in northern carnivores such as foxes and wolves, indicating that they obtained almost all their dietary protein from animal foods.

—*Scientific American, Special Edition: New Look at Human Evolution*, August, 2003, p. 69

The mood of the tribe was sour. Enga Dancing Flower could almost taste it hanging over the village. Banishing Doon last night was something they had all hated to do. But it was clear that someone who harmed others could not be allowed to stay in the tribe.

Enga sat just outside her door and watched her tribal brothers and sisters go about their day. Sister Sun warmed her face, but she didn't feel much warmth from the tribe, ever since Hama had made those wild and false accusations against her. Enga had hoped the tribe would accept her again after she and Jeek solved the mystery of the attack on Fee Long Thrower and the baby. But, if anything, they were angrier at her.

Did they think it was her fault Doon was expelled? She heard the thoughts flying around. Outsider, they said. Not really a Hamapa, they whispered. Enga wanted to scream. She was a true Hamapa, no matter what they thought.

Hama had not appeared since new sun. Earlier, Cabat the Thick had brought her some of the thin gruel that was their breakfast these days. Now he squatted at the fire pit, deep in conversation with Akkal, the Fire Tender, his birth son. Their faces looked serious and they kept their thoughts between them. Ung Strong Arm and Lakala Rippling Water, the Singer, sat near them, lingering near the warmth of the fire. Ung was so much better she could hobble about unassisted now. Lakala was straightening and braiding the hair of some of the younger females. Vala Golden Hair was helping with this, too. Tog Flint Shaper and Donik Tree Trunk and some young males had gone to check the fish weir, but there was not much hope for a catch.

Sannum Straight Hair caught her eye and lifted a hand to Enga in greeting. Sannum would always remain friendly to her, she knew. He knelt outside the male wipiti, chipping a new spear tip, the clinks of his stone tool ringing over the bustle of movement around him. Roh Lion Hunter and Ongu Small One, sitting together tearing leather into strips with their teeth, thought-whispered, putting their heads close together between rips. But soon Roh summoned her daughter, Gunda, and they left with their spears. Enga hoped they would bring something back to eat. She would have gone with them if they had invited her, but was glad they did not. She was so tired. The conflict in the tribe sapped her strength. Maybe Gunda was going to have target practice with her mother because Roh did not want Enga teaching her, or even near her.

Panan One Eye, the Storyteller, sat idle, having earned his rest by virtue of his fifty summers. A fly, late in the season, buzzed above his bald pate. As Enga followed its movements, Panan stood up and broadcast a message to the whole tribe.

We will start to think about the murder of our Aja Hama together now. We must question what happened there. The small footprints might not be real. If Doon could manufacture beaver prints, someone could manufacture those. At the next council we will meet and discuss everything we have thought of separately.

Enga was relieved that someone else was going to question the death of Aja Hama. If the whole tribe put their minds together, maybe they would discover the truth. But, before that happened, maybe everyone would return to suspecting each other. And her. She wondered if anyone would think she had faked the prints. Personally, she wondered if Nanno Green Eyes, as she was then, had had anything to do with them.

Then she noticed most of them were looking at her, some directly, some sneaking glances at her. They did! They suspected her. Enga could not breathe. She clenched her eyes closed and tightened her fists.

Enga Dancing Flower, my sister. Enga opened her mind to Ung. *What troubles you?*

Can you not feel the suspicions directed at me? The whole tribe thinks I killed Aja Hama. A tear leaked out of Enga's eye.

But you must not let them think that. You must find out who killed her.

Yes, you speak the truth, sister. I must. She drew a noisy, shaky breath.

She would find the killer herself.

She sent a private, tunneled message to Cabat and asked him to meet her behind the wipitis, near the stream. It was close to the village, but they wouldn't be seen there. He was one who could have killed her.

Why did you summon me here, Enga Dancing Flower? He seemed irritated that she had done so. It took some effort for him to descend the bank of the stream.

And now what would she say? Enga thought quickly. The stream murmured peacefully over its stones behind her. *I want to find out more. I am concerned about the last moments of Aja Hama.*

Cabat hung his head. *Yes, I am sorry we quarreled just before she died. But I could not know she would be killed. And that it would happen so soon after our argument.*

But what did you argue about?

Cabat regarded her for a moment. A black bird cried out above them. *It was a private matter.*

Was she returning to Panan One Eye as a mate? Did she no longer want you for her mate?

That is not true! Cabat stepped very close to Enga and stuck his round face in front of hers. She stumbled back a step, repelled and frightened by his anger. *You think I killed her. And I think you did.*

She wanted badly to accuse him more strongly. But he was an Elder. She watched Cabat struggle up the bank, then slowly followed him back to the Paved Place, no wiser than before. Who should she question next? Could she question Hama?

Zhoo of Still Waters, the Healer, emerged from her wipiti and crossed to check on Fee Long Thrower, who still lay unconscious. Enga knew Bahg Swiftfeet was there, too, unable to leave Fee alone, and trying to comfort his hungry son.

Enga started to enter her wipiti to try and rest, but halted when she heard a strange sound. As she listened more closely, she remembered hearing it many summers ago. She closed her eyes. It had been dark, yes, and the air had been hot. Enga, then a mere girl, had sought coolness and had scooted out of the nightly gathering to lay her cheek on a cool paving stone at the edge of the communal area. She had seen two figures, outlined against the night sky, and one had wept with an eerie, low-pitched tone. That was the sound she heard now.

She got to her feet to investigate, but had only gone two steps when Bahg burst from his doorway, throwing the flap back so hard it bounced and swung back at him. He laughed aloud, placed it back properly, and ran to the center of the gathering place.

Zhoo poked her head out of Bahg and Fee's wipiti, then emerged, too, her serene face beaming like Sister Sun.

Bahg jumped up and down, waving for everyone to come near, and sending out a clarion thought-call to all of them, a message the color of bright, leaping fire. Enga ran, her fatigue forgotten. The males, who were just returning from the fishing trap empty-handed, ran, too. Roh and Gunda rushed back and joined the gathering, breathless.

It is Fee! thought-spoke Bahg. *She opened her eyes.* He nodded to Zhoo, who stayed near the dwelling.

Yes, confirmed Zhoo. *Fee Long Thrower is well. She is nursing the baby. She knows who Bahg Swiftfeet is and who I am. I think she will recover fully.*

But where is Hama? wondered Enga. She didn't want to get her, remembering the last time she tried to summon a Hama. Nevertheless, she knew someone must see why Hama had not shown up.

Roh, the birth daughter of Hama, took it upon herself to check.

*****

Jeek moved as quietly as he could, hoping to sneak up on the beaver. He had worked hard during dark time. Brother Moon had kept him company throughout his labors, giving him faint silvery light from his slight, lopsided form, while Jeek dug a deep ditch at the edge of the pond. The first two he made filled with water soon after he started digging. That prompted him to search out a dry hillock for the third hole. His hands ached from scraping at the dirt for most of dark time.

He looked up now and saw that soon Sister Sun would greet Mother Sky and shed light through the thick trees onto this damp earth. He said goodbye to Brother Moon. He would be even smaller next time he appeared.

Now Jeek must locate the beaver and lure it to the trap he had covered with long pine branches. The vision of the celebration that would be held in his honor hung in his mind, spurring him on. There would be a true feast, on the meat of the beaver. The Hamapa would have to eat it. They were all so hungry, they would have to. Wouldn't they? He was hungry enough to eat almost anything. Its pelt would yield many new garments and much soft bedding.

There was evidence the beavers had begun rebuilding, close to their old lodge. A new dam lay across a narrow neck of the same stream, upstream from their old habitat. The beavers had collected a pile of twigs and had gnawed and felled a few trees.

Jeek crept away from his pit and explored the area, trying to see where the beavers had spent the dark time. He froze when he heard a stirring behind him.

He sniffed the air.

Beaver.

A slight swivel of his head revealed one of the smaller female beavers very near, five of his own body-lengths away.

He had debated with himself how to get one of the animals to the trap. Should he drive it, as they did caribou and bison? Or should he show himself and let it give chase, as they did with the large cats and peccaries? He assumed this animal would be too timid to chase him, so he had decided to try and drive it to his trap. The Spirit of the Hunt was with him; the trap lay beyond the creature. All Jeek had to do was drive it toward the hole.

The beaver had seen Jeek and stood still, studying him with its small eyes. Jeek straightened from his crouched position and walked slowly toward it. It backed away two steps. Then he let out a whoop and ran at it, hoping it wouldn't chomp on him with its long, shiny tusks, wouldn't bite off a limb as had happened to poor Kung. He would make sure it did not catch him if it came at him.

It turned away and crashed through the undergrowth. Jeek tore after it, veering from one side to the other, steering it toward the trap. It swerved just before the hole. It was going to miss! Jeek stood still, then maneuvered around the beast, now catching its wet fur scent full force. He screamed once more, "Yi-yi-yi-yi-yi!" and jumped at it.

It reversed, lumbered over the branches, and fell in! Now Jeek let out a cry of triumph. It had worked! He had trapped a beaver!

He sat beside the trap, grinning, panting, and savoring his victory for a moment. Then he crawled to the lip of the well and peered over.

No!

The beaver was tearing at the sides of the hole, her huge claws removing dirt many times faster than Jeek had when he'd dug it. The walls collapsed. The beaver kept clawing. More dirt tumbled down, piling up. Soon the beaver climbed, easily, out of the hole and scurried off through the trees.

Jeek wailed himself to sleep and slumbered while Sister Sun arose, traveled the length of Mother Sky, and headed toward Brother Earth. He awoke, cold and alone, saw his destroyed trap, and wept again for a short time. He was so hungry. A great ache crawled inside his belly. A new one welled up in his chest.

After his tears stopped, Jeek rose and trudged back to his village.

A cluster of people surrounded Roh Lion Hunter near the fire. Roh held something in her hand. Panan One Eye stepped over to take it as everyone looked at it, open-mouthed.

Chapter 18

The oldest positively dated musical instrument was discovered in a cave in Slovenia. It was a flute made by the Neanderthals out of the bone of a cave bear. It has been dated to 50,000 years ago.
—From: http://www.paleodirect.com/cavebear1.htm

Enga Dancing Flower thought Fee Long Thrower looked wonderful. True, she was wan and thin, but her eyes were bright and she was smiling at the ravenous baby boy smacking and gurgling at her breast. As much of the tribe as would fit crowded into the wipiti to see for themselves that Fee was back among them. No one's thoughts touched on the attack, on the baby's crippled hand, or on Doon, his treachery and disgrace. There would be plenty of time to tell her about that later.

One by one they drifted out the doorway, Enga lingering just a bit more to watch the happy baby. Her longing for one was intense.

When she emerged onto the Paved Place, it was dusk. She saw a small group gathered around Roh Lion Hunter. Hama stood nearby scowling. As Enga neared, she saw Roh was holding a figure in front of her with both hands, presenting it to the onlookers.

Enga made her way through the crowd, which was growing larger with every moment, and sucked her breath in when she saw it. The wooden carving, about as tall as a hand-length, and beautifully polished, was the image of Aja Hama, the beloved leader they had buried a few suns ago. The image was very much like the one Enga had seen the day Aja Hama died, only larger. That image had disappeared, then reappeared in the present Hama's possession. This new one could only be the work of Stitcher.

Tog Flint Shaper appeared beside Enga and took her hand. The beating inside Enga quickened. *Soon, soon I will approach Hama about our First Coupling.*

Yes, do. Soon. Tog's dark eyes shone in the firelight. Enga tore her gaze away to watch Panan.

Panan approached Roh and held out his hand for the carving. He took it gently and rubbed a finger over the belly. Then he held it up so all could see it clearly. His thought-speak was calm. *This is a most remarkable carving. It is as if Aja Hama were still with us.*

He turned it over in his hands and inspected it. A head poked up beside Enga. She looked down to see young Jeek beside her. Tog had moved closer to Panan. Jeek's hands were caked with dirt and his face was tear-streaked. *Are you all right?* she thought-whispered to him.

He nodded, but his face was somber, frowning.

Look, she thought-spoke to him. *Panan One Eye holds a carving Stitcher did of our Aja Hama. Isn't it beautiful?*

Yes, agreed Jeek. Enga noticed his distress lessen a bit and his eyebrows relax. But he was agitated about something. *The figure even has her hair braids carved into its head. How could he do that?*

Enga did not know, but neither did she know how he put garments together like he did. It could not be explained.

She sent a private message to Jeek. *If you come to my wipiti after this meeting, we can talk.*

I do not want anyone to know I am talking to you, I think.

After the meeting, everyone will be tired and ready to go home. No one will notice us.

He nodded at her eagerly and a small smile of relief lit his face.

Panan turned to Hama, who stood apart from the cluster, glaring at Stitcher.

Why do you despise it so? he asked her. She gave no answer, but her hatred radiated from her scowling face. Then he turned to Roh. *Where did you find this?*

I went to the wipiti of Hama to fetch her so she could share in the good news about Fee Long Thrower. Stitcher was just coming out. That carving was lying on the ground and the Hama was aiming dark wishes at Stitcher. She was refusing to accept the carving as a gift and wanted harm for him.

While she listened to Roh's thought-speak, Enga watched Stitcher. He still stood just outside the door of Hama's wipiti, looking unsure of his next move. Even though, as Enga knew, he did not read the thought-speak of Hama, they all knew he could tell she was displeased and angry. Anyone could. A kernel of sympathy for him began to grow in Enga. He was trying so hard to make the Hamapa like him. And Hama had been friendly with him until he had given her this carving. But it was of her birth sister, the one she had always been so jealous of. It wasn't an image of her. He should have given her an image of her own self.

This is something we could trade with the Mikino, thought-spoke Panan. *They would treasure items such as this. If Stitcher can make more of these, we will take them to their village on our next trading mission.*

Panan placed the carving on a large flat stone near the fire where it could be seen and admired. Then he astonished Enga, and the whole tribe, by making the Pronouncement Hama should have made.

"Hoody! Listen! The Storyteller speaks. At darkness the Hamapa tribe will give thanks to the Spirit of Healing. The Hamapa celebrate the good health of Fee Long Thrower and the carving of Stitcher."

Enga stole a quick look at the visage of Hama. It was now closed up tight, like her thoughts. Her face looked as if it, like the figure's face, were carved of wood.

Panan motioned for Stitcher to come close to him. Shrinking with distrust and timidity, Stitcher limped across the paving stones to stand next to the Storyteller. Panan put his hands on Stitcher's shoulders and smiled. He waved toward the carving and nodded his head up and down. Only then did Stitcher relax his shoulders, slightly, and smile back at Panan.

Tog had returned to Enga's side and caressed her shoulders. She leaned into him.

It is well you are seeking permission to couple soon, he thought-spoke.

Enga smiled. His desire was so easy to read.

It is best you do not gaze upon Stitcher too much. He pulled her closer.

She had thought she was keeping thoughts of Stitcher clamped down. Did he see them? She stiffened slightly.

He does not have good intentions toward you. You should stay far away from that one.

Enga nodded. *I agree with that. I am keeping away from him.* She stole one more glance at him, though. Those thin white hands, Enga marveled, those hands that carved such beauty, were the same ones that had torn at her clothing and assaulted her in the Holy Cave. *How can this be?*

*****

Before the celebration began, Panan One Eye, again preempting Hama, declared they would discuss the slaying of Aja Hama and try to determine what had happened.

He started by having each member of the tribe convey their actions that day. He went first.

Mother Sky wept small tears that morning. I stayed in the wipiti of the males, coming out only to eat, until the hunting party returned. I reviewed the Sagas to choose one for the gathering.

He waved a hand at Cabat the Thick. *I, too, stayed in most of the day.*

But you went to Hama's and quarreled with her, interrupted Panan.

Cabat frowned. *I was about to relate that. We quarreled and I became angry at her.*

Why? asked Panan.

Cabat shifted his weight where he sat. *It was trivial.*

And yet you became so angry.

I brought her something to eat. She did not want it. And we were all so hungry. She flung the gruel at me and I ripped her garment. The antler buttons popped off. Then I left.

Enga had seen no gruel on the ground. She didn't think she believed his reason for the quarrel. And it did not sound like something Hama would do.

Panan gestured toward Hama, who was then Nanno Green Eyes.

I lost my mate that day.

Our Hama was killed before the hunters returned with the news, Panan thought-spoke. *They did not broadcast it ahead.*

You cannot think I killed my birth sister. Hama had been sitting with the rest. Now she rose and looked down at Panan, menace in her eyes.

I am trying to understand what everyone did that day, where they were and what they saw. I am not saying you killed your sister. I am asking what you did that day.

Hama closed her eyes for a moment. Then she sat down, looking a little calmer. *I went into her wipiti after Cabat did. It was just as the hunters were returning. She was already dead. But when I found out Kokat had been killed on the hunt, I could not think of anything else. So I did not tell anyone. What of Stitcher? Does anyone know what he did that day? Where he went?*

Panan stared at Hama. *You have seen the carving he did of Aja Hama. He could not have killed her when he thought enough of her to carve her likeness.*

Panan turned to Roh Lion Hunter. *You were not on the hunt. What did you do that day?*

I pounded meal, Roh answered. *I tried a small hunt with my little girls, but could not walk very far. I was still weak from losing my last baby. We did not bring anything back from the hunt.*

I saw them leave and return, thought-spoke Sannum Straight Hair.

Most of the day I worked on a new spear head. I did not leave the village, but I did not go to Aja Hama's wipiti either.

Ongu Small One jumped to her feet. *This will not tell us what happened to Aja Hama. No one here killed her.*

Panan stood and faced her. *I fear you are right. This will not reveal who killed her. But we must think of a way to find out what happened. We will discuss it again another time.*

*****

The celebration was in full swing. Jeek's mood began to lift just a little. He would speak to Enga Dancing Flower after the meeting and hoped some weight would lift from his mind. Roh Lion Hunter had gone to the woods earlier with Gunda and, to his surprise, speared the cat of long-tooth he had seen on the caribou hunt. It turned out to be a medium-sized cat.

There was plenty to eat for this night, but one cat would not last all winter. If only he had been able to trap and kill a beaver; it was many times larger than the cat. He tried to darken his bleak thoughts and rejoice in the fact that his stomach was full for now.

Jeek was happy to see Tog Flint Shaper dancing very close to Enga Dancing Flower. He liked both of them and it looked like they would mate some day. That day would be a happy one, like this, but, he hoped, with even more to eat. He looked forward to sharing his thoughts with Enga later.

Panan One Eye, Storyteller, followed the singing of Lakala with the Saga of the Vanished Horses.

Once many small horses ran free on the plains. These horses were like the large ones that roam in herds now, like the mammoth also do, but were smaller than horses now and very fleet. They were eaten by large predators, and some were eaten by Hamapa, although we have always preferred slower, larger game. Our Ancient Ones began to notice there were fewer and fewer of these small horses over time. Large herds dwindled down to small ones. Then an Ancient One, who was a good tracker, saw a herd going toward the place where Sister Sun goes to sleep and followed them. Maybe this was a time when they needed food and he wanted to hunt them. I do not know why he followed them, just that he did. They ran for many suns, then many moons

The herd he tracked was joined by other small herds and grew large. It became a huge herd, but kept running in the same direction.

The good tracker finally had to turn around and return to his village. But he felt they would keep running. The Storyteller of his tribe had the opinion that the horses were going to the place where the Hamapa came from in ancient times. They would go, he said, far to the north and across a narrow land. Then they would be in a vast land, like the one we are in. They could live there. Maybe they would not be hunted by so many large hunting animals.

Jeek was spellbound by the picture of the tiny graceful horses. He had never seen one and now it seemed he never would, if they were all leaving this land. There were many things in life that Jeek had not seen, had not even dreamed of. Maybe he was not an important enough person to see and dream everything. Maybe it was not up to him to save the tribe. But someone must. They must have food.

Panan continued. *Others have said the small horses traveled in the direction away from the Guiding Bear who turns with the Seasons in Mother Sky, to a land where it is always warm.*

Wherever they went, they are no longer here. Sometimes creatures need to move in order to survive. This may be what the small horses have done. It is what our Ancient Ones did when they came here. And it is what we must do, as our Aja Hama has told us. We must all consider how to do this.

*****

Enga Dancing Flower, while she waited for her turn to dance, studied Jeek to see if she could figure out what had made him so distressed early in the day. And so dirty. Now he looked cleaner, but sat still and solemn. After the gathering she would make sure they met and she would see if he could share whatever burden he carried on his small shoulders.

The Storyteller's Saga of Vanished Horses had given them much to think about, but now they were celebrating noisily. They rejoiced in the recovery of Fee Long Thrower, and in the beautiful carving of Stitcher. Shouts and clapping urged the dancers on.

Lakala Rippling Water had helped Enga bring Ung Strong Arm out to the fireside and the two sat together, smiling and laughing softly. It would be awhile before Ung was able to dance.

Stitcher's carving stood in a place of honor and the dancers, in dancing around the fire, danced around it, too. The flames brought out the shine of the wood and the flickering light made the statue seem as if it, too, danced. Could there be good and bad, both, in Stitcher? Could she have just misunderstood him so badly, and he also misunderstood her, that he thought she wanted him to couple with her? Enga shuddered at the remembrance of his attack, then, at the rattle of Hama's gourd, flung herself into the dance, beckoning Tog Flint Shaper to dance beside her. There would be no harm in dancing for him instead of the spirits tonight.

Hama seemed to be enjoying the evening, but Enga thought she was forcing her good mood. She stood well away from where the carving shone, on the other side of the fire. Cabat the Thick stood near her, Sannum Straight Hair at their feet beating rhythm with his hollow log.

A startle washed over her and Enga turned to see Zhoo of Still Waters walking slowly toward the group, her son Teek Bearclaw at her side. A great cry of, "Ya, ya, ya, ya!" went up from the tribe. Teek was well enough to walk on his own!

Enga finished her turn dancing, following Tog out of the circle.

Tonight, he thought-spoke to her. *Will you ask permission for our First Coupling tonight?*

Enga wasn't sure. *Is this a good time?*

I don't want to wait any longer. He put his arm around her and drew her to his broad chest. Enga closed her eyes in pleasure as a little purring sound started up in her throat.

I will, Tog Flint Shaper. I will ask tonight.

Tog beamed like Sister Sun at the middle of the day.

Enga decided to do it now, before she could think about it too much longer. It would be good to get this done before any more discussion of the murder took place.

With a drum beating double-time in her breast and drops of moisture springing up on her palms, Enga marched over to Hama and knelt before her.

Most High Female of the Hamapa tribe, I, Enga Dancing Flower, seek permission to make a First Coupling in the Holy Cave with Tog Flint Shaper. Enga communicated this with her face toward the ground, then waited in that position for Hama to touch her shoulder, giving her consent.

Moments passed. There was no touch. Enga grew cold inside. What was wrong? Was Hama not going to give her permission?

Hama finally returned a thought to Enga, a bright, wide open thought for the whole tribe. *You have already had a First Coupling in the Holy Cave. Without my blessing. This would not be your first.*

Enga gasped and jerked her head up. She realized her tribal brothers and sisters all stood staring at her, silent. *No! I did not!*

Ah, but you did. I saw you leave the Holy Cave. And right after you left, THAT one followed you. She pointed to Stitcher, who sat with Ung and Lakala. *I saw you run from the cave and saw Stitcher walk out later. Your clothing was halfway off.* Hama sneered. She was enjoying this! *You have had your First Coupling, in the Holy Cave. Without my permission. You have defiled the Holy Cave.*

Something shrank inside Enga. She looked around frantically for Tog. He gave her a questioning look, then looked down.

Chapter 19

E nga Dancing Flower leapt to her feet.

Yes, yes, I was in the Holy Cave with Stitcher. But not for a coupling. It was not my choice to be there for that.

The heavy disapproval of her tribe took her breath away. Dark thoughts flew at her, weighed her down.

From Tog Flint Shaper, the one she loved, *Did you not think of what you were doing? Did you defile the Holy Cave with that one?*

From Sannum Straight-Hair, *My dear Enga Dancing Flower. You haven't done such a horrible deed, have you?*

Her birth sister, Ung, kept her thoughts to herself. Enga could feel no support from her, but only a shudder of fright.

No! We did NOT couple. He attacked me. Enga sank to her knees.

But Hama continued, standing over her, gloating. *You willingly followed him there. I watched you. Then I saw you emerge with your clothing displaced. This alone is a good reason to expel you from the tribe, Enga Dancing Flower. You have disrespected me and our Holy Cave. But there is another matter, even more serious.*

Hama drew herself up to her full height and looked down on Enga with a slight smile. *You defiled the Holy Cave with Stitcher. And you told no one, you kept it secret. What could be the reason for this? We all know Aja Hama disliked Stitcher. And you mated with him. What else have you done for him? What else has he bid you do?*

What do you mean? Hama's face blurred through the flood of Enga's tears. *I did not want to couple with him. He tried to force me. We did not couple.*

I am waiting to hear what else you have done for him.

Nothing! Why would I do anything for him! He attacked me. He hurt me.

As Enga watched, Hama's face distorted with hate, just for an instant. Her nostrils flared wide and her eyes, the white showing all around her dark center eye, frightened Enga. Hama drew her lips back from her teeth and her breath came fast.

Then she regained control and shut her face down. Hama radiated calmness and reason to the tribe. Her nasty smile was gone, her lips clamped in a thin, tight line. It was like she had become an animal for a brief moment.

Have you considered that Stitcher tried to harm me and he may have harmed Aja Hama? thought-spoke Enga in desperation.

What reason would he have for that? I saw you go into the wipiti of Aja Hama just before the rest of us found her dead. You killed her. You killed my dear birth sister, our beloved leader. You must be expelled. And your birth sister with you.

This could not be happening. Not to her. Enga worked hard with her mind, her fists opening and closing.

Look how frail Stitcher is, continued Hama. *You are strong.*

He was strong enough to attack me! He is much stronger than he looks.

That is what you say. I do not believe he attacked you.

If she were expelled she might survive. But if Ung were expelled with her they would both die. Ung was still a cripple. She could not move fast enough to escape predators. Enga could not find food enough for both of them. She could not hunt, and protect her sister at the same time. They would both die.

Enga tried to rise, but didn't have the strength. She fell back on the stones with a thud. Everyone stood staring at her, their backs to the fire. No one else saw Stitcher grab his carving and leave. Enga did not have the strength to send out a thought, to show this to the others.

Why did Hama accused her of murder? She could not think Enga had killed Aja Hama. Hama already said she wanted to expel her for unsanctioned coupling. So why accuse her of this? Her mind spun, then stopped at the point she had seen Hama, who was then still Nanno Green Eyes, right after Hama was found.

Enga stumbled to her feet, swiped her tears away with her cape, and faced Hama.

And you, Hama, she thought-spoke. *You were in the wipiti of the Aja Hama earlier, before I was. You said she was dead, then. Was she? Or did you kill her yourself? When you came out after I discovered her, your hands were dirty. What had you done in there? Did you disturb the footprints so they would look like those of the Mikino? Is that how your fingers picked up so much dirt? Did you make false footprints, like Doon did for the beaver? Did you do that so we would not accuse you?*

That look of anger and hot hatred flashed across Hama's face once more, and was gone just as quickly as it appeared. Hama turned to Cabat, who now stood at her elbow. *Do you hear what she says about me? What do you think of that?*

Cabat looked as though he wished he were far away. He did not want to answer the Hama. *I think,* he began, then stopped.

Panan stepped in front of Cabat. *That is enough, Hama. This girl did not murder Aja Hama. We have known her all of her life. She did not kill the woman who raised her. Enga Dancing Flower loved her very much and grieved with all of us when she died.*

But, interjected Cabat, *one of us killed her. I have come to a decision. Enga Dancing Flower is not a true Hamapa. She must be the one who killed Aja Hama.*

But where has Stitcher gone? thought-spoke Vala Golden Hair. *We should give him a chance to defend himself against what Enga Dancing Flower accuses him of.*

The others craned their heads, but Stitcher was not there.

Enga whirled around. Her birth sister had come to stand beside her.

Ung grabbed Enga's hand. Enga searched for Tog. He stood at the front of the crowd. His mind was closed, but she thought she saw fear and pity on his face. Enga's tears poured down her cheeks and dripped onto the stones.

My birth sister did not kill Aja Hama, declared Ung. *But neither did Hama. That is my thought. You will have to look elsewhere to find her slayer.*

Hama pointed at Enga and Ung with one hand and raised her gourd with the other.

"Hoody! Listen! The Most High Female Speaks. Enga Dancing Flower slew Aja Hama. Enga Dancing Flower is banished. Ung Strong Arm is banished. Mother Spirit of the Sky, Dakadaga, bless the Hamapa."

Hama rattled her gourd with extra violence.

*****

Ung Strong Arm slept, her breathing soft and even. Enga Dancing Flower, propped on one elbow, gazed upon her sister, wishing she, too, could fall asleep. There had been no reason for Hama to banish Ung. It had not been discussed, not even mentioned. But Hama and the Most High Male had overruled Panan One Eye.

An owl in the tree above them startled her with its low whistle. She shivered at the eerie sound and drew her cape close around her neck. The stiff breath of Mother Sky whipped through the bare branches above them. Enga clutched the flint knife she had been allowed to take with her tight in her fist. The two exiles had walked as far into the woods as they could, then bedded down in the underbrush. They had both agreed the woods would be better than the open plains. At new sun Enga would try and find a cave for them. And figure out a way back into the tribe.

As she had lined up her belongings in her warm wipiti, Enga tried to line her thoughts up in her head. But they would not stay in order and jumbled and tumbled about.

She had sent waves of appeals to Tog Flint Shaper, but his mind was still clenched tight against her. He had tried to warn her about Stitcher, she thought, but his warning had been too late. She guessed he had believed the lie of Hama, that Enga had coupled with Stitcher. But Enga had no more tears to cry over Tog. Now she must survive.

She had been taught that a spoken word was a powerful thing, meant to be heard by the Spirits. And once it was pronounced, it could not be un-pronounced. But, she reasoned, could not another Pronouncement be made? Panan had just made one. Maybe Panan could make a Pronouncement in her favor. Did she dare appeal to him? Probably not. He was outnumbered by Cabat and Hama. She would have to make the whole tribe see that she and Ung should not be banished.

Enga sat up and vowed to Dakadaga that she and Ung would not die out here. The wind stopped. The woods fell silent.

When Enga looked up, Dakadaga sent one of her flaming eyes down to Enga. She held her breath as it streaked across the sky. One lone tear fell from her own eye. Was this glowing eye a sign that the Spirits would take care of her?

The breath of Mother Sky blew again, colder and fiercer than before. Enga lay down, but did not sleep. She drifted into an old memory, one that replayed in her mind often.

One night, when Enga had been a part of the Hamapa tribe for eight summers, she had wandered to the edge of the Paved Place during the nightly gathering. It was the Warm Season. The breath of Dakadaga was soft and the fire was very hot. Enga sought a cool place and lay down with her cheek resting on a smooth paving stone far from the fire.

Two different trading parties had recently come by. First, several suns before, there had been the Cuva, the neighboring tribe of people like the Hamapa. They had traded tanned skins of camel and bear, and pieces of carved wood to blow through and create music. Then, during the same time of sun, that day, a strange-looking people had arrived. They were tall and dark, and their bodies were not sturdy like the Hamapa. They were called Tall Ones by the Hamapa tribe. It was the first time Enga had seen them. The Tall Ones traded intricately carved pieces of bone and antler, and woven cloth. At dark time they had moved a short way from the village and camped nearby.

Enga Dancing Flower started to get drowsy, lying on her cool stone away from the group, and heard voices in her head. A twig snapped in the forest beyond the village and Enga held her breath in a moment of fear. Maybe an animal was prowling for little girls who lay at the edge of their Paved Places. Then she heard other sounds. A person was weeping, a low, strange sound. She raised her head slightly and peered into the darkness, her fear gone.

Brother Moon, then at his fattest, showed her a female, standing on a rise, backing away from another being. That female figure looked like the new Hama. Jansa Wild Wind, Enga's foster mother, had become the new leader very recently when the old one, her mother, had died.

The other figure was tall and extremely thin. It looked like a Tall One and might have been a male, but Enga couldn't be sure. She strained to see them through the wavering moonlight, leaf shadows drifting across it. The Tall One stretched out two slender arms toward the female, but she kept moving away. The female was not the one crying. She shook her head to signify "no." The thin figure fell to its knees. Brother Moon drew a thick cloud cloak around himself then and, when he let it go, the two were gone.

"Ha," breathed Nanno Green Eyes, standing over her and pointing a finger at her.

It had made Enga jump.

There you are, Nanno thought-spoke. *Why are you so far from the gathering?*

Nanno ran back to tell the Elders that Enga Dancing Flower was where she should not be. Enga sighed and got up to return to the fire. Nanno constantly followed her around hoping to get her into trouble. There was no way for Enga to get along with Nanno. Kokat No Ear would always limp from his injuries the night Enga was rescued and brought into the tribe, and Nanno, his mate, would always blame Enga and her sister for that. On her way back to the gathering, she was met by Sannum Straight Hair, who had come looking for her. She remembered running into his strong, comforting arms.

Now, lying in the cold, dangerous forest, Enga's lower lip quivered at the memory of Sannum, missing him sorely. Nanno, now Hama, had finally gotten her way. She was rid of the twins.

Chapter 20

The earliest unequivocal manifestations of fire use—
stone hearths and burned animal bones from sites in
Europe—are only some 200,000 years old.
   —*Scientific American, Special Edition: New Look at
   Human Evolution*, August, 2003, p. 68

Enga Dancing Flower handed a piece of sharp-smelling raw flesh to
Ung Strong Arm. They both preferred cooked meat, but they had
no flint. They had no spears either, but Enga had fashioned an
implement she could use to skewer hares and voles. She had seen a
coyote near the cave several times and would try for one next time she
saw one. With her flint knife, the only tool she was allowed to bring into
exile, she had sharpened a long, sturdy pine branch, and it served as a
spear. She would not dare to try it on a larger animal, but so far, at least,
she and Ung had food.

   After the first night on the floor of the forest, Enga scouted until she
found shelter for them. She would never have noticed this cave if she
hadn't seen a pair of cawing ravens dart out of the thick branches that
obscured its mouth. She had investigated, hoping to find a fresh kill she
could snatch from the ravens. They were not feeding, but this cave was
a fortunate find.

   She and Ung had spent the next night dry and safe. Now that Enga
had found a place to leave Ung, she was ready for action. Ung would be

safer in the cave than out in the open. It was small enough that bears and large cats had not been there. In fact, she and Ung barely had room to lie down. But a large fallen spruce tree obscured the opening and it seemed safe. Their only companions were the ravens, and their nest was not inside the cave, but in the spruce branches.

Their shelter didn't remind them of their Holy Cave. No red streaks on the walls for decoration, and the interior was dark because of the branches. The only warmth was from their bodies, but the space was so small, they were comfortable there. It might be a place they could stay for a while. If only they had a fire. But they didn't.

Enga detected a faint odor that reminded her of Doon. She wondered if he had used this cave. He had not been in it recently, she could tell.

Now it was nearly high sun and she was going to attempt to get near the village. She wanted to try and listen in on unguarded minds so she could figure out who killed Aja Hama. Enga wrapped her feet carefully. The breath of Mother Sky was getting colder and colder, and Brother Earth would soon don a mantle of hard frozen dirt. For now, she was grateful the path was neither muddy nor frozen, although she would not follow the path for more than a few steps. She might be seen. Exile meant not coming near the tribe again. Enga had never known of a Hamapa tribe to put a member to death, but she imagined that was what would happen if the Hama's exile decree were defied.

And Enga was about to defy her Hama. Something she had had a great deal of difficulty justifying to herself. And something she would probably not be able to justify to the tribe. Her only hope was to make them see that the accusation had been wrong. She had not killed Aja Hama.

The small cave was only half a day's journey from the village. She planned to arrive around last sun and conceal herself to overhear the Hamapa. She would spend dark time outside the village, then get close to catch thoughts. If no one knew she was around, they might not shield conversations from her. Then there was scent. If her scent were detected, she hoped they would think the smell was left from when she lived there. She had no idea what she was seeking. Just something, anything, to clear her name.

She ran at a brisk trot through the woods, parallel to the main path, to make time as well as to stay warm. She slowed only for thick growth she had to push through or go around. If anyone from the village were in this part of the forest, she was fairly confident she would detect them before they detected her, but she remained on high alert, her nose quivering to detect scent, her mind stretching to catch thought feelers.

When she got near the village she stopped for breath and to calm her mind. It was crucial that she not betray her presence. Her thoughts must remain as black as a dark time without Brother Moon. She smelled the fire and the familiar odors of her fellow tribe members. Tears of loneliness sprang to her eyes.

In order to focus on single thoughts, she would have to get close. She wiped the tears away and approached with a tightness in her throat. Thoughts would be flying around, none of them directed at her, so she would have to filter them. Being nearer would help with that. Sister Sun sent up a few last flares across the stones of the Paved Place and sank into Brother Earth's vast form for their nightly tryst.

The dry leaves rustled under her feet and she slowed. There must be no sound. The breath of Mother Sky was in her favor, wafting her scent away from the village. A squirrel started in a tree above her, but did not chatter. She froze as it scampered away. Then she continued, putting each foot down carefully in the darkness, drawing nearer.

If two Hamapa conversed together and did not know another was trying to tune in, there was not a need to funnel thoughts between them. It occurred to Enga that she might overhear some things that would be hurtful to her. She must brace herself for that.

But she would start where she knew she was loved. She crept around the backs of the wipitis until she came to the large one that housed the males. It was at the opposite side of the village from Hama's wipiti. Here she hoped to catch some stray thoughts from Sannum Straight Hair, or maybe one of the Elders. Tog Flint Shaper also slept there, but Enga wasn't sure she wanted to know what he was thinking about her.

She could detect Sannum's scent, but no thoughts. Tog also seemed to be there. Some of the males were exchanging ideas on food, mostly thinking about how hungry and worried they were.

I do not know if I can eat another shrew, thought-spoke Akkal. *And the voles taste just as bad. I am so hungry for a good big bite of mammoth flesh.*

I would be happy with a rabbit, thought-spoke Tog.

The others agreed, then all was quiet.

Come on, she urged, to herself. *Thought-speak to each other. Let me know what's going on.*

But nothing came. Her mixed feelings for Tog swirled and threatened to give her away. If she knew what he genuinely thought of her now, she could decide what she thought of him. If only she could catch his thoughts. She waited until her feet and hands started to suffer from the cold and inactivity, then moved to the next wipiti. It was that of the Healer and her children, Jeek and Teek Bearclaw.

Enga basked in the serenity coming to her from Zhoo of Still Waters. She wished she could feel the Healer's hands on her forehead. She closed her eyes and imagined it. Zhoo and her sons sent thoughts back and forth, but they were about affairs of the tribe, mostly the trading mission Hama wanted. Jeek wished to be allowed on the trip, but his mother was against it. Teek boasted just a bit that he would probably go since he was older and had gone on the last one. Jeek still seemed anguished about something else, too, but he didn't let on what it was.

Zhoo told them to quit bickering. *You both know we are not trading until the leaders can agree on how to do it. There is no use thinking about it until it is decided.*

Enga wished she had had a chance to see what troubled Jeek before she left.

She crawled on past the wipiti where Nanno Green Eyes had lived before she became Hama. Her daughter, Vala Golden Hair, dwelt there now, but no one was present. The next one belonged to Roh Lion Hunter. Vala was inside with Roh, her sister. Their thoughts flew.

I know she is our mother, thought-spoke Roh, *but she will never make a good leader.*

It was a good thing they were not close to Hama's wipiti. These thoughts were light, and would not carry that far. But if Hama had been crouched outside their dwelling, instead of Enga, she would have heard them.

We miss Aja Hama so much, answered Vala. *We need her now.*

What will happen to us? I am afraid Cabat the Thick and Panan One Eye are not united against her. That is the only way to keep her foolish plans under control.

Yes, I agree. What will she want next? She will let her own whims destroy us.

Enga listened awhile longer, but they had no thoughts about who had killed Aja Hama. Enga felt certain neither of them had. Gunda and her two little sisters were playing a tossing game with their seed giver, Donik Tree Trunk. The wipiti must have been crowded inside, Enga thought.

The next wipiti was the one Enga and Ung had shared. It sat empty. She swallowed a sob and moved on to Fee Long Thrower's. Thoughts flowed freely between Fee and Bahg Swiftfeet, but they were all about the baby. This was the only wipiti brimming with joy. Enga gave a sigh. She wished she could stay here for all of dark time, letting their happiness course through her.

Ongu Small One was inside her dwelling with her three male children, busy untangling their hair and stopping quarrels between the two younger ones. Any other thoughts she may have had were not apparent.

Enga thought Lakala Ripping Water might be thinking of Ung, but nothing radiated from her place. If she was there, she was keeping her thoughts to herself.

The only one left was Hama's. It sat apart from the others, so Enga would have to expose herself when she crossed from the rear of Lakala's.

A sound behind her.

She quit breathing.

A footstep.

Her mind clamped shut as tightly as it ever had in her life. She could do nothing about her smell, though. The wind had died to almost nothing. Any passing Hamapa could smell her. She crouched as small as she could, next to the rocks surrounding Lakala's walls.

Stitcher came from the direction she had been. He took great care, with his lame foot, to tread softly. It looked like he did not want to be heard. He passed very close to Enga, but didn't see her. He stood outside the back of Hama's wipiti for a long time, then went back the way he had come. Enga assumed he would go to sleep now, where he stayed, in the wipiti of the males.

What had he been doing? Had he hoped to understand the thought-speak of Hama? Had he just wanted to be near her? Hama had favored him for a while, but didn't seem to anymore, since he had given her the large carving of Aja Hama.

She realized he had not smelled her. So he couldn't understand thought-speak and he couldn't smell. How did Tall Ones survive? Maybe the rest of them could do these things.

Enga waited a long time to make sure Stitcher didn't return, then crept to the place he had stood. She was surprised to find that Cabat and Panan were there with Hama.

Is it not beautiful? thought-spoke Hama.

Did Enga dare touch her mind to see what she referred to? She didn't have to. Cabat and Panan both filled their minds with it and sent thoughts to each other.

It is as good as the one he did of Aja Hama, agreed Cabat.

Yes, and bigger. Hama giggled. *It is better looking than that one.*

Enga saw, in their minds, a carving Stitcher must have made. It was of Hama and was, indeed, a bit larger than the last one. Hama sent out affection for Stitcher now. *He is such an asset to the tribe. And it is so good to have the twins gone. Our luck will change now.*

I am not certain you should have expelled them, thought-spoke Cabat.

You agreed with me. Hama shot coldness toward Cabat.

I did. But I am not sure now that I should have.

Then Enga noticed something odd. Panan and Cabat were sending thoughts back and forth but Panan was refusing to communicate with Hama. In shielding his thought from her, it bounced more readily to Enga. It shocked her that Panan was searching the Sagas in his mind for a time when a Hama was deposed. His thoughts reached Cabat and Cabat told him to quit doing that.

There is a mission we must do, thought-spoke Hama. *I must make certain the twins do not come back. We must send scouts to see where they went.*

Both males answered *No!*

Yes! They must not be allowed to live. We must make sure they are dead. The tribe must do as I wish!

Snowflakes started to drift down. Enga knew she had better leave now. If she stayed she might leave tracks and it would be obvious she had been there. The cold masked her scent, at least. She rose to her feet.

What is that? Hama sent out thought-probes. Enga stood as still as a rock and resisted with all her might, her eyes squeezed tight. Her whole body vibrated, threatening to betray her. *Someone is outside.*

There is no one there, answered Cabat. *It is late. I will not discuss that last idea with you. It will not happen. I am going to leave and go to sleep. Come, Panan.*

Enga didn't think Hama was convinced, but sprinted into the woods as quietly as she could. She would hide during dark time and leave at first sun. How would she ever find out the truth?

Chapter 21

...(An) indicator of strong social ties and social complexity is the survival of individuals with severe, sometimes crippling injuries; an individual's value was not solely based on his or her ability to obtain food or carry out physical work effectively.

—*The Neandertals*, Erik Trinkaus and Pat Shipman, p. 418

Sannum Straight Hair could not sleep. Enga Dancing Flower and Ung Strong Arm had been banished three suns ago. The more he dwelt on it, the more he was sure Enga had been telling the truth. She would not defile the Holy Cave. And he knew she had not slain the Aja Hama. Enga could never do a thing like that.

He was brought back to the night he and two other young males rescued Enga and her twin.

It was the time of the nightly gathering and the community was sharing their last meal of the day. That night they chewed on roasted peccary meat. Sannum Straight Hair remembered thinking the pig was especially fat and succulent. He had grinned at the taste and surveyed his fellow tribe members, crouched around the fire in a half circle, pig fat glistening on most of their faces. How he would love to have some of that fat pig now!

Their leader at that time was the mother of the now Aja Hama.

Sannum thought her still a handsome woman even if she had lived forty-two summers. Her long gray hair hung in two plaits down her back, which was straight and proud. She stood and cocked her head at a distant sound.

She made a sharp hand motion and the singing and eating and commotion stopped. Silence fell. Then Sannum heard the sound too, the cry of a small creature. *A child?* he wondered.

Hama picked out Sannum and two other robust males, focusing on each of them with her dark, wide-set eyes. The trio rose and left the warmth of the fire to search for the origin of the sounds, understanding their mission from the thoughts she sent them. They were to see if a small creature was in distress or trapped. If it turned out to be a young peccary they would stab it and bring it back to eat. If it were larger, they would call the females to throw their spears. Or, if it were not an animal, they would rescue it.

Kokat No Ear tucked his piece of meat into the rabbit-skin pouch at his waist and drew his cloak of coarse mammoth fur tight around his shoulders. Sannum led the way through the dark woods surrounding the village, half wishing he were still at the dancing fire eating the roast peccary. Kokat, giving nervous glances around him, followed very closely behind Sannum. Mahk Long Eye, a male in his early twenties, named for his excellent eyesight, trailed behind.

When Kokat trod on his heel, Sannum turned, grasped his shoulders, and thought-spoke to him. *Do not fear, Kokat No Ear. It is dark time and many dangerous animals roam now, this is true, but we are three. We will be safe. Whatever cries out here may need us.*

Kokat swallowed and bowed his head. Sannum and Mahk heard his thoughts of shame that he, Kokat, had thought of himself and not whatever small creature they were after to kill or rescue.

Sannum silently urged them to be attentive. They could, he reminded them, smell if the source of the sound was animal or not. He was beginning to think it was not an animal at all. The wind was not in their favor, though.

The small mewlings rose and fell on the wind as the males peered into the shadowy swaying ferns and willow bushes and lifted spruce branches that reached to the dark forest floor.

Eventually, after the village was well out of sight, Sannum almost stumbled over them. He heard the incredulous thought-speak of Kokat behind him. *Are they children? Alone at night in the forest?*

Sannum nodded, then stooped to assess their condition. A shaft of light from Brother Moon shot through the spruce branches and rested on two very young females, naked, cold, and very frightened. They could not be more than three summers old, maybe less. They looked the same age, twins. They sat in the fragrant needles, clutching each other's small hands and staring defiantly at the three large males who bent toward them.

We must be careful and not frighten them further, Sannum thought-spoke to his two companions. *Do you think they have been abandoned by their tribe?*

Our own tribe would never do that, shot back Mahk. *The Hamapa do not abandon children. Do you think another tribe would?*

We do not know the ways of all tribes, answered Sannum. *But we must help them. We can carry these little ones to the warm fire where they can get food and drink.*

Kokat smiled at the girls and knelt down to their level. But when he reached for them, one recoiled and screamed at the sight of his scarred face. Kokat jumped up and backed away.

Sannum tried next. The one who screamed seemed fascinated with his shiny dark locks, looking almost black in the darkness and worn loose tonight, falling like raven's wings beside his face. She quieted her screeching and reached for his hair, then pulled at his wispy beard.

A low growl sounded, close by. The three males froze. They caught the scent of a cat. A large cat with the long, curved tusks.

Mahk Long Eye spotted the gleam of yellow eyes in the moonlight. The cat crouched in the willow bushes at a good distance behind the infants, perfectly still. Mahk sent its location to Sannum Straight Hair and Kokat No Ear.

Sannum slowly reached his arms around the small, shivering girls, careful not to look in the cat's direction. Smoothly, carefully, he straightened up with a child in each arm, his chest thumping loudly in his ears.

Meanwhile, Kokat reached into the pouch slung around his waist and pulled out a piece of meat, the roast peccary he had been eating when Hama summoned him on this mission. Step by deliberate step, he drew forward with the meat as Sannum drew backward with the babies. When Sannum was back far enough he handed them to Mahk, who turned and fled with them in his arms.

After Mahk sent a mental signal to Kokat that the children were well on their way down the trail, Kokat flung the meat into the willow bush and he and Sannum backed away from the cat. They heard the cat chewing and ripping the meat.

Sannum breathed out his relief and turned to Kokat. *Now the animal is occupied and the girls are safe,* Sannum thought-spoke. *We can return.*

I am glad I had the meat with me. It's not a very big piece. We'd better get out of here before the cat finishes it.

They had only gone a few steps, Kokat in the lead, when Kokat turned his head to check on the cat. His eyes shouted out his fear. Sannum sensed the leap of the cat. Kokat whirled toward them, drawing his flint knife from his pouch.

Sannum felt the claws bite into his back and fell to the ground with the attack to try and lessen its impact. As they hit the ground, the claws loosened and Sannum rolled, attempting to draw his knife. It stuck in his pouch. The animal came after him.

Kokat jumped on its back and stabbed it in the neck. The beast shook his head and fastened his great teeth on Kokat's leg. He cried out, then brought his blade down again and again on the top of the cat's head.

By this time Sannum had gotten his knife out and circled the melee, searching for an opening. Kokat managed to land a stab into the ear of the cat. It loosened its grip and raised its head in pain.

Sannum sprang and stabbed at its eye. For a moment its horrible fangs came toward him, grazed his arm. Then its essence, the Red of the beast, spattered Sannum and flowed down onto Kokat, still beneath it. The cat howled in rage, sprang away, and limped off into the dark.

It took a long time for their breathing to return to normal. Sannum knelt over Kokat and examined his wound. Taking his own cloak in his teeth, he bit off a strip and bound it around the gash. He helped his wounded tribe mate to his feet and Kokat found that he could hobble if he put an arm around Sannum's sturdy shoulder. They returned to the settlement.

By the time they drew near, the tribe was cooing and murmuring softly over the two infants who sat in Jansa Wild Wind's lap.

Nanno Green Eyes, Jansa's birth sister, however, was waiting tensely, pacing, having sensed her mate, Kokat's, pain. She cried out and ran to them. Sannum helped Kokat to the group, then set him down. Nanno wailed at the sight of her mate's injured leg and tore at her garments.

When Sannum straightened up, however, he could tell they saw the claw marks on his own back. Jansa sent thoughts of empathy to him and to his mate, who ran to him and started inspecting his injuries.

The Healer did her best for Kokat, tending and binding his wound. It hurt too much for him to put weight on it, but the Healer thought he would be able to walk when it healed.

While the Healer treated his back, Sannum joked about Kokat being tastier to this cat than himself, but Kokat's mate kept a frown on her face.

When she finished tending the two males, the Healer brought two brown bearskins from her dwelling to wrap the girls in. Jansa Wild Wind requested to have them in her dwelling that first night and the Hama granted Jansa that permission.

Look. Hama directed a thought to the whole group. *The children come with flowers.* Her thought was colored with surprise. Sannum looked at the hands of the babies.

One clutched a red flower in her chubby fist and the other a yellow one. Sannum marveled that the flowers were blooming this late. The one with the red flower stood up and shoved her flower at Hama, uttering a word, "Ung."

Nanno snickered. But when the tribe burst into laughter, the child burst into tears of embarrassment. Jansa grabbed her up and cradled her until her sobs quieted. Jansa directed a stern look and a disapproving thought to her birth sister for upsetting the children.

Do not be so serious, Nanno thought-spoke to Jansa. *These are just two stray creatures. We don't need to keep them. Besides, they appear to be twins. Twins are bad luck. They will bring hardship to the tribe.*

Thoughts flew: *We are Hamapa, not savages. When did we ever turn away orphans? How can you think like that, Nanno Green Eyes? There is no reason to turn them away, just because they are twins. Where did you get such an idea?*

Sannum was grateful the tribe uniformly objected to Nanno's opinion. He already liked them.

Hama quieted them. *We will shelter these two. It is our way.* She shot a stab of disapproval at Nanno Green Eyes, who lowered her head, but retained a stubborn set to her shoulders.

Every member of the Hamapa tribe was affected by the injuries of both Kokat and Sannum, but Nanno could only think of her mate, Kokat, and his injured leg. She also stubbornly held the little girls to blame for the injury to her mate.

Nanno had never gotten over that feeling. And now, with Enga and Ung banished, she finally had her revenge.

Sannum could not lie in his wipiti with Enga and Ung out in the cold. They had been gone for three suns. Soon Enga would be too hungry to hunt. It was not time for first sun yet. But he arose, put a few dry pieces of peccary meat in his pouch and, careful not to disturb his sleeping tent mates, went to find them. He was weary from keeping his thoughts about Enga and Ung from the others. He wasn't used to hiding anything.

No one stirred in the dim light from Brother Moon. The fire sent sparks onto the stones when the breath of Dakadaga, Mother Sky, whistled by. Sannum pulled his fur about him and stole into the woods, in the direction he had seen Enga and Ung go.

He had not gone far when hail and sleet began to pummel his weathered cheeks. Ice soon coated his beard and his long hair. Sannum walked on. He knew the two young females were also out in this storm, alone

Chapter 22

Enga Dancing Flower had slept, but not much. She felt insecure in the open, this close to the village. Sister Sun had not arisen yet, but Enga brushed the snow off her cape and stood to shake it out of her hair.

A brittle sound rattled through the branches above.

She looked up. A hollow space gaped inside her, then filled with dread.

Mother Sky sent hard, cold tears—hail, mixed with sleet—to make her task difficult. But she could not wait for Sister Sun to join Mother Sky. Afraid someone would find her, she started trotting back through the woods toward the cave where she had left Ung Strong Arm.

The sleet cut like slashing obsidian knives. Enga knew which direction the cave lay, but could not retrace her steps since she hadn't used a path. She sprinted when she could, slogged through thick undergrowth when she had to, and at last spied, through the trees, the spruce branches that concealed the small cave.

She was halted by a sudden feeling of dizziness. Was it because she hadn't eaten recently? No, an instant later Enga understood what was happening. She had heard Panan One Eye tell of this in a Saga once. When things are out of harmony, it upsets Brother Earth and he reacts, Panan had said.

Brother Earth was moving.

Something had greatly angered him. He was roaring. Heaving up and down.

A huge crack appeared in Brother Earth's skin beside Enga and she barely avoided falling into it.

She dove to the ground to avoid being knocked over. The trees around her clanked their trunks together. Some of them succumbed to Brother Earth's rage, crashing to earth. She crawled toward a thicket of fern trees.

Her hand encountered warmth, flesh. She parted the underbrush. Lakala Rippling Water, the special friend of Ung, lay there. Unconscious.

Quickly Enga rolled her over and put her fingers on Lakala's neck. Her life rhythm beat in her throat. Lakala was alive. Enga lay next to her to wait for Brother Earth's fury to abate. Lakala must have been looking for them. Enga was sure she missed Ung. No wonder Enga hadn't detected her presence in the village. She hadn't been there.

Tall trees tumbled down around her, startling a short scream out of her with each one.

She wondered if the cave where she had left Ung would collapse.

*****

Sannum Straight Hair had journeyed almost half a day. He did not understand what was happening at first, but quickly realized Brother Earth had become angry and was throwing his skin around to express himself.

A crack in the earth opened before him with a boom. He dodged aside to avoid being swallowed up by Brother Earth. The crack expanded.

He ran.

The crevasse yawned wider, then lengthened toward him.

He zigged and the opening followed him.

Was Brother Earth trying to kill him? Had he made Brother Earth angry somehow? Maybe by being away from the tribe during dark time? Or did Brother Earth disapprove of defying the Hama? His love for Enga and Ung was stronger than his fear of either Hama or Brother

Earth. Even though the wipiti would probably withstand the quaking, maybe the tribe was being punished, not just him.

Hail fell harder, pummeling him like a cold, hard waterfall. It had been falling his whole journey and now coated the ground beneath his feet. His feet slipped as he tried to avoid the crack coming toward him. He grabbed the trunk of a huge spruce.

The opening gaped, came closer. It tore at the roots of the spruce, exposing them. The trunk started to topple.

Sannum shoved himself away from it and ran harder. Why was Brother Earth so irate with him?

Sannum fell.

He skidded on the hailstones, couldn't regain his footing.

He slid toward the widening crevasse.

*****

Jeek lost his balance and fell on the wet ground, pebbled with the hard, icy tears of Mother Sky. What was happening?

The bits of dried hare he had clutched in his hand flew up, then landed in the growth at the side of the trail.

He had hoped he could track Enga Dancing Flower and Ung Strong Arm and bring them something to eat, but the ice had made it difficult to get their scent. And now Brother Earth was shaking as Jeek had never experienced. He remembered the Saga of Brother Earth Shaking, but could this be one of those times? Did Brother Earth shake this violently? Was Brother Earth dying? Was Mother Sky weeping her sleet tears for her dying son?

As the suns had passed Jeek had become more and more worried about the twins, Enga and Ung, out on their own in the cold forest. He kept expecting Hama to reverse her decision. Most of the tribe agreed it had not been a good one. But, so far, Cabat the Thick had backed her up and if two Elders agreed on something, the tribe followed their wishes.

But Panan One Eye had been fomenting a resistance, trying to cajole Hama into changing her mind. Jeek had observed both Cabat and

Panan visiting the wipiti of Hama many times a day. He did not think they had been summoned to couple. In fact, he did not think they had been summoned at all, but were each petitioning her for his own purpose.

He shuddered with each shake.

A new idea occurred to him now. Were Mother Sky and Brother Earth angry at the tribe because of their dissention? Had Brother Earth removed the large animals from their reach to punish them? No, the animals had been disappearing before the animosity began. But this upheaval, this shaking. What was it? Would it injure him?

A whimper escaped his trembling lips.

Jeek rolled out of the way as a huge aspen whooshed through the air and crashed down to the spot he had just left. It would have crushed him! Brother Earth was angry, he was certain of it. Maybe Brother Earth was as upset as Jeek was about the banishment. Maybe, if Jeek found Enga and Ung and brought them back, it would appease the Spirits.

But how could he find them? Brother Earth thundered like Mother Sky and kept heaving. Jeek slipped.

*****

Jeek awoke. He was cold. The sight he saw when he sat up amazed him. Huge trees lay on their sides, their roots dangling in the air. The rushing of a nearby stream surprised him. He hadn't been near a stream. Why had Brother Earth put this new one here? Was he trying to drown him? He would be careful not to fall into the rapid waters.

When he lifted his head a sudden wave of nausea rose in his throat. He clunked his head back down. It struck a rock. And it was sore!

He must have fallen and hit his head on that rock. He knew a head injury could put someone to sleep for a while. That must have been what happened. He rubbed the knot on the back of his scalp. The bump was not too large and no Red flowed. He sat for a while and the nausea subsided.

Gingerly, Jeek tested the ground as he stood. It seemed to be staying in place. Brother Earth's fit must be over. The angry, hard tears of

212

Mother Sky had quit pelting down, too. The forest floor was strewn with them.

The blow to his head had not made him forget his mission. And now it seemed more urgent than ever. He hoped Enga Dancing Flower and Ung Strong Arm had survived the storm. He searched for a short time but could not find the dried meat he had meant to bring them. But maybe he could at least find them.

He found he could still follow the path he had been on. It was partially blocked by fallen trees and uprooted shrubbery, but he could get over and around those. He continued, although he could no longer catch the scent of the two females. They had to have headed this way. There weren't that many paths through the forest.

But, just ahead and a little to his right, a new canyon gaped. It had never been there before. He caught the wave of distress just before he heard the cry. Then he stopped and sniffed. Sannum Straight Hair! He was in the new chasm.

Jeek crept to the edge of it, being careful not to dislodge anything into it. A falling log might injure Sannum. If he wasn't injured already. He peered over the edge. Sannum greeted him with a huge smile.

Young Jeek! I am extremely happy to see you. I do not think I can get out of this hole.

But why are you here?

I am searching for Enga Dancing Flower and Ung Strong Arm. What are you doing here?

The same thing. I do not want them to die.

We can help each other, but I must get out of here first.

Jeek sat back on his heels and pondered the situation. Sannum was stuck in the hole. The hole was a little like the one Jeek had dug when he had hoped to trap a giant beaver. The beaver had clawed her way out, collapsing the walls and climbing up them.

Stand back from this side, he thought-spoke to Sannum. *I have an idea.*

As he shoved some of the dirt into the abyss, the side started to crumble. The dirt was wet and moved easily. Too easily. With a whoosh, the mud slid down, and Jeek with it.

He screamed all the way down.

The mud stopped moving. Jeek flexed his limbs. He was unhurt.

But where was Sannum? Under the mud?

Chapter 23

The woodland musk ox (Symbos cavifrons) was a wide-ranging animal that apparently preferred warmer and more wooded climates than other musk oxen species did.

—*Ice Age Mammals of North America: A Guide to the Big, the Hairy, and the Bizarre,* Ian M. Lange, p. 148–149

At last Brother Earth lay still. Bahg Swiftfeet rose to his feet inside his wipiti. He had hovered over his infant son and Fee Long Thrower during the shaking, but nothing had fallen apart inside their dwelling.

Cabat the Thick and Panan One Eye had each taken his own quick assessment and now conveyed it to everyone. Some of the tribe convened at the Paved Place. Now, poking his head out his doorway and looking around, as far as Bahg could tell, no real damage had been done. He had heard trees clanking their trunks together, and some falling, in the forest, but their village looked like it had survived intact. There were cracks running through the Paved Place that had not been there before, but they could refill them with gravel. All the wipiti were standing. Although a few mammoth bone supports would need to be set back to their upright position, none had collapsed.

The light wind carried the scent of dirt, maybe from the uprooted vegetation, Bahg thought.

Cabat and Panan both withdrew into the wipiti of the single males. Bahg was glad he was not in that dwelling to witness the hostility between those two.

Fee spoke to Bahg. *It may be that we can find animals that perished in the storm and the quaking.*

She called the young girls together, and, leaving their baby with Bahg, led them into the forest.

Bahg had never been so happy in his life. Or so distressed. He waved a stick above his baby boy so the infant could follow it with his eyes. One day he would grab for a stick. It looked like he was trying now. This boy would grow to be a fine Hamapa male.

And it seemed that Fee was fully recovered. It was a good sign she felt well enough to lead the young females.

Intense joy filled this warm, comfortable wipiti. But there was no joy outside of it. Hama had been seeing both Panan and Cabat in her dwelling. Was she mating with both? All Hamapa knew this was not a good idea. If a female lay with two males, the two males would quarrel.

The last attempted hunt had fallen apart before it started because two of the females would not go if the others went on the hunt. Half the tribe agreed with the thinking of Hama, especially regarding Enga Dancing Flower. The other half disagreed. They suspected each other of having killed the Aja Hama. And all hunters were needed to succeed in a kill, so no hunt was made.

And the Elders were no help. If Panan squatted by the fire chipping a spear head, Cabat made a wide circle around him to go down to the stream. And if Cabat was drinking at the stream, Panan would go far upstream to take a drink for himself. Bahg was afraid one of them would push the other one into the water soon. The air between those two was thick with rancor. How could the Elders make decisions like this?

What could be done? The tribe could not continue this way. The anger between Panan and Cabat had been raging for three suns now, ever since Enga and Ung had left.

Hama had told them about the Gata tribe whose leader recently died of a sickness. There was so much dissension among the Gata afterwards that they could not organize a hunt. Part of the tribe had left and traveled far away to start a new tribe. The remnants might not make it through the next season.

And the two tribes he and his brothers had encountered on their recent failed trading mission had been even worse. One completely gone, the other, the Cuva, almost all starved to death.

Would the Hamapa make it through the Cold Season themselves? They had to. There had to be a way to mend the relationships of the Elders. Bahg was afraid that Cabat and Panan each suspected the other of killing the Aja Hama. Maybe one of them had. He knew Enga had not. And Ung hadn't even been accused, just expelled because she was Enga's sister. That was not right. The Hama's decision was not good, not wise.

Bahg picked up his sleeping infant, bent to drink in his sweet smell, and carried him outside. Stitcher sat near the fire but, for once, he was not working on a garment. There were probably no more skins for him to use. The fire had melted the ice pellets and dried the stones near it. Tog Flint Shaper sat cross-legged on the paving not far away, unenthusiastically chipping at a piece of flint. Bahg greeted him.

Tog Flint Shaper, what are you making?

I am shaping a scraper, but when will it be used to scrape a skin? When will we have a good hunt? And I am not able to care about the hunt now. I will never see her again. Tog dropped his stones with a clatter and held his head in his hands. *I miss Enga Dancing Flower so much.* He looked up at Bahg and despair dragged tears down his face. *Did you know we were to couple? Enga Dancing Flower had already asked permission of the Aja Hama. It would have been given that night. The night Enga found her slain.*

Bahg laid a hand on his shoulder. *My brother. I am so sorry.*

It was wrong of me to close myself to her, but I did not know what to do when she was accused in front of the tribe. I could have supported her and I did not. And now she may be hurt somewhere from the shaking of Brother Earth.

Bahg squatted next to Tog for a while and let his mind work. An idea came to him.

Do you remember how Enga Dancing Flower figured out Doon's treachery? That Doon had attacked my family and not the beaver?

Tog nodded and gave him a puzzled look.

Enga Dancing Flower is a very clever female, Bahg continued. *She might be able to figure out who really killed Aja Hama. Then we could all stop suspecting each other. Besides, the Spirits might pay more attention to our hunts if Enga were here dancing. And if Ung were on the hunts throwing her spear. We never went hungry when Ung Strong Arm hunted with us.*

Enga Dancing Flower and Ung Strong Arm are banished. Enga is not here. Mourning dripped through the thought-speak of Tog. *If someone had spoken up for her she might still be here.*

Yes, they should both be here. You do not want to be without her any longer. Maybe we could go find her and bring her back.

Yes, she may need a rescue. But would not Hama expel us also if we did that?

Maybe not. Many of the brothers and sisters are against what Hama did. They do not think she should have expelled them.

And none of them spoke up either. I will ponder this, Bahg Swiftfeet. Would you go with me if I went to seek her?

Can you not send her a thought-feeler and find out where she is?

Tog shook his head, hard, and a tear flew onto the ground. *I closed my mind to her when she first left. Now she has closed her mind to me. Either that or she cannot communicate because harm has come to her. I cannot get through.*

Then we will have to go find her.

At dark time?

Yes, at next dark time. After the council.

The two males looked into each other's eyes, knowing what they planned was a grave trespass. But before their own welfare must come the good of the tribe. Always.

*****

Lakala Rippling Water opened her eyes. Enga Dancing Flower had been able to shoulder-carry her back to the cave. Enga was overjoyed to find it intact. Ung Strong Arm rushed to the opening to help Enga lift Lakala over and through the branches at the cave's mouth. The inside of the shelter was a bit warmer than the air outside. Ung quickly stripped off her own cloak and laid it over Lakala, then bent and planted kisses all over her face.

Lakala's eyes flew open. *My Ung! I have found you!*

Ung smiled. *Were you looking for me?*

Of course. I have searched every day. Look, I have brought you something to eat. She reached into her pouch and pulled out two pieces of jerky. *I found the place where you spent the first night, but then could not find where you went. Why have you closed your mind to me?*

The two sisters looked at each other.

That was my doing, thought-spoke Enga. *I thought it better to make a clean break. Also, I....* Enga did not know if she should tell Lakala her plan. But Lakala and Ung were special friends. If Lakala had risked her life, and the censure of the tribe, by seeking them, she should trust her. *I sneaked back to the village to see if I could overhear enough thought-speak to figure out who killed our leader. I have just returned, without success, but I plan to do it again as soon as there is no snow. I do not want to leave tracks.*

If anyone could figure out who killed her, you could, thought-spoke Lakala. *You and clever Jeek. Did you know that he has gone to seek you, too? I saw him leave the village just before I did. I hope he was not hurt in Brother Earth's rage.*

Enga hoped so, too. *I will go see if I can find him. I will open my mind to him and maybe, maybe this time he will receive my thoughts.*

*****

There was another scent here besides Sannum Straight Hair's. Jeek twitched his nose and looked around as he stood up from the mud slide. There were musk oxen very near. But before he concerned himself with them, he must find Sannum. Jeek closed his mind to all but Sannum. He crawled to the top of the mudslide, careful not to dislodge the pile. Sannum lay on the other side, at the bottom, buried to his waist.

I will be right there, he thought-shouted, and scrambled down the slope. *Are you injured?*

Not badly, answered Sannum. *My ankle twisted when I fell. I do not think this mud has hurt me, but it is heavy.*

Jeek spread his legs and leaned over, then shoved the dirt off Sannum, throwing it behind him between his legs. Jeek soon had him free and Sannum stood up, testing his ankle.

My ankle is sore, but it will hold me, he thought-spoke. *I can walk. But can we climb out of here?*

I do not think it will be difficult to crawl up the mudslide. As long as it does not slide again. But what is that odor? Are there musk oxen here with you?

Sannum looked surprised. He tested the air. *I believe you are right. They must be farther along in this trench. My smeller is not as good as it used to be when I was your age.*

Jeek crept down the narrow canyon until he spotted the small group of oxen, trapped just as Sannum and he were. They did not have the large claws of the beaver to collapse the sides and climb out. He counted six females and four half-grown young. They milled around, bumping into each other. The young ones bawled when they saw Jeek. He ran back to Sannum, who sat rubbing his ankle.

I saw them! There are oxen farther down there, thought-spoke Jeek. *All females and young, no large males. I have an idea.* His eyes lit up and he bounced on his heels. *The mudslide made this pile. Let us climb over it, then mound the mud up as high as we can behind us. We can get out of here the way I saw a beaver do it once, by caving in the sides until we can climb out.*

Why do you want to pile the dirt up behind us?

That will trap the musk ox and maybe someone can return and kill some for the tribe.

Ah, you are a clever lad, Jeek.

He basked in the approval of Sannum for a moment, then they got busy.

Jeek helped Sannum struggle over the mud pile. Then they started to work clawing dirt from the sides of the gully, carrying it, and dumping it to make a barrier for the animals. Brother Earth gave a few little shakes but did not seem so angry anymore. They both broke out in heavy sweat, working with the wet earth. It slid and stuck where they did not want it and made their task harder.

Chapter 24

Enga Dancing Flower paused outside the cave before she started trying to find Jeek. Ung Strong Arm and Lakala Rippling Water were inside and she thought they would be safe there. But was any place safe when Brother Earth was acting up?

A shiver lifted the ground under her feet and threw her into a stumble. She caught herself with one hand and one knee. A clatter had come from the cave. Brother Earth was not done.

Enga! We must leave! Ung parted the dead branches between them. *A shower of rock just rained down from the top of this cave. What if the whole roof falls in?*

The two females scrambled over the downed tree. Enga looked inside. Small rocks now littered the floor of the cave and new cracks criss-crossed the top. One was as wide as her hand.

She knew Ung was right. If Brother Earth continued to rage, the cave might collapse. They would have to spend the dark time outside again.

I think the walking we did to get here was good for my injury, thought-spoke Ung. *And with the rest I have just had, I feel I can walk a long distance now.*

This is good, birth sister. Enga was relieved to hear that. They might have to walk a long while. *Lakala Rippling Water, do you feel well enough to travel also?*

Lakala gave a grim nod. *But where will we go?*

Brother Earth gave another shake and they started to walk. Enga knew she could not return to the village; at least, not before dark time. And it would be hard to be stealthy when there were now three of them.

*****

Young Jeek, thought-spoke Sannum Straight Hair. *This pile is big enough to hold the oxen. Sister Sun is almost down to Brother Earth. We must think about where we will spend the night.*

Not here, answered Jeek.

I agree. I want to leave this hole.

It was hard going slogging up the wet earth that had slid down on top of Sannum, but the side of the gully, now gently sloping, made it easier than it would have been before the mudslide. When they reached the top Sannum paused to catch his breath. He sat and rubbed his ankle.

Do you think you can walk back to the village? asked Jeek.

Sannum shook his head. *I do not know. We should not spend the rest of dark time out here in the forest, but my ankle is sore. The climbing we just did—it hurts more now.*

Jeek squatted beside him and looked at his ankle. Sister Sun had gone to sleep, but a thin Brother Moon was starting to throw off his dense cloud garments, peeking around them enough to give some help. When Jeek put his hand on Sannum's ankle he could feel heat inside. He frowned and considered what his mother, the Healer, would do. He thought she would wrap the ankle tightly with a poultice. Jeek smeared some of the mud onto it as a poultice. He had seen his mother do this once. He tore a strip off his tattered cape with his teeth and wrapped it around the ankle, tucking the ends in so it would stay. Then he got up and kicked through the downed branches lying all over the forest floor, finally finding a stout walking stick with a crook that Sannum could tuck under his shoulder.

I always say you are a clever young lad, thought-spoke Sannum. *See how resourceful you are! I think I will be able to hobble about. But we still have to find a place to spend the night. The distance back to the village is too great for me.*

They both cocked their heads. A message was being funneled to Jeek, but Sannum could read it, too.

It is Enga Dancing Flower! exclaimed Jeek, with a yelp. *She is contacting me!* He closed his eyes and became still to hear Enga better.

Jeek, Jeek. I need your help. Jeek, Jeek. We need your help.

I am here, Enga Dancing Flower. I am in the forest. Where are you?

Enga sent him a picture of the cave and her surroundings, also letting him know that Ung and Lakala were with her.

He was surprised Lakala was there, but would find out more about that later. He had never seen the pictured cave before.

What part of the trail are you near? he asked.

We are far off the trail, but we are heading toward it. Send me a picture of where you are.

It is much different after the earth-shaking than it was before. There is a new valley and a new stream. He sent her the vision of the land before the earthquake.

I know where you are, she answered. *We can be there soon. Before first sun. Can you stay where you are?*

Jeek looked at Sannum. Sannum had been hobbling around, poking at the fallen trees with his stick. *These three trees might make a shelter,* he told Jeek. *If we were inside the space they enclose we would be somewhat protected.*

And these trees cannot fall on us. They have already fallen. And I have a knife, added Jeek.

As do I. Sannum touched his pouch to make sure it was still there.

Yes, Enga Dancing Flower, Sannum and I will find a place to hide until you approach.

Sannum Straight Hair is with you? The joy rang in Enga's thought. *Keep safe until we reach you.*

*****

Bahg Swiftfeet tried not to fidget. The evening meeting should have started long ago. Where was everyone? The Singer, Lakala Rippling Water, was not here to start the blessing. Sannum Straight Hair wasn't even here to beat the drum. Panan One Eye fingered his flute and pushed his lips in and out, ready to begin.

The snow and sleet of yesterday were gone. Sister Sun had smiled today for a brief period. And Brother Earth had remained mostly calm, giving off just a few minor shakings.

Bahg wished the meeting would start so it could finish. He knew he wouldn't be able to pay attention to the proceedings. All he could think about—he must cloak this thought tightly in the most dusky hues of night—was stealing away with Tog after the meeting.

But now, before it even started, the meeting halted. The mental chattering stopped and all fell silent. Once again, their Hama had not shown up. Memories of the dead Aja Hama filled everyone. The vision of her bloody, lifeless body haunted their minds. This time an Elder should go to her wipiti.

Cabat the Thick, who had been sitting as far from Panan One Eye as he could, lumbered to his feet and ambled to the largest wipiti. Bahg tried to peer into Cabat's mind, but he could not. After Cabat lifted the flap and entered the dwelling he opened his mind wide and let everyone see that the wipiti was empty. Hama was not there.

Bahg joined Cabat and the others in sending vibrant scarlet thought-shouts out to her, but they all went unanswered. *Hama! Answer us! Come!*

Where was she? Had the Mikino sneaked in and taken her? Had she been right to suspect them?

Cabat stuck his neck out and sniffed outside the wipiti. *A recent scent trail leads toward the Sacred Hill. Bahg Swiftfeet and Tog Flint Shaper, go, follow this trail.*

Bahg gave his mate a private signal of trepidation, the hair on the back of his neck prickling. Fee Long Thrower, their infant cradled in a sling hanging from her shoulder, replied with encouragement. *You will find her. And she will be alive. I will send hopes that she will be alive.*

The two males left the circle of firelight and headed toward the hill. They sniffed the air. Yes, she had come this way. Maybe she had wanted to visit the Holy Cave. Sometimes Aja Hama used to do that. She would often sit and try to receive the thoughts of the Spirits. This Hama had not been known to do that, but maybe she had decided it might help the tribe.

The path up the hill seemed alien in the dark. The familiar shrubs and trees assumed sinister shapes, seemed larger than they were when Sister Sun was out. They knew the daytime animals were asleep and night predators roamed. Bahg and Tog stayed close together.

They tracked Hama to the Holy Cave, as Bahg had expected they might.

Let us go in together, thought-spoke Tog. *Let us discover whatever there is to discover with each other.*

Bahg agreed and they entered side by side. The permanent fire burned just inside the overhang. The crackle of the fire was the only sound. The Holy Cave seemed empty. And warmer than usual.

Bahg walked to a side wall and felt his way around the edges, but was halted just beyond the ring of firelight when his knuckles brushed rock that shouldn't be there.

There was a new wall of rubble. Half the cave was gone!

Tog read his alarm and ran to his side. *The tremors of Brother Earth have collapsed our Holy Cave!*

Bahg stood speechless, thoughtless. Then he looked down and saw her hand. Hama's hair bracelet encircled her wrist. The males sprang into action, throwing aside rocks and debris until they uncovered the rest of her. They grabbed her shoulders and pulled her free. Dragged her beside the fire.

Look! She breathes.

Bahg leaned down and saw it was true. Her chest rose and fell. But her eyes remained closed and no thoughts came from her. She lay as Fee had lain for many suns after Doon's attack.

They hoisted her up and carried her back down the hill to the waiting group.

Zhoo of Still Waters came running and tried to summon her son Jeek, but could not get a response. *It does not matter,* she thought-spoke. *There is nothing much I can do for her. She will either awaken or she will not. We can only keep her warm and trickle water into her mouth, like we did for Fee Long Thrower, and hope she will come back to us.*

Bahg and Tog carried her to the Healer's wipiti. Despair covered the tribe like a shroud.

Chapter 25

After Bahg and Tog brought Hama back and reported the condition of the Holy Cave to the others, Panan One Eye had tried to lead a Song of Asking for the healing of Hama. But with only Panan on the flute, the Hamapa chanting was feeble. Bahg feared the song did not reach to the ears of the Spirit of Healing.

Cabat the Thick and Panan both agreed the tribe should meet at first sun.

The dark time was long and anxious. Hama still lay unseeing and unhearing in the Healer's wipiti. One by one each Hamapa had gone to her to try and elicit a response, but none was given.

Now Sister Sun, veiled in thick, cold, gray garments, had barely greeted a pale Mother Sky. It was strange to start the council with no singing, but Lakala Rippling Water could not be found. Sannum Straight Hair was absent also. Bahg Swiftfeet feared the missing Hamapa might have perished in the jerkings of Brother Earth.

Panan One Eye began telling a Saga. *The quaking of Brother Earth is frightening to behold. He must remind us, at times, that he has wondrous powers. Shaking is only one of them. He can also push the top off a mountain and blow it to Mother Sky. Our Ancient Ones saw this happen and handed down the tales. The anger of Brother Earth is so fierce when this happens that the rock melts. He becomes angry when the Hamapa are not living in harmony.*

Bahg sat with his tribe and received Panan's broadcast picture of scarlet, liquid rock flowing down the sides of a mountain. A black plume of cloud lifted to Mother Sky and the daytime was dark. Sister Sun and all of Mother Sky hid from the wrath of Brother Earth.

This shaking is a warning. Brother Earth is angry with us. We must determine what we have done to anger him. And what we can do to appease him.

Young Gunda, sitting very near Bahg, broke into his thoughts. *Bahg Swiftfeet*, she thought-spoke, directly to him. *Have you seen Jeek? He is not here.*

He looked around. She was right, Jeek was absent.

Do you think he was injured in the shaking? I fear for him.

Bahg could tell she was on the edge of tears. He reached over to pat her hand. *Have you tried to reach him with thought-speak?*

Yes, but there is no response. Do you think he is asleep like the Hama?

I do not know, little one.

He looked up as a dim shadow passed. As Vala Golden Hair stood and watched with worry on her brow, Stitcher hurried from the gathering and disappeared into the woods.

A vibrant scarlet announcement startled Bahg.

Panan One Eye and I have made a decision, declared Cabat the Thick. *It is best that we have three to make official decisions for the tribe. But now we are two, so we must make a decision without Hama. We need someone to take the place of Hama while she sleeps. Panan and I appoint Roh Lion Hunter as Hama.*

Bahg stiffened. There was to be no discussion? No election?

But only until Hama awakes, continued Cabat. *She will be the temporary Hama, Hama Dy.*

Is this a good thing? wondered Bahg. One thing was good, though. The two Elders had agreed on something. Maybe they could stop their feud now. Would that appease Brother Earth?

But Bahg was of the opinion that the Hamapa's bad fortune had started long before these two began to quarrel. He thought it started with the death of the Aja Hama. Or maybe with the election of Nanno Green Eyes.

Ongu Small One jumped to her feet. *No!* Her thoughts screeched. *I should be the Hama Dy. I was the other one voted on in the election. If Nanno, I mean Hama, is not able, it should be me!*

A few Hamapa nodded their heads and sent out their agreement with Ongu.

Roh Lion Hunter is the birth daughter of Hama, explained Panan. *That is why Cabat the Thick and I gave her the position. If anyone can get thoughts from Hama it should be Roh Lion Hunter.*

It is because she can slay a lion and I am too small to hunt, argued Ongu. *Just because she is a mighty huntress will not make her a good leader.*

Cabat gave her a withering look and she sat, tears dashing down her cheeks. Bahg saw Panan give her a look of pity.

This had not helped the tribe. Now some of them were in favor of Roh as Hama Dy, and others would prefer Ongu. The tribe was still split. Bahg feared the bad fortune would continue. Brother Earth would remain angry. Maybe the other Spirits would become angry, too. Mother Sky had pelted them with hail tears earlier. He knew she could do much worse.

*****

Enga Dancing Flower returned from the edge of the village, where she had spied on the council, to the glade a short distance off the trail where Ung Strong Arm, Lakala Rippling Water, Sannum Straight Hair, and Jeek all huddled, waiting.

The thoughts of the tribe are open and plain, she told them. *I could read them with no difficulty. I was able to use very dark masking colors to hold in my own thoughts. I do not think anyone detected me. Several things have happened. The back of the Holy Cave collapsed and Hama was injured. I could see this in the mind of Bahg Swiftfeet most clearly. I could even see into the mind of Tog Flint Shaper in a dim way. Before this his mind has been closed to me. It was they who found her.*

Enga gave this picture to the others. Sannum began to weep. Enga did not know if he wept for the cave or for the Hama.

They have just had a daytime meeting. Cabat the Thick and Panan One Eye appointed Roh Lion Hunter as Hama Dy so the tribe will have three Elders. But some think Ongu Small One should have been given the position.

The dissention troubled her. She could tell it also worried the others squatting with her under the sheltering branches of dense willow shrubs. Mother Sky hid behind capes of dark clouds, making it dark and cold. The tears on the leathery cheeks of Sannum, running into his grizzled beard, were joined by the tears of the others.

I did overhear Gunda talk about you, she thought-spoke to Jeek.

He sat up straight and a spark lit behind his eyes. *What did she say?*

She is worried about you. She has been trying to contact you.

The ember in his eyes went out. *I had better not let her. We are in hiding, are we not?*

Yes, that is correct, answered Enga. *It is the only way we will get the information we need. But the minds of the tribe are not on the murder now. Besides being very hungry, they are all worried about Hama. I will return and see if I can find out more about that.*

But, my birth sister, thought-spoke Ung. *Jeek has trapped all those musk ox. Surely I could kill some for the tribe and at least alleviate their hunger.*

Without a spear? asked Lakala.

Ung had forgotten she had no weapon.

I may be able to get one, put in Jeek.

The others asked how, but he just replied, *Leave it to me.*

*****

Spear practice was usually noisy. The girls gave shouts to encourage each other and gave pitying sounds when the throws went wide. This practice, however, was quiet. When Jeek peered between the fern branches that hid him, he could see a hard, serious look on Gunda's face. She was consumed with her task. Her spear did not hit the target often, though. She was the oldest student, and the others did even worse.

Jeek pondered what to do. He could do it two ways. He could steal their spears when they took a break. Or he could contact Gunda and appeal to her for help. Roh Lion Hunter had been made Hama Dy and Roh was the birth mother of Gunda. He did not know if that had influenced Gunda or not. Or if it had changed her feelings about him. Although he wasn't always sure what her feelings were for him.

He squared his shoulders with decision. He would not confide in anyone. He would do this himself.

Fee Long Thrower called a halt and told them to follow her to the stream to get a drink. The girls laid their spears in a pile in the middle of the clearing and departed.

This is perfect, Jeek thought to himself. He stepped out of the ferns and started for the pile. Then he heard a set of footsteps returning to the clearing. He could not make it back to the ferns. He flattened himself onto the ground. Gunda's youngest sister dashed to the place where the throwers stood and picked up a carved toy. Jeek could not see what it was, but it looked like something Stitcher had carved for her. She didn't glance his way, but skipped away, leaving him to snatch some spears and run back through the woods.

Jeek had reached the place where he had practiced throwing Gunda's spear at the softberries when he smelled someone ahead of him. He stopped and slowed his breathing. He had been running hard and his panting was loud. Surely whoever was ahead would have smelled and heard him. But no thoughts came.

He set the spears down and crept forward. Stitcher knelt beside the softberry bush, reached into it, and pulled something out. Jeek remembered then. This was the bush he had hidden his stick in, the one that sheltered a pile of antlers. These antlers belonged to Stitcher. He watched as Stitcher selected one, stuck the others back, and left to head toward the trail.

That is strange, Jeek mused. *Why does he keep them all the way out here? Why not closer to the village?*

Jeek gave a shrug and, when he could no longer hear Stitcher, resumed speeding back to the others in hiding.

Chapter 26

Ung Strong Arm held the spear like it was her own, even though it was shorter. She bounced it on her palms a couple of times, then sighted along the stick. She moved her arm back and forth, feeling the weight and balance. Then she scrambled over the mud pile that held the musk ox captive and led the charge. Enga Dancing Flower ran behind Ung, carrying one of the stolen spears herself. Enga grinned to see Ung running. Her leg was much better.

Sleeping in the open had been easier with more people. Enga felt safer. And the warmth of the collective body heat had warded off the frosty night air. Sister Sun sparkled today, but gave off less heat every day.

Their task was going to be easy. The frightened musk ox huddled together, protecting their young, in the narrow space at the end of the gulch. The sharp scent of their animal fear assailed them. Ung drew her arm back and waited until one of the oxen faced her. She held her breath, squinted, and let the spear fly. It flew true to the nearest female and pierced the center of her eye. The cow jerked her head up, lowed and stumbled, then fell onto her side, lifeless. Enga whooped. This was a fat animal. It would be welcome in the village.

Enga cocked her spear back and waited for the herd to settle a bit. They milled about, bawling and sniffing the fallen cow. A half grown calf presented his flank, then turned his head. Enga shot. Her spear tip glanced off the bone next to his eye, then went in.

Ung turned to her and smiled. Enga grinned back. This would be easy. Ung retrieved their spears from the dead animals while Enga distracted the herd, then the two continued to pick off more of them. When they had killed enough for the tribe, they dragged the carcasses slightly aside so they would not be trampled. With those out of the way, they ran to the side of the ravine and let the other oxen flee. They must not kill all of them or there would be no more of this herd. This herd would produce more babies who would grow large enough for them to eat.

The twins gave each other quick hugs. Then they trotted after the herd, signaling ahead to the others that the hunt had been a success.

Jeek, Sannum Straight Hair, and Lakala Rippling Water had been digging a trench so the oxen could get through and escape up the sloping side. As Enga and Ung reached them, the last of the oxen were pounding up the muddy hill, leaving an odor of feces and terror in their wake.

Now that we have the kill, thought-spoke Enga, *how do we get it to the village?*

You and Ung Strong Arm stay here, answered Sannum. *Let Lakala Rippling Water and Jeek and myself go tell the tribe of your feat. We will return with hides and knives to cut and carry the meat and skins. You stay here to guard the kill until we return.*

*****

Enga Dancing Flower had never loved her sister more than at this moment. They were nearing the village, coming in triumph, bearing meat and fur skins. The males, including Tog Flint Shaper, lugged the hunting skins, piled with meat. Roh Lion Hunter, Ongu Small One, and Fee Long Thrower followed, their arms laden with fresh fur skins.

There will be a dance tonight, thought-spoke Enga. *And I will dance my best.*

Tog had tried to approach her when the males came to the gully to butcher the oxen, but she had avoided him. The way he had avoided her eyes when Hama accused her of coupling with Stitcher still stung. He was being persistent about trying to get into her mind, but she kept him out for now. Maybe later.

It was full dark time. Panan One Eye and Cabat the Thick stood at the middle of the Paved Place to officially welcome Enga and Ung back into the tribe. Roh Lion Hunter quickly joined them after she had put her bundle of skins down.

I cannot recall a time when this has happened, thought-spoke Cabat. *A Hamapa does not come back from being expelled. But you two have saved the tribe for the Dark Season.*

He fell back and Roh, Hama Dy, stepped forward. She gave Enga and Ung solemn nods, rattled the gourd of her office, and extended her short arms toward Mother Sky.

"Hoody! Listen! The Most High Female, Temporary, Speaks. Enga Dancing Flower is a true Hamapa. Ung Strong Arm is a true Hamapa. Dakadaga, bless Enga Dancing Flower. Dakadaga, bless Ung Strong Arm. Mother Spirit of the Sky, Dakadaga, bless the Hamapa."

Enga noticed the tribe staring at Roh for delivering such a lengthy speech. Who would have thought she could do that?

Panan added his comments also. *We accept you back as Hamapa. We give you thanks for the bounty you bring.*

At that moment a light snow began to fall from a dark Mother Sky. Her cloud garments usually started shedding these beautiful, cold, white flakes at this season. Brother Moon slept tonight, but the snow made it seem as though he shone on them.

Enga turned her gaze to Mother Sky, thanking her for letting them reunite with their adopted tribe. Her cool breath washed over Enga's face, smelling clean.

Enga tried to feel sorrow that Hama was not awake, but could not. It meant that the celebration was unmarred by her bitterness and hatred.

This dark time, Lakala's sweet voice led many songs. First, a Song of Asking for healing for the Hama, then a Song of Thanks to all the Spirits for the bounty, another of thanks for bringing all the lost Hamapa back, then one of sheer joy. Sannum pounded his log drum with exuberance, and Panan trilled on the flute, sending shrill music into the night sky, all the way to the Spirits.

As she entered the circle of dancers, Enga shot a look at Stitcher where he stood at the edge of the gathering. Vala Golden Hair stood near him, reaching her hand up to rest on his tall shoulder.

Enga danced until her feet were sore. Tog danced next to her but she ignored him until the end of the dancing.

Do you want me to walk with you to your wipiti? he asked.

Why do you want to walk with one who has coupled with Stitcher? Maybe I should walk with him. She turned and started for her dwelling through the thickening flurry.

You said you did not couple with him.

Did you believe me? She stopped and looked straight at him for the first time that day. Snowflakes caught on his eyelashes and dusted his hair.

Tog focused on the ground between them. *I want to believe you. But I did know the intentions of Stitcher and he wanted to couple with you. And the Hama thought you did. It is hard to doubt the word of a Hama. But...*

Yes?

This Hama has not proven herself a wise leader. She had been wrong about other things. She was wrong about you. I am sure of that now. Tog raised his head. His blue eyes brimmed with unshed tears. *Bahg Swiftfeet and I were on our way to look for you when we were sent to look for Hama. Then we found her and could not leave.*

A movement behind Enga made her whirl. Was someone behind her wipiti? Was Stitcher there again? She let Tog see her thought.

I cannot tell him anything, she thought-spoke. *He does not hear that I want to couple with you, and not with him.*

I will let him know, answered Tog. *But I need to know for certain. You do not want to?*

Enga smiled and showed Tog her dimples. *Of course not, doon-doon.*

She shivered as soon as the thought left her mind, the term recalling the fate of Doon to her. She lifted a quick thanks to Dakadaga that she and Ung did not suffer the fate of Doon. Then she yielded to Tog's strong and gentle and warm embrace.

*****

Something woke Jeek from a deep sleep. At first he did not know where he was. He thought he was still hiding in the woods. But no, he was in his home, the wipiti of Zhoo of Still Waters, where he belonged, sleeping beside Teek. Zhoo was resting beside Hama so that she would notice if Hama awoke. Everyone should be sleeping now.

But something was not right. He sniffed the air, smelling the comforting odor of his fellow tribe members, all near. He listened and heard only an owl in the forest and loud snoring from the wipiti of the single males. The snow that had fallen all evening deadened most sounds. He put out thought-feelers, but could not touch anyone. All were asleep.

Then he singled out an odor. It was a familiar one, but was too close and did not belong here. Stitcher was very near. He did dwell in the next wipiti, but he was much nearer than that. The night was moonless, but the central fire cast a shadow on the doorflap. Jeek saw a tall, narrow silhouette. Stitcher stood motionless in front of the wipiti. He held something that had sharp points.

Jeek tried not to move, not to breathe. But his head buzzed. Something was very wrong.

He put out a quiet call for help. He called Enga Dancing Flower.

239

Chapter 27

Enga Dancing Flower received the call for help from Jeek. She puckered her brow. He would not contact her in the middle of sleep time if it were not urgent. She rose from her sleeping fur slowly so she would not awaken Ung. Then she remembered that Ung was spending this dark time in Lakala Rippling Water's wipiti. Enga thought Ung might stay there permanently soon.

She wrapped her feet quickly and grabbed her worn mammoth cape. Pulling it around herself, she smiled to think that soon they would all have new musk ox capes. Females and males alike would be scraping skins for a while. And with full stomachs.

The brightness of the Paved Place surprised her. She had forgotten how the snow makes dark time light. Flurries drifted down, swirling on a gentle wind. It was strange how snow, such cold stuff, made her feel warm.

The embers of the central fire sputtered. Enga lifted her face to Mother Sky again and gave thanks that the fire in the Holy Cave had not gone out when the rear part of it caved in.

Then she hurried to Zhoo's wipiti, where Jeek had summoned her.

He was standing outside, shivering.

Go put on a wrap, she scolded. *It is too cold for your bare skin.*

But look. He pointed to the tracks, unmistakable in the new snow, that led away from his dwelling. *Stitcher was just here. Why is he sneaking around when everyone is asleep?*

What was he doing? She pulled Jeek close to her and wrapped her fur around him to stop his shivering.

I sensed him here, smelled him. Then, after I called you, I crawled to the doorway and saw him leaving.

But what did he look like? Was he distressed?

Jeek shrugged. He gave Enga the picture of Stitcher he had seen.

What was that, in his hand? she exclaimed. *It looked like an antler prong.* It looked very much like the piece of caribou antler that had been used to stab Aja Hama.

Now she knelt to study the footprints in the snow. They were the size of the footprints that had been found outside Aja Hama's wipiti, the footprints the Elders assumed Mikino made. Stitcher's feet were slender, like those of the Mikino. Stitcher wrapped his feet differently than the Hamapa, though, and, unlike them, kept them wrapped all the time. The Mikino did not wrap theirs at all. Had he killed Aja Hama? But why would he? And he would have had to remove his foot wrappings at that time. Why would he do that? To disguise his footprints? Was he that clever?

But now the new Hama lay sleeping, unable to wake, here in this wipiti, tended by Zhoo of Still Waters. It seemed Stitcher was coming after someone. Jeek thought he might want to kill Hama with his piece of antler.

Should we follow him? asked Jeek. *He headed for the Sacred Hill.*

Enga wanted to follow him. But she could not make her feet move toward the Sacred Hill. That was where Stitcher had attacked her in the Holy Cave. Her mind worked quickly.

Go inside, she told Jeek. *Get warm wrappings and come back out. I will summon Tog Flint Shaper. We will follow him together.*

Tog arrived just as Jeek emerged from his dwelling, this time dressed for the cold breath of Mother Sky. Enga filled Tog in on what Jeek had told her. Jeek helped with his mental images of Stitcher.

Tog told them to wait and shut his eyes.

What on Brother Earth is he doing? wondered Enga.

When he opened his eyes he smiled. *Stitcher is sad and is going to the Sacred Hill to weep, but he is not thinking of harming anyone. He may have been thinking of it before, outside this wipiti, but I have told him he must not.* He patted Jeek on the head. *Now you should both go and get some rest.*

Enga's eyes widened and her mouth dropped open. She snapped her jaw shut and told Tog to go back to sleep, that she and Jeek would follow.

Make sure that you do. It is not good to be out at dark time.

Tog ran back to his warm sleeping skin.

She turned to Jeek, her mind reeling. *He can thought-speak with Stitcher? How can that be?*

Jeek chewed a thick hank of his hair. She could feel him thinking furiously, but not drawing any conclusions. *We must follow Stitcher by ourselves.*

Enga ground her teeth, furious with Tog. And bewildered by him, too. Then she remembered Tog telling her Stitcher meant her harm. Did Tog know that or was he guessing?

She must see for herself if Stitcher was actually weeping on the Sacred Hill, if Tog could really tell that.

At this moment she trusted Jeek more than Tog. She was glad Tog had left and she and Jeek were free to discover what Stitcher was doing.

They hurried toward the Sacred Hill, following the narrow footprints.

I remember something, thought-spoke Jeek. *Right after Aja Hama was killed, Stitcher came to the gathering. He was called the New One then. And he was wet. Dripping. He had been to the stream. The day was not warm, but it looked like he had been in the water.*

Do you think he washed off the Red of Aja Hama after he killed her? Enga shook her head as soon as she asked the question. *Why would he kill her, though? I know she did not like him. But to kill her!*

Jeek gave her no answer, just plunged ahead up the hill.

Enga followed, fighting the rising wind that whipped her garments and her hair in all directions. Snow fell harder. She pondered what it meant, if Tog could indeed thought-speak with Stitcher. Kin could always understand kin.

Stitcher was taller than any Hamapa, but not as tall as most Tall Ones. Was he truly a Tall One? Could he be kin to Tog? How could that be?

They approached the Holy Cave, still tracking Stitcher. Enga's mind whirled like the wild wind, which tossed snow into the air from the ground and stung her cheeks. If Stitcher did do harm to Aja Hama, did Tog know about it? Did he help him? But Aja Hama was the birth mother of Tog. Nothing made any sense.

The wind had blown the new fallen snow off the side of the hill. The ground was bare. The footprints ended just before they reached the Holy Cave.

I remember something else, too, thought-spoke Jeek again. *Stitcher hides antlers under a bush in the woods. But after he carved the buttons for Aja Hama, he never carved anything else from antler. He has done many carvings, but always from wood.* He frowned in concentration, puzzling as he thought it out. *I saw him in the woods with the antlers and wondered why he kept them there, in the forest. I saw him take an antler from the pile when I went to get the spears for the musk-ox kill.* His eyes bulged. *It must be the antler he has now.*

He hides antlers? Are they caribou antlers?

Jeek screwed up his face, bringing the picture back. He nodded. He was sure they were caribou and that Stitcher had hidden them.

That means he does not want us to see them. Or to know he has them.

Yes, that is what I think, answered Jeek.

Enga wondered if Tog knew about the antlers. She wondered what exactly he knew about Stitcher.

Chapter 28

The wind carried a sound to Enga Dancing Flower's ears. It could have been the sound of a small trapped hare, but Enga knew what it was. She had heard that quiet keening before. It was a sound she had heard long ago. When she had attained the age of eight summers, she had heard it.

She had left the group to lie on a cool stone at the edge of the village. Two figures had appeared on a rise behind the wipiti. One had made this noise. It had sounded like weeping, but was a different sound than a Hamapa would make. Had that long-ago Tall One been Stitcher? He had been imploring someone, someone who had been backing away from him, refusing something to him. Had that been Jansa Wild Wind, as Enga thought at the time? Her adopted mother and later Hama of the tribe?

The alien weeping did not come from the Holy Cave, though. She cocked her head, then looked at Jeek. They agreed they should find the source. It was hard to hear above the roar of the wind, blowing more and more fiercely.

It comes from the Burying Place, Enga Dancing Flower.

Yes, you are right. I think Stitcher makes the sound. But let us go there quietly. I have never known Stitcher to detect scent. We can get close to him without him knowing we are near.

She waved her hand for Jeek to follow and they crept through the woods, keeping to the soft fir needles and avoiding the crunchy poplar leaves, to the edge of the clear space that was the Burying Place. Stitcher sat cross-legged on top of Aja Hama's grave. He sobbed and made soft sounds, like speech, that Enga could not understand. His sounds mixed with the moan of the wind. While they watched, he threw himself face down onto the grave and pounded the ground with his fist.

Enga and Jeek together wished they could tell what was bothering him. Enga held her breath and concentrated as hard as she could.

But I can understand him. Tog's close thought-speak made Enga jump. He was behind them. She had been trying so hard to read Stitcher she had not sensed his approach.

I thought you went to your wipiti. Why was he here?

No, I wanted to see if I could help Stitcher. I felt his distress.

You can see his thoughts? asked Enga. *How?*

And he sees mine. Look.

Stitcher stopped wailing and scrambled to his feet, facing them. The thoughts that ran between Tog and Stitcher were private ones and Enga couldn't overhear them. She didn't understand what was happening. She grew anxious, not being able to catch their thoughts.

Tog walked over to Sticher. They appeared to be communicating. What private thoughts were these? She strained her mind to the utmost, but could not overhear anything. She watched their actions and concentrated.

The two males gestured toward Enga. Tog's gestures were angry. Stitcher hung his head, then looked at Tog and nodded.

The events of the last few suns finally fell into place and formed a nice, neat line in her mind. Enga grabbed Jeek's shoulder and drew him into the trees to confer.

*****

What is it, Enga Dancing Flower?

I think I have figured this out, but I am not certain. You are clever, Jeek. Help me.

Jeek waited for her to go on. Enga Dancing Flower had called him clever. A bright glow lit up inside his chest.

Tog Flint Shaper and Stitcher can understand each other. Kin can always understand kin. So is Tog Flint Shaper kin to Stitcher? How can that be?

Tog Flint Shaper, kin to Stitcher? Tog Flint Shaper is not a Tall One. Stitcher is not a Hamapa. But, when he pictured Stitcher next to the Tall Ones in his mind, he could see that Stitcher was not as tall as most of them. He was slender like them, but his face sometimes looked a little more like a Hamapa face than a Tall One's face. And his eyes were wide set, like Aja Hama's. Jeek gazed at Enga. His brows rose as understanding began to dawn.

But why does Stitcher hide antlers in the woods? And why did he hold one at our wipiti? asked Jeek.

Do you know that Hama was killed with a caribou antler? Stabbed with it?

Jeek gulped and grabbed his elbows, hugging himself hard. *Stitcher hid the antlers there so we would not know he killed Aja Hama? Was he going to kill Hama tonight? But why?*

*****

Let us think just a bit more. When he first arrived, Hama announced that the New One had been cast out of his tribe, thought-spoke Enga Dancing Flower.

So she understood him, too?

She must have. How else would she know that? He must have told her. Scenes from the past ran through her head.

The young Tall One, arguing and crying with Jansa Wild Wind right after she became Hama.

The New One, showing up a few years later and asking admittance into the tribe. He had not been admitted as a full member until after the death of Aja Hama, the one who hated him, but he was fed and given shelter.

But that Hama never wanted him here. She had even spurned the beautiful gift he had given her, the carving of herself. She had never shown it to the tribe.

And Aja Hama and Tog Flint Shaper, the birth son of the Aja Hama, could both understand his thoughts.

Tog left Stitcher and walked back to Enga and Jeek.

We have reached an understanding, Tog thought-spoke. *He will not bother you again, Enga Dancing Flower.* Then he paused, watching her closely. *What is it? Something else is bothering both of you.*

Enga stood tall, took a deep breath, and answered him over the drum beating inside her head. *If you can read Stitcher's thoughts, and Aja Hama could also read them, then he is kin to you as you are kin to Aja Hama.*

Tog looked at Enga, sending her amazement. *Kin? Stitcher, my kin?* He looked back at the Tall One, then again to Enga.

A jay screamed nearby and took wing. Did he sense their distress?

And the kin of Aja Hama, added Enga.

Jeek hunkered down quietly, watching them.

Enga thought-spoke, *His tribe cast him out because he is different from them. He is only partly a Tall One. Our tribe accepted him because that is what we do. But Aja Hama did not want him to stay. She tried to cast him out again. And she is his birth mother.*

My birth mother coupled with a Tall One? Tog looked bewildered.

Enga tried to picture the coupling of Aja Hama and a Tall One.

Then she whirled around. Stitcher had come near and was watching the trio. He still held the piece of sharp antler. They stood just inside the shadow of the woods that surrounded the clearing for the Burying Place. A flock of squawking geese flew high overhead and the wind stirred the branches of the poplars, raining snow onto them.

You are my birth brother, thought-spoke Tog to Stitcher, opening his mind to all of them. *Is this true? We have the same birth mother?*

Stitcher was catching Tog's thought-speak. Stitcher nodded. Then Tog nodded. Enga waited impatiently for Tog to report their conversation to her.

They kept conversing. Finally, she could wait no more. *Did Stitcher kill Aja Hama, his birth mother?*

No, Enga Dancing Flower, answered Tog, *although he confesses he wanted to at times.*

Then who killed her? asked Jeek.

Yes, who? echoed Enga.

Tog gave his half-brother a steady look, then answered. *Stitcher saw Nanno Green Eyes slay her own sister. Nanno Green Eyes could not stand for Jansa Wild Wind to be Hama. She never liked her sister. Nanno Green Eyes held hate for many. For Jansa Wild Wind who was the Aja Hama, for you and your birth sister, and for Stitcher.*

Why did she hate Stitcher? asked Enga.

Because he carved figures of Aja Hama, but never would carve one of her.

Is that a reason to hate someone?

She didn't need good reasons.

Ask him if her feet were wrapped when she killed Aja Hama, thought-spoke Enga to Tog.

Tog turned back to Stitcher and they had a short conversation.

Yes, Tog reported. *He saw her come out of the wipiti and strip off her foot wrappings. They were bloodied. He went inside to see what had happened and stepped in her Red. He stripped his own foot wrappings off before he left the wipiti and threw them into the stream while he was getting rid of the rest of her Red that clung to him, then made new ones. He had touched her all over to see if he could revive her, but he could not.*

I saw him return from the stream, thought-spoke Jeek. *He was all wet.*

Stitcher wanted to kill Nanno Green Eyes tonight, thought-spoke Tog. *But he found he could not do it. Even thought he knew she killed his mother.*

Stitcher limped back to the Burying Place of Aja Hama and drew a carved figure from his pouch. This one was newly carved, similar to the one of Aja Hama he had first carved, but even more beautiful. He laid the figure on her grave. The lush female curves were worked in smooth, loving strokes, and the wood was polished so it glowed in the sunlight.

Then he collapsed on the grave and started sobbing again. He stabbed the antler into the ground over and over. Tog sank to the ground beside him and buried his face in his hands.

Enga thought she could feel Stitcher's sorrow. He had loved his mother even though she had never shown love for him. Tears sprang to her eyes. Enga knelt and stroked Stitcher's head until his sobs quieted. Tog rose and nodded to Enga. They left Stitcher to mourn in his own fashion.

Chapter 29

We came from beneath the ground, the legends say, we came from the sunrise of the east, or the sunset of the west. We climbed up to the light from the bowels of our holy mountain, we climbed down from the sky by a ladder of arrows.
—*Indians*, William Brandon, p. 20

There had been too many unpleasant council gatherings recently, Bahg Swiftfeet thought, hoping this would be a good one. Roh Lion Hunter, as Hama Dy, stood and started the meeting at dark time.

We have an unpleasant task tonight. Let us start with a Song of Mourning. We have lost our Hama once more. We will do one last act of grieving.

Hama had died during the dark time, two nights ago. Bahg had gotten the message from Zhoo of Still Waters as soon as it happened. The tribe had mourned her at first sun and buried her at high sun, that same sun time. Some of the mourning had been sincere, some had not. There had been no council that night. Now another sun time had passed and the tribe was ready to deal with the future.

Having a full stomach is a wonderful thing, thought Bahg. He gave a loud belch. Their night meal had pleasantly filled his belly.

The wind blew past, cold tonight, reminding Bahg that Cold Season was upon them. At least the Hamapa would be able to make it through until next Seed Season.

Lakala Rippling Water started a slow dirge, her voice sweet and pure on the wintry air. Sannum Straight Hair beat a melancholy rhythm on his drum. Even the high flute notes of Panan One Eye dripped with sorrow. Bahg feared whatever the unpleasant task would turn out to be. He watched as Enga Dancing Flower did a slow turn. Her feet, usually so nimble and sure, dragged through the steps. A few of the other females joined her, and a couple of males. But the mourning dance and song did not last long. They had sat with the ashes on their faces for Hama during most of the sun time yesterday.

Bahg grimaced, thinking about mourning. There were other reasons to mourn at this meeting.

After the song, Panan offered a Saga.

I will tell of the Saga of Fire and Brother Moon. When Brother Earth was very young, when Sister Sun had just been born of Mother Sky, there was no Brother Moon yet. The dark time terrified the Hamapa. They could not see anything in the dark. But the dark time predators could see them. They had no wipiti yet, but had to huddle together every time Sister Sun disappeared, and stay like that until she arose.

The Hamapa did not yet understand that Sister Sun needed to sleep.

Bahg closed his eyes and enjoyed the Saga. This was one he knew well, but some of the younger Hamapa had not yet heard it. He tried to imagine seeing the distant, mystic times with their young minds.

The Hamapa cried to Mother Sky, Dakadaga, give us light so we may not all be killed at night. Mother Sky gave birth to Brother Moon and he shone forth with fullness, but only for a short time. He was weaker than Sister Sun. He could not shine fully all of the time. He grew thin and soon he disappeared. The dark was complete again when Sister Sun was gone.

The fire crackled and spit while the tribe, in silence, received the Saga.

The Hamapa danced and sang and cried for a long time until Mother Sky took pity. She gave a tremendous shout and shot light from her terrible brow and fire began to consume a tree. The tree burned in the sun time and in the dark time. It burned for many suns. Then the fire went out.

Bahg flinched at the cold mental picture. He glanced at their bright, warm fire, grateful he lived in an enlightened time, a time when the Hamapa had fire under their control.

Mother Sky scolded the Hamapa for not taking care of her gift. It was a long time before she sent another shot of light. But this time the Hamapa were ready. They gathered the fire with sticks and stored it in a fire pit. And now we have fire to keep us warm and cook our food. But, most importantly, fire keeps away the large beasts at dark time.

The Hamapa also came to understand that Brother Moon would always get fatter, then thinner, and would always need to take a period of rest when he was at his thinnest.

Bahg grunted and nodded with the others as Panan finished. It was wise of the Storyteller to give a message of light and warmth this night. This meeting's event would make them all feel cold and dark.

Cabat the Thick, the Most High Male, stood and broadcast to all that the tribe would now vote to accept Roh Lion Hunter, Hama Dy, as permanent Hama. Bahg threw Ongu Small One a look, wondering if she would compete for the position. But Ongu sat quiet.

Roh stood alone, facing the fire with her back to her tribe. Each Hamapa clinked down a stone on the ground behind her back, voting Roh as their new Hama.

It was a good choice, Bahg felt. This Hama would not make rash, unwise decisions, even though she was the birth daughter of the one who did. Her first task was a particularly odious ordeal.

Roh, now Hama, turned around, took a deep breath, then plunged ahead. She picked up the gourd and rattled it. Bahg put one arm around Fee Long Thrower, who held their son, and squeezed them both tight.

"Hoody! Listen! The Most High Female Speaks. Nanno Green Eyes slew our leader, the Aja Hama."

Startled looks and gasps went around the circle from those who were hearing this verdict for the first time.

"Nanno Green Eyes is banished from our memories. Mother Spirit of the Sky, Dakadaga, bless the Hamapa."

Her voice cracked on the last words. Nanno was her birth mother, after all. She rattled her gourd once more.

"Hoody! Listen! The Most High Female Speaks. Stitcher is allowed to remain with the tribe as long as he chooses. He is allowed to pick a mate. Mother Spirit of the Sky, Dakadaga, bless the Hamapa."

Stitcher was summoned. He walked into the full firelight, limping on his twisted foot, his shoulders and head held high. Cabat handed him an obsidian knife blade. Roh reached to touch the pouch around his neck, the pouch containing his sewing bones. She smiled at him.

These are your belongings, in this pouch, Cabat said. *No one else knows how to use them, and the Hamapa wish you to continue to gift us with your talents.*

Bahg caught sight of Tog Flint Shaper. He appeared to be shooting thoughts to Stitcher. Bahg wondered what the brothers were conversing about. And if the rest of the tribe would ever be able to communicate with Stitcher.

Vala Golden Hair gave Stitcher a shy smile when he turned away to take his place beside her.

Something very good had happened, though, Bahg remembered, in spite of the pain of banishing a leader from their memories and their lore. Now they knew who had killed Aja Hama. They need not to worry that the Mikino had done it. The tribe could now work together for survival.

But they now knew that one of them had slain another. This was something Bahg had never thought could happen. He hoped it could never happen again.

*****

Enga Dancing Flower watched Stitcher limp with enthusiasm to Vala Golden Hair's side. He looked so joyful. He had been a lonely stranger most of his time with the Hamapa, despised by his own birth mother.

His life had not been easy with the tribe. She would try to make it up to him and hoped the rest of the tribe would, too.

Enga Dancing Flower took comfort in the new Hama. Now, she thought, the tribe might be saved. A slight smile touched her lips.

Hama took up her next task.

Now, she thought-spoke, *we must decide on a trading mission. Shall we trade with the Mikino or not?*

There is no need now, was the opinion of Panan. Cabat agreed with him and the rest nodded their heads. They had plenty of meat for the near future. Ung Strong Arm and Fee Long Thrower would be fully able to hunt by the time they needed food again.

Then we must decide, together, whether to move the village when Dark Season is over, was the next thought from the new Hama.

Enga was proud of her. She was not shirking the hard decisions, but facing them. And getting input instead of deciding on her own. Her hope for the Hamapa swelled.

The last business of the council was to decide on a flint hunting trip for next new sun.

Enga walked to her wipiti after the meeting. She was alone most nights now. Ung and Lakala had decided to live together. Enga was happy for them, but didn't like being alone.

Tog Flint Shaper ran after her and caught her arm just before she entered the door flap. *Enga Dancing Flower. I want to see you before I travel to get flint.*

She turned and strolled with him behind the wipiti, out of sight of the others. It was dark back there, out of the circle of light. Deep shadows filled the hollows of Tog's strong face. His birth mother's sister had been proven a killer. Enga reached out and trailed her hand down his cheek, from his eyes to his lips. He turned his head and kissed her fingers. Enga fell into his warm embrace and gave Tog a proper farewell.

Hurry back, she thought-spoke to his retreating form. He turned and grinned, and answered that he would.

Inside the wipiti, nestling into her fur sleeping skin, she pondered Tog. He was not all good and not all bad. But, for the most part, she liked the way he was. She would be happy with him.

A new thought came. Aja Hama was not all good either. She was a bad mother to Stitcher. She should have accepted her own son and nurtured him, no matter how he had been born. Stitcher was not all bad, but like everyone else, a combination of good and bad. He had had terrible thoughts, thoughts of killing Nanno Green Eyes while she was Hama. But there had been much good in him. He had not killed her, even though she had done such a horrible deed. What was there good in Nanno Green Eyes, though? There must have been something. Her mate, Kokat No Ear, had stayed with her always and treated her well. And she had been kind to him, also. They had even raised a wise daughter, the present leader. Life was very complicated.

Chapter 30

Tog Flint Shaper took Enga Dancing Flower's hand and led her out of the village.

I am too happy to sit still, thought-spoke Tog. *I have to move!*

Enga smiled. *Then let us run.* They trotted through the woods, then came to the open spaces. They raced across the flat, grassy plain, still holding hands. Enga thrilled at the speed. Her hair, worn loose today, felt good streaming behind her. Sister Sun smiled on them with just the right amount of warmth.

In a few moons I will not be able to do this, thought-spoke Enga. *Your seed grows quickly in me. Soon it will be too large for me to run fast.*

The grass, just beginning to turn a tender shade of green, waved in the gentle, sighing breath of Mother Sky. Her Spirit was in a good mood today. A flock of geese flew overhead, honking on their way to their colder nesting places. Back on the Sacred Hill, flowers were blooming and the poplars were leafing out.

Enga and Tog ran until they were out of breath, then fell to the ground and lay admiring the wispy clothing of Mother Sky. Soon they got up and started walking back to the village. Tog reached over and ran his hand over her swelling belly. Soon there would be a newborn Hamapa.

In five suns the tribe would move to a warmer place where they hoped to find more game. The couple strolled into the village and plunked down onto the stones of their beloved Paved Place. Enga spread her hands on the paving. They could not take the stones with them, but hoped to find similar flat ones so they could build a new center in their new village.

It had taken so long for the snow to melt, and for Sister Sun's warmth to thaw Mother Sky's frigid breath, Enga had thought Cold Season would never end. But it was finally Seed Season, and the Hamapa had made it through the cold alive, thanks to the many strips of musk ox meat, dried by the fire before the worst of the Cold Season descended upon them. And thanks to the ox skins, scraped and cut to sleep on and wear.

Hama came out of the largest wipiti and greeted Enga and Tog. *I hope the seed of Tog Flint Shaper is growing well inside you, Enga Dancing Flower. It is important to have more Hamapa.*

Yes, answered Enga. *The youngest of Ongu has now passed seven summers. Too long a time passed with too few surviving Hamapa babies. Now we have the baby of Vala Golden Hair, and ours is coming.*

Enga was in marvelous health. She sensed that her seed was growing just fine. Sometimes it kicked so hard it took her breath away. She laughed aloud when that happened.

She watched Hama, whom she sometimes still thought of as Roh Lion Hunter, cross to the wipiti of the single males, probably to confer about the next council meeting. This Hama was much different than the previous two. She even looked different. She was shorter and stockier, besides being less serious.

Enga sent a private, dark blue message to Tog. *It is good she can rejoice with us about the coming baby.*

Yes, she seems recovered from the sorrow of losing her last one. As recovered as one gets. She takes pleasure in the little one of Vala Golden Hair and Stitcher, too.

Sometimes Enga wondered how it would be now if the Aja Hama who was the mother of Tog had not been killed. To Enga, Aja Hama had stood for her ideal, the person she would most like to be. But she often pondered that there were aspects of Aja Hama that were not good. She had not even loved her son, Stitcher, although he had always loved her.

Enga no longer wanted to be just like Aja Hama, but she would always love her. Aja Hama had consisted of good parts and bad parts, just like all beings.

Ung Strong Arm came running up to Enga and Tog, Lakala Rippling Water trailing behind her.

Look what I just caught! Ung held up a slain baby llama. *This will make a fine wrap for your baby.*

Vala Golden Hair or Stitcher may be able to do some stitching, thought-spoke Lakala. *Stitcher is teaching her how to use his stitching bones.*

Vala joined them holding her new daughter at her breast. They all cooed for a moment, then Ung showed her the llama. Vala touched it. *It's so very soft. It will make good baby garments. I can make one for Sooka. I watch Stitcher very closely when he makes garments. I haven't tried to make one for someone to wear, but I have practiced on scraps of skin.*

Stitcher came out of their wipiti and smiled on his mate and child. Enga could tell, ever since Sooka had been born, that Stitcher had given the seed for her. They would be able to tell more when Sooka was older, but her tiny limbs were slim and long for a baby.

I would like to make one for your baby when it comes, too, continued Vala. *If I can do it, that is. I may not be able to, but I'll try. If I cannot, Stitcher will.*

Tears sprang to Enga's eyes. She was affected by the kindness of Ung and Lakala, and also by the kindness of Vala and Stitcher. *However it turns out, I will use it and the baby will love it.*

She recited very private pleas to Dakadaga, each night just before she went to sleep, pleas to watch over the tribe and to never let another Hamapa bring harm to a tribal brother or sister, ever. But if Dakadaga watched over them carefully, maybe this would never happen again. No

Hamapa ever heard these pleas. Not even Ung. But maybe Dakadaga did.

Ung and Lakala retreated to the wipiti they now shared.

Do you still long to throw a spear as well as Ung Strong Arm? asked Tog.

Enga smiled again. She could tell from Tog's sparkling eyes that her dimples were showing. He always liked that. *No. Ung Strong Arm was given the ability to throw spears. I was given the ability to dance.* She no longer wanted to be just like anyone else. Enga Dancing Flower liked who she was.

And maybe to have many Hamapa babies, added Tog.

They entered the wipiti they shared and closed their door flap

.

Author's Note

Thirty thousand years ago, near the end of the existence of the Neanderthals, a world of incredible fauna, flora, and landscape flourished in North America. The last Ice Age was approaching, threatening the way they had lived since migrating from Asia.

It can be debated whether or not Neanderthals ever made it to the American continents, whether or not they were able to throw spears to bring down game, even whether or not they could speak. But, since their brains are known to have been larger than ours, it's possible some of their senses were keener also. Maybe they even had room for telepathy.

Because fiction can second-guess history, and because Neanderthals may have existed side by side with Cro-Magnons, referred to here as Tall Ones, and in the same time period as the little Hobbit people discovered in Indonesia, named Homo floresiensis, and called Mikino here, I have taken out an artistic license to move them all to North America.

www.ingramcontent.com/pod-product-compliance
Lightning Source LLC
Chambersburg PA
CBHW020313200626
46814CB00006BA/2229